WHERE SEAGULLS FLY

WHERE SEAGULLS FLY

Edwin Page

JANUS PUBLISHING
London, England

First published in Great Britain 2009
by Janus Publishing Company Ltd,
105-107 Gloucester Place,
London W1U 6BY

www.januspublishing.co.uk

British Library Cataloguing-in-Publication Data
A catalogue record for this book is available from the British Library

ISBN 978-1-85756-715-1

Cover Design: Edwin Page

Printed and bound in Great Britain

This book is dedicated to

my wife, Charlotte

and

my mother, Ellen

With thanks for all your support throughout the years

With a special mention for

Armorel and Sue

and for the inspiring music of Rebecca Clamp and Selena Cross, which set the mood for the redraughting process

1

The beast watched in shadowy silence as the small figure of Jebbit Cutler wandered along the ridge of the hill in the gathering dusk. The farmhand's grizzled black hound plodded by his side as the sound of his worn, leather boots rose into the stillness. He walked along the familiar, muddy track at the edge of the ploughed field. His shadow was long in the evening hush as puddles which had collected in the furrows reflected the sky like the broken shards of a mirror.

Stopping, he pulled back the hood of his long, grey tunic to reveal his thinning curls, the deep lines upon his face accentuated by the growing gloom. He looked out over the town of Marghas Byghan to the bay beyond, staring out at the Isle of Ictis which rose from the waters of high tide as Tinker halted beside him, the aged hound panting, breath misty in the late autumn chill.

The western walls of the priory at the Isle's summit shone in the fading light and the sails of a fishing boat returning to the island's harbour glowed with a golden aura as they caught the last rays of sunlight. The sound of the ocean lapping on the shore washed over the rooftops and treetops beneath Jebbit's vantage point and came to him like gentle breathing as stars winked into existence above, the western horizon softly shaded in pastel hues as the sun sank from view. Smoke rose lazily from soot-blackened holes in thatched roofs, the smell of burning wood mingling with the musty scent of fallen leaves and dank earth.

He took in the familiar view with weary eyes. The dull ache of arthritis in his knees intruded upon his mind as his gaze remained fixed on the darkened priory atop the Holy Isle. Pale yellow light issued from a few of the small windows and in his mind's eye Jebbit saw the monks kneeling in silent prayer in the chapel built upon the Isle's highest rocks.

Tinker suddenly turned towards the hedgerow to the right. A growl rose from deep within her as the hairs on her back prickled in a primitive response to the faint scent she had caught on the breeze. She took a step towards the barren bushes with teeth bared.

Jebbit turned, the western sky beyond the hedgerow now a deep, rich blue touched with a pale, golden yellow where it met the horizon. 'What be it, Tink?' he asked, glancing down at his faithful companion.

Tinker growled again and a shiver ran the length of Jebbit's spine. The hairs on the nape of his neck tingled. A sense of dread reared up within, arising from some latent instinct, some deep, primal pit of his being, a murky swamp the depth of which reached back to the dawn of life itself, its sluggish waters disturbed by images of demons and devils, of foul creatures filled with shadows harbouring a malady of fear.

He scanned the hedgerow carefully, eyes narrowing. His pulse quickened and he felt perspiration upon his upper lip despite the chill in the air. Every nerve and fibre spoke of warning, the murky pool deep within stirring in reaction to some hidden presence.

There. He spied a faint movement. His heart became thunderous as he saw a fearful shadow beyond the lower branches of the hedge. Something large was lurking on the far side. It was trying to remain still in order to avoid detection, and from what Jebbit could make out it seemed to be a man of sorts.

'Who be it?' he called, his voice tremulous despite his attempt at courageous authority.

No answer came.

Tinker's growling continued, hackles raised and head lowered as if about to leap forward. The muscles in her shoulders were tense and trembling, but something within held the hound in place, her claws digging into slick mud.

'Who be there?' He reiterated his question.

The shadow was substantial and he could make out the shape of a head atop wide shoulders. It then struck him with horror that whatever the fiend may be, it was looking back at him. Its eyes were upon him and beneath the gaze he felt all remnants of courage wither.

The figure of gathered darkness slowly began to move away to the left, following the line of the hedge towards the slope of the hill and the town below. It kept itself low, but despite this Jebbit could see its size was substantial, unnatural for any man.

Tinker took a backward step, her growls dying away in her throat.

Jebbit looked down at his dog and felt the rising urge to flee.

A branch snapped, its sound cutting through the night. The figure became still, hunkering down beside the concealing hedgerow.

The old dog barked uncertainly as she took another step back and looked up at her master, eyes questioning and fearful, sensing the apprehension of the farmhand beside her.

Jebbit reached down and scratched her head in an attempt at reassurance. 'Do not fret, Tink,' he whispered.

Turning, all the while feeling the presence of the dark shadow on the far side of the hedgerow, Jebbit quickly walked away. His boots slipped in the mud due to his haste, right foot splashing into a puddle, the ripples warping the darkened heavens reflected in the water.

He glanced over his shoulder as Tinker fell in step beside him and then began to trot ahead, grateful to be away from the hill's brow. They began to descend a grassy path, trees looming before them on the slope above the town.

Taking one last glance at the hedgerow on the other side of the ploughed field, Jebbit wiped away the perspiration on his upper lip. The farmhand then set off at a brisk pace, he and his hound consumed by the dark maw of the woodland which masked the town below from view. His nerves jangled and his eyes were wide as he stared to the right, his sight unable to pierce the gloom beneath the boughs and his mind conjuring images of a large devil lurking amidst the gathered trunks.

The undergrowth beside the path seemed to reach out towards him with shadowed, spindly arms and long fingers. It snagged on the dark, woollen stockings he wore to ward off the chill as his pace quickened. He felt as though the twisted trees to either side were about to pounce and devour him, their branches reaching overhead, black against the starry heavens.

There was a sudden disturbance beside the path and his heart leapt. He halted and stared into the pitch, but could see nothing as the undergrowth rustled. His breath held and heart pounding against his ribcage, Jebbit prayed for deliverance.

The source of the disturbance wandered onto the steep path descending before him, its snout muddied after rooting in the woods. The farmhand stared at the pig and felt a flood of relief. 'Only one of John's sows,' he whispered as he exhaled deeply and collected himself, hands trembling.

He then continued the journey back to the town, muscles coiled in readiness should the beast he witnessed on the brow of the hill suddenly come shambling through the darkness.

Jebbit breathed deep in the hope of bolstering his courage, the cold night air adding an immediacy to the heat of his fear. With a sense of being spied upon by the unnatural fiend, he hurried for the security of Marghas Byghan, the sound of waves washing over him, but unable to cleanse his mind of trepidation.

2

A thin veil of smoke hung in the air of the King's Arms. A knot of local men were gathered about the bar in the right-hand corner, regulars comfortable with their drinking silence. To the right of the bar crackled a fire, its flames dancing and trails of smoke rising into the small, musty establishment as they escaped from the weak pull of the darkened chimney, crudely built from red-brown rocks taken from the hillside. Thick, squat candles burned upon shelves in various nooks and crannies, old wax drippings surrounding them and marking the passage of time. Sawdust lay scattered on the stone floor, like so many teeth after drunken brawls.

The atmosphere inside the tavern was subdued by the preceding day of hard labour. Often pilgrims or sailors were present, but on this night the rest of the establishment's small, dingy interior was empty of patrons. The crackling of the fire filled the silence and then the sound of a dull, rhythmic thud arose from one of the rooms adjacent to the bar area.

'Mary with one of her regulars,' stated Richard Buckley, the landlord, as he stood behind the bar, the other men familiar with the sound and Morgan the blacksmith having found pleasure between her thighs from time to time.

Richard filled his tin cup with brandy, his rounded cheeks reddened by alcohol and left hand upon the bar in order to steady himself as he swayed slightly under the weight of his inebriation. His large stomach rubbed against the bar as he scratched his beard, which was black and shot with grey.

There was a brief moan of male pleasure and then the knocking stopped. Mervin Sallows, the carpenter who was the junior amongst those gathered in the tavern, placed his cup on the bar and walked over to the back door, stepping out into the night and turning right towards the outhouse before the door swung shut.

The front door opened and all the men turned to the activity. Jebbit entered with his hound at his side and the pall of smoke was disturbed by the new arrival. Tinker trotted to the slatted cellar door opposite and began to lap at the water placed in a bowl beside it.

'What be wrong with ye, Jebbit?' asked John Hadden, taller than the other men at nearly 6 foot, his face long, skin brown and leathery, weathered by working in the fields and with his livestock. 'It looks as though ye has seen a ghost.'

Jebbit shut the door and joined the men at the bar with a nod of greeting. Richard put a cup on the bar and pulled the stopper from a large, earthenware jug, pouring a brandy for the new arrival.

'It were worse than a ghost, I tell ye,' replied Jebbit as he gratefully lifted the drink from the bar and took a welcoming swig of its warmth. 'There be something unspeakable upon the hill this night.'

'Unspeakable?' John raised an eyebrow.

'A creature of darkness lurking above the town.'

'It sounds as though ye have been drinking at home again, Jebbit,' said George Pascoe, a farmer who had lost his left eye in an accident fifteen years prior, the socket now sunken and filled with shadows in the candle and firelight.

'If only,' said Jebbit with a shake of his head, 'but this be my first drink of the day.' He held up the cup and then drank the rest of his brandy, putting the vessel on the bar, Richard refilling it without a word.

'What did this creature appear to be?' asked John as the brothers Tupp looked over his shoulders, the twins standing near the back door as usual, the deep lines around their mouths giving the appearance of permanent frowns.

Jebbit wiped his lips and glanced at Tinker as she made her way to the fire and lay before the hearth. Morgan Pengelly was sitting at the table by the fire, as was his habit. He ran a hand through his unruly brown curls and then bent down to rub Tinker behind the ears, his sleeves rolled up to the elbows and thick forearms marked with burns in various stages of healing, signs of his labours in the smithy. His pale shirt was loosely laced with cord and his broad chest revealed despite the chill in the night beyond the hostel's dingy interior.

Jebbit turned to the farmers and other men at the bar. 'It was a creature of shadow. It skulked behind the hedgerow and I feared it would have come for me if it were not for the bushes blocking its path.'

'A shadow, ye say? Be ye sure it was not some brock or deer, maybe one of my pigs?'

'It were nothing like any animal I ever saw. Its shape was like a man, but a man of unnatural size. It were a beast of evil tidings, I tell ye.'

The men gathered at the bar shared looks of concern.

'Evil tidings,' echoed John.

'Aye, evil tidings. I felt its foulness as I feel the heat from the fire.' Jebbit glanced at the flames.

'I say we go find this beast and put it to the knife,' said Morgan from his seat beside the fire as he halted his attentions to the dog and straightened, Tinker looking up expectantly after a moment.

The other men turned to the dark-haired blacksmith.

'If evil it be, then we cannot allow its presence here. Though it did not attack Jebbit, there is no way to be sure that our women and children will remain safe.'

'Aye,' said Walter Hyne, though he was a little unnerved by Jebbit's obvious agitation. He was the local butcher, his face rounded and large nose discoloured by broken veins.

There were nods of silent agreement amongst the other men.

'I say we do as Morgan says. We go to the hill and flush out this evil,' said John, putting his cup on the bar with his hand over it, the sign that Richard should not refill. 'Are you with us?' he asked the Tupp twins along the bar.

The brothers looked into each other's eyes for a moment as if sharing some silent communication and then Jack nodded. He was the eldest and rarely spoke, his brother, James, never uttering a single word and many suspecting he was incapable of speech.

'We will meet back here after fetching weapons and torches by which to light our way. Then this damned beast will meet its end,' said Morgan, rising to his feet purposefully.

'What do ye mean by "weapons"?' asked Jebbit with apparent nervousness.

'Anything ye may have suited to such a purpose. A knife or hammer will do.' Morgan pulled down his sleeves and donned his felt cap.

'What if this beast cannot be harmed by normal weapons?'

The blacksmith fixed the old farmhand with a hard stare and then looked past him to the twins by the back door. 'Jack, go to the church and collect some holy water in one of Richard's cups. Even the devil himself would feel its burn.'

Mervin re-entered the King's Arms through the rear door. He stopped just inside and looked at the faces of the men gathered before him, all bearing expressions of utmost gravity. 'What?' he asked with slight uneasiness, his pulse quickening in reaction to the touch of fear he saw in Jebbit's eyes.

3

The group of eight men walked along a small track which rose through Marghas Byghan, passing the cob cottages of farm and harbour workers, candle and firelight glowing in the humble abodes as they passed in silence. Their torches flickered, flames fluttering in the darkness and casting their yellow light upon the weapons they carried and the puddles collected on the rutted path. They passed the last ramshackle homes on the upper outskirts of the settlement, the sound of children wailing arising from the building to their left as a black dog strained at its chain and barked at them, the sound fracturing the hush.

The men arrived at the thin strip of woodland which clung to the side of the hill at its steepest incline. They came to a halt and stood with eyes upon the thick darkness beneath the boughs, the path ahead veiled in pitch and so thin as to allow only a single-file ascent.

'The creature is upon the brow of the hill,' said Jebbit with an unenthusiastic nod ahead.

'Ye should lead the way,' said Morgan, smith's hammer grasped tightly in his right hand.

'Aye,' nodded Mervin, the young carpenter wielding a short length of wood and a smaller hammer than the muscular blacksmith.

'Why should I take the lead? Ye all know the route as well as I,' answered the aged farmhand as his gaze lingered on the pitch waiting for them and his mind conjured images of the demon hunkered within its concealment.

'Ye are the one who saw the beast,' said John, his tall frame slightly hunched as he fought the chill and his own sense of fear.

'The longer we linger the greater the chance that the beast will have moved on,' said Morgan curtly.

'Maybe that is no bad thing,' said Jebbit under his breath, which drifted away on the breeze like a diminishing ghost.

The smith stared at him as the bark of a fox rose into the night and Tinker looked up the hill. There was a moment of stillness as indecision held them bound and they stared up the slope, the security of the small town at their backs and the engulfing darkness before them.

'I will lead the way,' said Morgan eventually with a hint of annoyance. He stepped forward, angling his torch ahead as he ducked beneath a branch and moved up the track into the trees.

The others gratefully followed his lead. They were made more confident by Morgan's large frame at their head as the dancing light of their torches illuminated the tangled undergrowth of fading autumn greens and browns, the branches of the trees all but bare in readiness for the long sleep of winter.

They soon left the darkness beneath the trees to arrive at the brow of the hill and the ploughed field in which Jebbit had stood when spying the beast of shadow.

'Over there,' said the farmhand, pointing across the field.

They stared at the hedge on the far side of the muddy furrows in pensive silence.

'I see no sign of a lurking beast,' said Morgan without turning, his breath an apparition in the night, knuckles white as he gripped the hammer tightly, filled with the expectation of a confrontation with whatever foulness awaited them.

The men advanced, their steps measured as they watched for any sign of movement, barely daring to blink for fear the beast would come at them from some hiding place. Their weapons were raised in readiness as they approached the place of sighting and braced themselves.

Reaching the hedgerow, they stared through its knotted branches at the darkness of the field beyond.

'I see nothing,' stated Walter, the blade of the cleaver in his hand glinting in the light of the torch flames.

'As do I,' said John, his eyes narrowed as he crouched and peered through the hedge.

Morgan began to walk over the hill's brow.

'What have ye seen, Morgan?' asked George, the deep shadow within his empty eye socket moving in the flickering light of the torch in his left hand, shifting as if alive and the depth of the hollow revealed in its vacant paleness from time to time.

'Nothing,' replied the smith over his wide shoulder. 'I search for a passage through to the next field.'

The others followed close, eyes scanning the surrounding countryside, the outlines of hills to the north and west black against the starry sky.

The blacksmith passed through the hedgerow, thorns scraping against his leather jerkin like claws. John followed next with Tinker impatient behind.

'Are ye sure we should pursue the creature?' asked Jebbit, standing before the gap through the hedgerow, staring at Tinker as she disappeared from sight into the adjacent field.

'Come on, Jebbit. We do not want to leave Morgan and John to find the beast alone,' said Walter as he waited beside the farmhand.

Jebbit stepped aside. 'Then ye can go before me.'

Walter and Mervin made their way through the grasping hedge.

'Ye will be left on this side alone,' commented George as the Tupp twins passed by.

Jebbit looked at him with fear in his eyes. The farmhand glanced about the ploughed field and then passed through the hedge with the one-eyed farmer close on his heels.

Cauliflowers grew in the next field and the men stayed upon the grass between the crop and hedgerow. Morgan walked with back bent and torch lowered as he sought any sign of the beast's passage through the thick grass and dock leaves which grew beside the hedge.

'Here,' he called, feeling a chill settle upon him as he crouched and his companions gathered close, his gaze quickly roaming ahead as he felt watching eyes upon him.

The men looked at the area of flattened grass before the blacksmith, two indents clear where large feet had rested.

'I told ye I had not been drinking. What my eyes saw was true. There were a demon upon this hill,' said Jebbit, looking about with a growing sense of unease.

George Pascoe glanced over his shoulder nervously, his solitary eye wide as his gaze took in the treeline which began 20 yards away and held the potential of nightmarish creatures within its gloom.

'Maybe we should go back to town, the beast must have moved on by now,' said Jebbit.

'Aye, Jebbit may well be right,' concurred George as the group became increasingly restless, shifting on their feet as they adjusted the grips on their weapons, eyes unsettled and darting.

Morgan rose to his full height and looked at the one-eyed farmer. 'We came to flush it out, to kill it or ward the beast away,' he said firmly. 'Where did you last witness it? In which direction was it moving?' he asked, turning to Jebbit

'It was travelling towards the trees along the hedgerow a little further ahead of our position,' answered the farmhand, the tension in his lined face echoing the fear evident in the other men's expressions.

Taking the lead once again, Morgan walked slowly beside the hedgerow, his torch low, but gaze moving from the ground to the treeline which loomed ominously ahead of them on the slope of the hill above Marghas Byghan. Despite his apparent courage in the face of the unidentified danger, he could feel his heart racing and the chill that had come over him remained, along with the sense of being spied upon.

'Here, another sign of the creature's passing,' he stated after a few moments, the distant sound of waves and the flutter of torch flame accompanying the soft footfalls of the other men's steps upon the grass as they drew alongside him. Before Morgan was a rotted branch snapped at its centre, the wood crushed as if beneath great weight.

The tension grew as the men approached the trees, the light of their torches barely penetrating the darkness before them. The blacksmith studied the ground and saw a large footprint in a patch of mud at the edge of the woods which marked the beast's point of entry. It was flat and bore no marks of identity.

'It entered here,' he stated, raising his torch and staring into the woodland, his hammer raised, the muscles in his shoulders knotted, chest tight.

'What should we do?' asked John.

'I say we leave it be. We are too few and should come back reinforced with others from the town,' said Jebbit.

'I agree,' said Walter, his butcher's cleaver at the ready and trembling slightly in his apprehensive grasp.

Morgan turned and looked at the faces of the seven men who shifted nervously before him. 'If we stay close and watchful there be nothing to fear. We will flush it out for the sake of our women and children.'

The others looked at him, fear shining in their eyes, dancing with the flickering flames reflected from the torches they bore.

'Are ye with me?' asked Morgan.

The men shared glances of nervous trepidation, but eventually nodded their confirmation.

'Good, then we best set to it before the hour grows late and the beast escapes our purpose.'

Morgan turned and entered the trees, Tinker at his heels. The other men paused a moment, Jebbit taking a deep breath. They slowly crept into the trees in search of the dark fiend with hearts pounding and eyes wide against the darkness, the shadows cast by the torchlight dancing like lithe creatures in the tangled undergrowth, like demons calling them to their doom.

4

It crouched in the dunes west of the town. Silence hung heavy in the folds of its black cloak. It stared up at the torch flames moving through the distant trees upon the hill behind Marghas Byghan. Its dark eyes glittered with starlight as it turned its gaze skyward for a moment and then turned its attention to the Isle of Ictis rising in the wide bay, the trees on its northern lea appearing like a dark shadow creeping up towards the priory which rested at its summit.

The sound of gentle waves upon sand filled the air and the smell of the sea drifted over the dunes as a slight breeze lifted from the south-west. The tall grasses helping to conceal the creature swayed slightly, marking the wind's passage. It remained motionless, narrowed eyes fixed on the vague outlines of the priory buildings atop the Isle.

It had spent weeks travelling under darkened skies, sleeping in barns and hedgerows during daylight hours. What food it had scavenged had been meagre; rotting vegetables spilled from torn sacks in farmers' sheds or the leaves of wild plants which sometimes set its stomach to heaving and left it pale and sickly for days or brought about bouts of stomach cramps that gave rise to moments of fearful delirium.

The wind grew in gusting strength and loose sand blew across the undulating dunes, grasses swaying with increased violence, bending to the will of the elements as the beast's unkempt curls were tossed to and fro. Clouds began to mask the stars on the southern horizon and promised rain in the early hours.

It turned its gaze westward, briefly glancing at the scattering of ramshackle houses of another settlement, which was couched in thick woodland some distance away. All the buildings were masked in shadow and there were no signs of stirring.

The creature turned back to stare at the hill above the larger town to the east, eyes in pools of shadow cast by its protruding brow, and saw that the torches remained in the trees through which it had recently made its way. Then the creature rose, keeping its frame low, back bent as it crept slowly through the dunes with measured steps, cloth-wrapped feet sinking deep into the pale sands.

It moved onto the wide beach, its gentle curve stretching to the west as white-capped breakers rolled in from the ocean. Skirting the edge of the dunes, the fear of discovery rising with every footfall, it moved eastward, back towards the town of Marghas Byghan which rested atop cliffs rising 20 feet into the air, a promontory of rocks cutting into the waters 100 yards ahead where the small harbour of the settlement rested.

A large, dark rock jutted from the sands to the right, a third of the way to the Isle, the receding tide lapping at its most southerly point. With pace quickening, the beast passed across the beach, a shadowy wraith upon the sands which grew firmer beneath its feet. It loped across the beach towards the solid darkness of the rock, seeking refuge from prying eyes, the flutter of its black cloak like the wings of bats leaving their roost to hunt in the darkness.

The beast reached the large rock and discovered carved steps ascending its permanence. Climbing them with care, the shadows of the crags deep and impenetrable, it made its way to a small chapel nestled in the rock's summit. The building was barely more than a stone shed, such was its size, but it would serve well enough as shelter until the sea receded from the bar of sand and shingle that supposedly joined the Isle to the mainland at times of low tide.

Ducking its head, the creature passed inside, the wind whistling with growing intensity. An altar which was no more than a shelf rested opposite the entrance. Two candles in simple lanterns flickered wildly to either side of a carving of Christ upon the cross which glowed softly as if some divine spirit emanated from its grain, an appearance afforded by the thick lacquer with which it had been coated.

The creature knelt in the confines of the stone walls, knees cracking, pain flaring in tired joints which could barely carry such inhuman bulk and size after so long with so little food. Its bearded face was covered in grime, cheeks hollow, features masked by deep shadow as it kept its head bowed.

The wind rose into a sudden gust and the candles were blown out in an instant, their wicks glowing a faint red before they darkened and brief wisps of smoke rose like lost souls. The beast watched the ghostly trails rise in the deep gloom for a moment, the wind then ripping them asunder as it again rushed into the tiny chapel.

Pulling its hood over its head, the creature turned to look from the door, hoping to remain undiscovered until it could vacate the rock and make its way across the sand bar to the Isle that rose in the darkness. It stared up at the Mount, a sneer upon its lips as it lurked in the gloom of the small chapel, the glint of its eyes visible in the pitch gathered beneath its brow.

5

The old monk woke beneath the dark bedcover on his simple, wooden cot. Brother Elwin's eyes opened and he took a breath, the cold air invigorating as it filled his lungs. He stared at the beams above as starlight faintly illuminated his small room from a window over his bed which was no more than a slit in the granite wall. His thoughts chased after the dark dream he had been experiencing, but it evaded his wakefulness and vanished into the realms of the forgotten.

His body ached as he stretched beneath the cover, his feet chilled and verging on numbness as they poked from the bottom, even though thick woollen socks hid them from the night. There was silence outside after the passing rainstorm which had woken him during earlier hours.

With a look of determination on his gaunt face, he swung his scrawny legs over the side of the cot, feet settling upon the cold stone floor. He yawned before rising, robed in a simple nightgown of pale linen, looking like a white-haired ghost in the gloom of his small room, the crown of his head cleanly shaven.

Stepping to a wooden table beside the head of the bed, he picked up his tinderbox and lit a white candle which rested next to a small basin of water, the flame reflected in its dented tin as the candle, which was barely a stub, cast a murky pool of yellow light. He cupped his hands and collected water from the basin, which sparkled as he leant forwards and splashed it upon his lined face. His eyes were closed, wrinkles about them deepening as droplets fell to rejoin the pool within the basin, creating ripples that distorted the image of his aged visage.

Brother Elwin picked up a damp piece of cloth from beside the basin and slowly wiped his face, every movement conducted with care and meditation as he felt the sensation of the material upon the contours of his face and the jowls which hung loosely beneath his chin. Moving to the tiny window above his bed, he laid the towel on the granite ledge before it so that it may dry when the sun finally brought its vague autumnal warmth to the world.

He took off his nightgown and stood naked in the chill, his body frail, skin sagging from his thin frame, the shadows of his ribs clear in the candlelight. With care, he folded the gown and placed it upon a wooden shelf above the table, taking down woollen undergarments from beside it and putting them on in a concession to the growing cold of coming winter.

From a wooden peg on the back of the door to his room, he took down his brown monastic robe and put it on with the calm assurance of familiarity after many years of routine. It was as if his whole life had become a contemplation, a calmness apparent in his demeanour. There was no urgency, only a sense of tranquillity in all that he did in the soft light that illuminated the room and held back the darkness which still held sway beyond the window.

The old monk tied the cowl about his waist with a pale cord, its ends hanging to his knees. He took off his socks and slipped on the leather sandals that were resting beside the door. Then Brother Elwin stepped back to the wooden table and bent to blow out the candle. His gaze fell on his bed and he was surprised to note he had neglected to tidy the cover.

With brow furrowed, he straightened. There was the faintest trace of concern in his expression. Never before had he forgotten this task in the many years spent in service of the Lord.

Neatening the cover with the same calmness with which he had previously conducted himself, the old monk ascribed his forgetfulness to the strange dream which had disturbed his sleep and distracted his waking mind. Coughing, he placed his right hand before his thin, pale lips and then stepped to the table, blowing out the candle and plunging the room into darkness.

After waiting a few moments for his sight to adjust to the meagre light afforded by the stars, he walked to the door and left his cell, stepping into the cold corridor beyond, his breath hanging in clouds and marking his passage. He looked in both directions and saw no sign of light from beneath the other doors which were set into the granite wall on the left-hand side of the long corridor. He then set off to the left, passing six other doors, faint sounds of snoring issuing from behind the penultimate one.

He stepped out of the corridor and into the entrance hall. Two wooden chairs were placed against the wall to his right, beside which was the rear door of the hall that led to a footpath climbing to the chapel. He crossed the small room with its vaulted roof to the front door located opposite the rear.

Brother Elwin walked out onto the Mount's summit and into the chilled morn. He stopped to look south across the ocean, low cloud hugging the horizon. The dark swells of waves crested by white horses could be seen as they moved towards the Mount of St Michael and the mainland beyond. He could see land to the west where the fishing village of Mousehole nestled against the coastal hills in the darkness and the old monk drank in the beauty of the surroundings of which he never tired.

He turned and walked to the right, his sandals upon bare rock and patches of grass which found purchase in shallow hollows where earth had collected. Soon he reached the stone steps which curved in descent around the north side of the Mount.

He stopped at the top of the steps and looked northward, seeing the island's harbour below, its wooden jetty in dark contrast to the sands revealed by low tide. Tethered fishing boats listed upon their sides to the right of the jetty in the protective lea of the island as they rested on the sands. Lying inland were granite warehouses, their slate roofs visible over the trees gathered on the slope below the old monk's vantage point.

Beyond the harbour he could see the sand and shingle of Marghas Byghan's western beach, the sand bar that linked the Mount to the mainland like a pale ribbon parting the gentle waves as the tide rose, Chapel Rock a dark shadow at the bar's far end. The haphazard cottages of Marghas Byghan clung to the coastline opposite. They rested in silence upon the lower slopes of a long hill rising behind the westerly dunes and stretching eastward, the thoroughfares darkened and without signs of life. To the west he could vaguely make out the sparse dwellings of Marghas Yow, a small settlement hidden in trees.

The monk drank in the sights afforded him by starlight and then began his descent, the stone steps glistening with moisture as he took every care not to slip, trees rising to his left and the rocky crags of the Mount looming to his right, the priory above soon hidden from view by their enormity. He walked in silence, his mind uncluttered by thoughts as he made his way to the gardens below. The descent was arduous, the chill always setting pain in his joints.

Near the bottom of the steps, he peered between the trunks gathered to the left, spying the line of warehouses below which were filled with goods such as copper and tin ready to be shipped to the far climes of the Mediterranean. He stepped down onto a cobbled path that led straight ahead and walked peacefully along it with his hands clasped together, the long sleeves of his cowl sheltering them from the cold. He passed a small flight of stone steps to the left which marked the start of the path to the harbour, a path he had often followed in order to obtain supplies for the priory.

After another 20 yards Brother Elwin arrived at a simple wooden gate flanked by trees. He entered the priory's gardens, a gentle creaking of hinges marking his passage. He stood a moment and looked down the slope, a stone wall running to his left down its incline to meet with another which protected the south-eastern border of the terraced gardens from the sea that lay beyond. Upon each terrace were small vegetable plots and a herb garden nestled in the far right corner, gathered in the protection of the southern wall. A little higher on the slope above the herb garden was a small orchard of apple and pear trees which he had helped to plant many, many moons ago. Rocky crags rose beyond, wild shrubs and ivy clinging in crevices filled with deep shadow, the priory's chapel visible high above.

The smells of the shore, of seaweed and salt water, mingled with the scents of late autumn and he breathed deeply. Above, in the priory, his Brothers would be stirring in preparation for the first psalms of the day, but, as was his habit, he liked to take in the glories of the Lord's creation before going to the first duty of the day.

The old monk walked along the path, which followed the gentle incline of the eastern wall to his left. His sandals padded on the soft grass as his gaze took in the view out to sea, evergreens planted within the bounds of the south wall obscuring it as he descended, their branches serving as additional coastal protection for the plants which the monks nurtured in the walled confines of the small gardens.

He arrived at the lower climbs of the gardens and turned right to follow the south wall, the branches of the evergreens reaching overhead towards the mainland after years of being sculpted by the wind.

He wandered along the path in peace, his mind still as he looked at the ocean when a view was afforded between the trunks of the evergreens. Peering over the wall, he could make out the Greeb, a formation of rocks which rose from the waves beyond the eastern curves of the mainland like the scaled back of a sea monster. White clouds of spray passed over it like apparitions in the darkness as high Atlantic rollers crashed against its southern side, their waters boiling and angry upon the dark stone which would not yield.

As Brother Elwin continued he raised his head to look at the rocks ahead, which climbed steadily to the priory. The chapel upon the summit was silhouetted against the stars and it was there that he would soon be attending the first psalms.

A sense of foreboding suddenly came upon him. The old monk came to a halt on the grass and lowered his gaze to peer ahead in the gloom. Narrowing his eyes, he tried to spy what lay in the shadows beneath the evergreens that lined the wall to his left.

He could see nothing of threat within the deep shadows, but still his being warned of something hidden in the night. He noticed that his hands were trembling and felt his pulse quicken.

The pale glide of a barn owl overhead gave him a start and he scolded himself for being so easily disturbed, though he still could not bring himself to resume his walking. The warning within was firm and came from some hidden depth of his being.

He stood and stared at the path ahead and the trunks of the trees which rose beside the stone wall. He tried to penetrate the darkness with his gaze despite the knowledge that his eyesight was not equal to the task. Glancing up at the chapel, he could make out a faint light shining from within, the stained-glass windows taking on an inner glow.

With one last look ahead, Brother Elwin turned and made his way towards the easterly wall and the steady climb back to the gate at the gardens' entrance. He did not give in to his fear and peer behind him, though the urge to do so was strong.

As he walked, he felt as though eyes were upon him and his pace quickened. His sense of calm vanished into the night with his misted breath as he hurried along the grassy ascent to the gate. He made his way onto the cobbles beyond and then began the climb back up the stone steps to the priory.

Beneath the evergreens at the southern edge of the gardens the dark figure listened to the diminishing sounds of the monk's rapid retreat. It sat huddled beside one of the tree trunks, leaning against the rough bark, body wrapped tightly in its dark cloak and pulled close for warmth in the cold night.

6

The gate creaked softly as Brother Elwin led the five monks in his charge into the gardens, the sky above heavy with cloud. To his surprise he found a sense of mild trepidation lingering after his experience earlier that morn. His gaze scanned the far wall and the evergreens beside it, but he could see nothing untoward.

In silence the others moved onto the terraces to attend to their duties in tending the fruit trees and vegetable plots. Brother Elwin watched them distractedly for a while as he idly paced along the northern terrace that abutted the rocky climbs of the Mount. His gaze continued to return to the southern wall, kept seeking the source of his previous feelings of alarm. Times too numerous to count he had wandered there prior to the first psalms of the day and never had he felt such things. His sojourns along the edges of the gardens had always been filled with meditative inner peace, even during inhospitable weather.

As the other monks busied themselves with the tasks at hand, two of them pruning the apple trees at the far end of the gardens and the three others scattered amidst the vegetable plots, kneeling on the grass as they pulled weeds from the sodden earth, Brother Elwin slowly made his way along a path which split the gardens, descending along the gentle gradient to the southern wall which masked the shoreline.

As he drew closer he noted a growing tension in his neck and shoulders, a stiffness of knotted muscles that he tried to relieve by rolling his head, hearing the internal crunch of tendons tightly strung. His blue eyes remained fixed ahead, scanning the length of the wall, but still sighting nothing of alarm and no sign of recent disturbance.

Folk tales of knockers and green-skinned boekkas drifted into his mind, of the faerie kin who were said to inhabit those western lands, to be found in the depths of tin mines or dancing in stone circles during starlit nights. They cavorted through his thoughts and Brother Elwin tried to banish them, push them from his mind as he searched for any sign of what had unsettled him during the hours of darkness.

Reaching the southern wall and the trees whose boughs arced above his head, the old monk turned right and began to walk in the direction he had been travelling when the sense of foreboding had welled up from within. In the greyness of the overcast day the old monk stepped with a considered pace as he studied the needle-scattered earth beside the wall and between the tree trunks.

Then he saw it. He stopped and turned to the wall. Taking a small step from the path, he crouched and studied the compacted earth and flattened tufts of grass beside the trunk of an evergreen. Something of considerable weight had rested there and, if he were any judge, its presence had not been long departed as the grass had yet to begin rising back to its usual lush fullness.

A shiver ran the length of his spine as he glanced about the gardens. The five Brothers continued with their work and there were no signs of anyone else present in the walled confines.

Looking back to where the unknown had taken rest, his mind turned to his walk that morning. Something inside him had known of the creature's presence as it skulked in the darkness along his intended path. Maybe the Lord had been watching over him and sent His spirit to disturb his mortal mind with a sense of alarm. He was in no doubt that he had been warned from approaching the place where the creature had hidden itself, possibly lying in wait and he its intended victim.

Taking a deep breath to calm the beating of his heart, Brother Elwin straightened. He stepped up to the wall and peered over, seeing the white-capped rollers swelling beyond the shoreline rocks. He glanced in both directions and saw nothing of note amidst the thick grasses and brown skeletons of bracken.

Satisfied that whatever had lain in wait beside the wall had moved on, the aged monk turned back to the gardens and moved onto the path. He was about to make his way up to the small orchard to help with the pruning when a sensation of being watched halted him and stilled his heart momentarily. His gaze darted to the crags which rose to the priory atop the Mount. Scanning the lichen-covered rocks and the undergrowth gathered in their folds, he could spy nothing amiss.

The feeling persisted. For long moments he stood as if rooted to the spot, eyes watching for the slightest movement amidst the rocks. A gull called out as it passed the crags, wings stretched as it glided out to sea in search of food.

'Brother Elwin,' called one of the monks who had accompanied him to the gardens.

He continued to look to the rocks.

'Brother Elwin,' came the call once again.

He blinked and shook his head in order to free himself of the impressions of being watched which had settled so heavily and with such suddenness. He turned to the Brother whose face was rounded by youthful weight, his complexion without the blemishes that age would bring, freckles gathered upon the bridge of his nose. The young monk stood beside one of the vegetable plots looking at his senior as he awaited an answer and assistance.

'What is it, Brother Thomas?' asked Brother Elwin as he began to walk over to the diminutive monk and tried to shake off the feelings which so unbalanced his usually calm interior.

7

After Mass Brother Elwin decided to return to the gardens, determined to find the source of his disturbance and banish the feelings from within. The Lord was with him and he felt certain that he would find no true cause for concern or alarm. The compacted earth and bent blades of grass could have been caused by a fox from the mainland lying in wait for the rabbits which regularly found their way into the gardens, possibly even a brock which had wandered across the sand bar during low tide.

He walked through the gate with a sense of purpose and confidence in his stride. He had decided the best place to begin the purging of his distress was at the site where evidence of a presence had been detected.

Brother Elwin soon arrived at the spot and stared at the ground. Though he was loath to admit it, the area of occupation was larger than he would have expected from a mere fox. Even a large brock would not have made such an indent in all probability, and this thought served to lessen his resolve.

Turning to the rocks that rose to the priory, he again felt as if he were being watched by something hidden in the crags. He glanced around the gardens and found their emptiness unsettling, his Brothers all gathered within the shelter of the refectory above, choosing not to venture out as low, dark clouds were ushered across the sky by strengthening winds.

Brother Elwin briefly contemplated walking along the southern side of the island at the foot of the high bluffs to see if he could detect what it was that had set such a chill within his soul. The idea was soon cast aside, his body being far from the nimbleness of youth and without the strength to flee should there be any danger.

His resolve faltered and then collapsed. He wanted nothing more than to return to his Brothers and the shelter of the priory. There, behind the oak doors and granite walls, he would find safety and the security of companionship. He felt vulnerable alone in the gardens, a feeling that grew with every moment he remained.

Moving with a quickness that betrayed his inner fear, Brother Elwin made his way up the gardens towards the entrance gate and the stone steps beyond which would lead him back to the priory. The hairs on his arms stood on end and tingled and he berated himself for being so easily unnerved, like a child jumping at shadows. Despite this the sensations continued to haunt him and he glanced over at the high crags, feeling the pressure of a hidden gaze upon him.

His bony hand settled on the top bar of the gate and he hastily pulled it open, his pulse racing with adrenalin and exertion. The first drops of rain began to fall, their patter soft as he retained the presence of mind to close the gate and raised the hood of his cowl.

Setting off along the cobbled path, the rain became more incessant and beat down upon the stones. Brother Elwin soon arrived at the steps wrought into the side of the Mount, warning himself against haste as his sandals slipped in the growing dampness. The rain grew heavier and the strength of the wind increased, whipping at his hood so that he had to hold it in place with his left hand.

His ascent was steady, hips complaining with mild stabs of pain as the day became darkened by the threatening clouds. His lungs strained and his mouth was dry. As he followed the curve of the steps up the side of the Mount the rain drove into his lined face and his vision was impaired. He wiped his eyes with his right sleeve and continued to hold his hood in place as the squall held the island in its grasp.

Left foot slipping, he stumbled forward in the wind-whipped deluge. His knees clashed violently with the edge of the next step, the stone jarring him to the bone and sending shooting pains through his nerves. He stifled a yell and tried to compose himself as he knelt upon the steps, now slick with rainwater which cascaded down them in small streams.

Bracing himself for the pain he knew would flare when he attempted to rise, Brother Elwin wiped his eyes and looked up the curving flight of stone steps.

His heart leapt. A dark figure stood 10 yards up the steps and towered into the grey sky. The storm clouds were its backdrop as its black cloak snapped angrily in the wind, a grey tunic beneath tied with frayed cord. It seemed to him like some nightmare image drawn from the primitive depths of his mind, his body trembling in response.

The old monk raised his right arm before his face in an attempt at protection as the dark creature came closer, its height well over 7 feet. It descended to within a couple of steps as the wind rose further, howling like anguished souls in purgatory as the trees on the slope to the right bent under its rushing weight.

'O Lord, preserve and protect your humble servant, I beseech you,' said Brother Elwin, clasping his hands together quickly, eyes closing for a moment as he offered up his prayer for divine protection. 'Deliver me from evil, for thine is the glory in which I place my faith,' he added as he knelt like a supplicant before the huge beast.

8

The old monk, water matting the white ring of hair about his shaven crown and streaming down his lined face, opened his eyes and stared wide-eyed at the giant looming over him.

It raised its hands and Brother Elwin awaited a fatal blow which would surely come as the storm raged about the Mount.

Slowly, the towering form pulled back its hood to reveal its face. It was the face of a man in middle age, his brow large and protruding, cheeks sunken, the paleness of his skin accentuated by black curls that hung about his face and the dark, straggly beard which gave him a wild appearance. His nose was crooked, evidence of a break at some point in the past. There was a pale scar that curled his upper lip, giving the appearance of a slight sneer, something which aided in unsettling the old monk.

The giant's curls glistened in the dull light and his eyes were hidden in large pools of shadow cast by his brow. Despite this, Brother Elwin could see their light shining from within the darkness in which they rested. In that light he at once discerned no malice and a kindly desperation, a tragic longing.

'Friend.'

The solitary word was almost a whisper, but the aged monk heard it above the wind. His pulse began to slow as he stared up at the figure and felt his fear rush out of him as if torn from him in a sudden gust of wind that passed through his very being. There was no threat from the dishevelled wretch before him. All sense of alarm and foreboding was vanquished and he felt a strange serenity in the wake of these feelings which had haunted him since the early morn.

The giant stepped closer and bent over, holding out his huge right hand to the old monk kneeling before him in the storm.

Brother Elwin took it after only a brief hesitation, his hand as a child's in comparison with the stranger's. With a gentle tug, the giant pulled him to his feet, though he nearly toppled back upon the glistening steps, severe pain erupting in his knees.

The giant held him steady with hands resting firmly on Brother Elwin's shoulders.

'Thank you,' said the old monk before turning his attention downward, dizziness overcoming him and his body feeling weak.

He raised the sodden hem of the cowl and before his damaged knees were revealed he spied trails of blood making their way down his shins, the crimson diluting in the rainwater upon his sandalled feet.

'Will you help me to the priory? I fear I cannot make it alone,' he said slowly and clearly, blinking water and tears of pain from his eyes.

The black clad stranger studied him for a moment and Brother Elwin was unsure as to whether he had been able to comprehend what had been said. He was about to reiterate the request, a feeling of faintness growing and his mind increasingly indistinct, when the giant suddenly gathered him up in his arms.

The stranger turned to the ascent and, like a child cradled in the arms of an adult, Brother Elwin was slowly conveyed up the slippery steps to the priory. He felt himself overcome by frailty as the stranger took great care with each step, the progress slow. He tried to block the pain from his mind, but it was so great that it made his head swim and the world began to shift and blur about him.

Brother Elwin looked up at the face of the giant carrying him up the side of the Mount as the wind and rain continued to sweep in from the west. He blinked in an attempt to gain clarity, but all he could see was a blur of light and shadow, noting the darkness beneath the giant's large brow. He felt as if removed from reality, caught in a place of myth and legend, a half-world like that of dreams. In the arms of a giant he rested, a monster from childhood tales come to life, living and breathing.

He closed his eyes a moment and then tried once more to focus on the stranger, thinking that perhaps his mind was playing tricks on him. The pain flared. His mind struggled to retain consciousness as the periphery of his world darkened, the pitch spreading inwards as the sounds of the storm seemed to fade from his hearing.

Brother Elwin's eyes rolled back and closed as he slipped into unconsciousness, his blood seeping into the rain-soaked cloak of the unnaturally tall stranger. With the white-haired monk held securely in his arms, the giant made his way up the stone steps, the rocks to the left giving way to a view of the priory buildings as he reached the Mount's summit in the gloomy squall.

9

Jebbit stood with the other local men at the bar as they talked in low mumbles and drank brandy from tin cups. The fire crackled and danced to their right, a log collapsing into bright, glowing ashes and releasing a shower of sparks which rose like fireflies to disappear up the chimney into the night beyond. The wind howled against the thick and uneven glass of the windows as the accompanying rain beat incessantly, as it had without abatement for two days.

Sat at a bench on the far side of the King's Arms were a couple of men dressed in simple, grey robes. They were pilgrims and their faces were alive with moving shadows as the pair of candles placed between them flickered in strong draughts circulating around the tavern's interior. Before each was a wooden bowl of steaming gruel at which they sipped with spoons, the long and ardious journey fading into memory now they had found rest and sustenance at their intended destination. Such folk were a regular sight in the old tavern, where they found food and lodging. Many came to visit the holy Isle of Ictis and found shelter at the hostelry, though few mingled with the locals, remaining somewhat aloof, unlike the sailors who called in during shore leave and drank their fill, the alcohol loosening their tongues and their inhibitions.

'It will blow over by the morn, ye mark my words,' said John, who was in a sullen mood, something which was a regular occurrence since the death of his wife during childbirth and was not helped by the inclement weather. The high, howling winds of autumn and winter always brought with them a deep melancholy which sometimes verged on a bleak madness that he could not shake from his mind.

'I hope ye be right,' said Jebbit. 'Such miserable days of windswept chill bite to my very bones.'

'I thought ye would have been used to this after so many years of toil upon the land,' said Morgan as he sat at the table beside the fire, feeling more at home seated near the flames than standing at the bar with the other men. Mary sat beside him wearing a green dress which accentuated her ample curves. She was draped against his muscular body, head resting upon him as her long, black hair cascaded to her bare shoulders. Her softly lined eyes sparkled, skin like snow, lips full and filled with temptation.

'At least the smithy has warmth,' responded the farmhand. 'Maybe we should join ye there until the rains and wind pass.'

Morgan frowned and raised his cup, taking a swig of his brandy. He wiped his lips with the back of his hand as Mary nuzzled his neck, her hand upon his thigh beneath the table.

'I am not so certain these storms will pass by the morrow,' said George Pascoe, looking at the other farmer with his one eye. 'The cattle have settled and tis a sure sign of more to come.'

'Aye, and did ye also check the consistency of their dung in your predictions of the weather?' asked Richard as he topped up his own cup from an earthenware jug, the landlord's face flushed by his consumption.

The group erupted into laughter as George looked sullenly at the landlord and drank his brandy, filled with a sense of injustice as the battered cup was raised to his lips.

The front door opened and a man in a deep blue cloak entered with the swirling winds of the gale, his face hidden by a leather hood. The eyes of the local men and two pilgrims assessed the newcomer who had braved the stormy night as he shut the door and the winds that had reached in were barred from further entry. His clothes were of fine material and well tailored. There was a walking cane in his left hand and Jebbit noticed the sparkle of a blue jewel atop its carved handle. He was clearly a man of some wealth.

The man turned to those gathered at the bar and lowered his hood with purposeful slowness. The face beneath was of good bearing, with high cheekbones and unblemished skin, well fed and his beard well groomed. His hair and eyes were dark, and his confident gaze held the spectators for an instant before his pale lips curled slightly, the smile they created neither friendly nor malicious, more akin to a statement of intent.

He untied the cloak from about his neck and took it off with a gentle flourish, hanging it with others on a pillar near the cellar door, water dripping from its hem to darken the sawdust on the floor. Stepping over to the bar, his cane clipping on the flagstones beneath the wood shavings, the local men silently parted. He untied a weighty purse of black velvet from the cord about the waist of his pale blue tunic, the sound of coins audible to all as he allowed its weight to shift on the palm of his right hand.

'Brandy please, innkeep,' he stated simply as he looked at Richard, noting with satisfaction that he had been staring at the bulging purse.

Richard uncorked an earthenware jug after putting a tin cup on the bar. The regulars gathered to either side of the man remained wordless as the drink was poured. As soon as the cup was filled the stranger lifted it and drank every last drop, putting the vessel back on the bar and wiping his lips with the back of his hand before sighing with contentment.

'Another,' he instructed, Richard still holding the uncorked jug, his large eyes a little bloodshot and pot belly resting against the bar.

The stranger's cup was refilled and the man looked at each curious face in turn. 'Would anyone care to join me in a drink?'

'That be a kind offer from someone travelled so far,' said Morgan as he sat at the table beside the fire, his words spoken in the hope the man would reveal his origins.

The man's smile grew almost imperceptibly. He found people easy to manipulate and to read, something which never ceased to amaze him considering the apparent complexity of the human animal at first sight. 'I have journeyed from Winchester and the road has been long,' he stated, his words steady and filled with self-assurance.

The locals shared a few glances.

'Winchester,' nodded John knowingly. 'I hear of a new cathedral being built there. How goes the work?'

The man shrugged. 'As well as can be expected in such inclement weather, but my affairs do not involve me in such a magnificent task.'

There was a pregnant pause as the stranger picked up his tin cup and Richard topped up the vessels of the locals who stood along the bar.

'What be your affairs?' asked Morgan, stilling Mary's hand with his own as it stroked his thigh.

The man's eyes sparkled. He noted that the landlord had completed the task of filling the other men's cups and raised his into the air. 'Here's to your good health, gentlemen,' he toasted.

The locals raised their cups and all drank of the brandy which had been poured.

The man waited until all attention was again centred upon him. 'My name is Baines and I come here on business,' he stated, resting his drink on the bar.

'John Hadden,' the farmer said in introduction, taking Baines' hand in a firm grasp as they shook their greeting. 'What be the business that has brought ye all the way from Winchester?'

Baines allowed a short pause as the local men waited expectantly for his reply. 'I am searching for lost property.'

'Lost property?' said John with a questioning look.

'I seek a creature bound to me by law and a father's disregard. This is no ordinary creature, mind. This is a beast the likes of which you will rarely see.'

'A beast you say?' said George, his eye widening as he cast a sideways glance towards Jebbit.

Baines looked from face-to-face and it was plain that his audience were captive. 'Aye, a beast. A wretched beast of such height as to be a monstrous giant.'

John looked at Jebbit, whose weathered face drained of colour. 'Jebbit there saw a creature not three nights past.'

Baines turned his attention to the stocky farmhand. 'I would have you tell me of its appearance, but before you

35

answer, know that I shall reward well the man whose words or actions lead me to the beast.'

Jebbit looked at the man, his eyes sparkling with the promise of reward. 'I did not see the beast's face, but it were larger than any man I ever set eyes on.'

Baines studied the expression on Jebbit's face and noted the fear in his grey eyes. 'Where did you come across this beast?'

'Atop the hill behind the town. It were lurking with malice behind a hedgerow. A demon of some kind I thought.' Jebbit glanced down at the dog which lay before the fire with grey muzzle resting on its front paws and eyes closed, back legs kicking a little as it dreamed. 'My dog was as disturbed as I by its presence.'

The gathered men bore expressions of seriousness as Baines remained thoughtful and silent, turning to stare at his cup momentarily.

'Do ye think it were the beast ye searches for?' asked Jebbit quietly.

Baines lifted his cup and took a swig of his brandy. 'There is no way to be sure. Can you take me to the site where this monster was seen?'

Jebbit frowned. 'We sought out the beast, but found little evidence of its passing. With the storms, all trace will now have been lost.'

'There were marks in the grass and mud, and it had trodden heavily upon a rotted branch,' said John. 'Morgan led our party as we tried to seek the creature out.' He nodded at the blacksmith by the fire.

The wealthy newcomer turned to the muscular man, the firelight dancing upon the smith's chiselled features as he gently pushed Mary from his shoulder and she sat up straight upon her chair. 'Did you discover the direction in which it travelled?'

'West,' replied Morgan, holding the other man's gaze.

Baines nodded and swigged his brandy again.

'Do ye think this beast ye seek be the same as that which Jebbit saw?' asked Richard, his left hand once more upon the bar to act as a support.

Baines studied the men before him as they awaited his reply, their faces alive with shadows and skin overlaid with yellow light. 'I cannot answer, for without sight of the beast or some token of its passing there is no true way to tell.' He downed the last of his drink and placed the cup on the bar, nodding at Richard. 'But there is one thing of which you can be sure,' he stated as his cup was refilled, leaving a brief silence before continuing, the fire crackling and the wind and rain buffeting the windows. 'I will find this wayward creature, even if I must winter in these western lands.'

'Is it truly of such worth as to expend so much time and effort?' asked John, curious as to how such a beast could be of so much importance to a man who clearly had wealth.

'No creature who is bound to me can release itself from servitude without my decree. Only my own hand or that of death can release it so,' replied Baines with a firmness to his tone.

The local men fell silent as they noted the conviction in Baines' tone, his eyes steely with resolve to track down the beast which had fled its master.

'Do you have rooms here where a traveller may rest for the night?'

'Aye,' replied Richard with a nod. 'Do ye intend to stay long?'

'I shall stay but one night. Then I shall head west if that is truly the direction in which it departed,' said Baines, looking at the blacksmith.

'It is,' confirmed Morgan with a curt nod.

'I will leave details of my Winchester residence so that if any of you happen upon the beast or evidence of its location you may contact me, but I must leave you with a stern warning.'

The local men stared at Baines in expectation, the tone of the stranger's voice giving rise to a touch of apprehension as the wind rose and howled outside and the candles about the tavern's interior flickered wildly in the ensuing draughts. A few nervous glances were exchanged, the Tupp twins leaning closer from their usual position by the back door and Jebbit holding his breath with wide-eyed anticipation.

'Do not approach this creature. Do not go near its vile existence, for it is evil through and through,' whispered the man who had everyone's full attention. 'My leg ...' he said with a glance at his left leg. 'It was disabled by the beast when I let my guard down. I had begun to trust it, to treat it almost as a real man, but my trust was greatly misplaced. It deceived me and not a day goes by that I am not reminded of such.' He raised his walking cane in the air to illustrate his last point.

'What did it do?' asked Jebbit quietly.

'It grabbed me with great violence, its large hands leaving dark bruises upon my body. Into my shin it sank its teeth, so deep that the bone shattered in the grip of its powerful jaw and it has ne'er fully healed, infected as it was by the beast's utter foulness.

'There was no provocation. It attacked me as I brought it food, as I showed it kindness. I tell you now, it is an evil which may try to take on the guise of a man without malice, but malice is the blood in its veins. It is the spawn of the devil and because of this is cursed in appearance. You mark my words, its unnaturalness is no accident. It has been marked out by God in order that we should know the blackness of its heart.'

Baines raised his cup to his lips and swigged the brandy as Jebbit looked at his left leg. The stranger noted the direction of the farmhand's gaze and placed his cup upon the bar. He bent down, the eyes of the regulars following his every move, the Tupp twins straining to look over George Pascoe's shoulders.

With deliberate slowness, he lifted the hem of his long tunic to reveal the scars of a deep bite upon his shin. Each scar was an indent marked with shadows which gathered beyond the light of the candles and open fire.

Baines looked up at the peering faces and then hid the old wound, straightening and grasping his tin cup. 'Heed my warning. No matter how it may appear, the beast is utterly evil.'

10

Brother Elwin woke, mind filled with a groggy lethargy. He opened his blue eyes and found the indistinct world about him coated in a warm yellow glow. He blinked in an attempt to focus, but all remained blurred and without definition.

Trying to raise his head, he felt a palm press softly upon his brow and force it gently back to the pillow.

'Do not try to move, you must first regain your strength.' The words drifted into his mind as though part of a fading dream.

'Brother Cook?' he asked weakly, his voice rasping.

'Yes,' came the reply.

There was a moment of silence and the sound of high winds seemed to emanate from some distant quarter.

'I dreamt of evil coming,' said Brother Elwin quietly, closing his eyes and relaxing against the pillow and the vague firmness of the cot beneath him. 'Is he ...?'

Sitting at the old man's side, the youthful monk nodded despite his Brother being unable to see the confirmation. 'Yes. Prior Vargas granted him sanctuary. If it were not for the stranger's actions we fear you may have been lost,' he said as Mrs Hyne, the butcher's wife, stood silently beside him and regarded the patient after being summoned from the mainland due to her knowledge and stores of medicinal herbs.

A vision of the giant filled Brother Elwin's mind, his features viewed as if underwater, shadows collected beneath his protruding brow and from within them the sparkle of dark eyes clearly visible. His cloak flapped in a gale which was strangely silent, black curls matted with grease and rain.

'How long have I been here?' he asked, the words taking great effort as he tried to concentrate his thoughts.

'It has been two full days, but it will be many more until you are fit to rise and rejoin us,' replied Brother Cook as he took hold of Brother Elwin's withered left hand, holding it tightly within his hands as he looked upon the drawn face of his friend. 'Though we are all grateful that the Lord saw fit to preserve you.'

Brother Elwin forced a thin smile as pain began to intrude. 'Thank you,' he whispered, managing to squeeze Brother Cook's hands with a gentleness born of frailty.

The pain grew. He winced, eyes tightening. His muscles were filled with aches and stiffness, but a constant, throbbing pain arose from his wounded knees, his teeth clenching as he fought against the agonies in his nerves.

'No!' exclaimed Brother Elwin with a surprising strength of voice and feeling, his eyes remaining shut.

Brother Cook looked upon his charge and thought the outburst was related to the dream the old monk had mentioned, one which still floated in his delirious mind. He saw the sheen of perspiration building upon the monk's forehead, the droplets capturing the candlelight as a solitary flame on the bedside table flickered in hidden draughts. He released the hand that had grown limp in his and then took a cloth from the table which rested to his right. Dipping it in the bowl of cool water beside the white candle, he then leant forward and mopped his patient's brow.

'Do you think he will recover fully, Mrs Hyne?' he asked the rotund woman with ruddy cheeks.

'I fear he will be left with a permanent limp. At his age such injuries are rarely sustained without some lasting impediment.' Mrs Hyne rubbed the side of her bulbous nose.

'Do you think he will still find the strength to descend to the priory's gardens?'

'In time,' nodded the herbalist.

'Good,' replied Brother Cook, knowing how precious the gardens were to the old monk before him. 'Thank you once again for taking the trouble to come to our aid. Our stores of herbs are much depleted and I fear we would not have had enough if it were not for your kind assistance.'

'It is of no bother,' she assured the monk.

'Could you please pass on our regards to your husband and thank him for the side of pork he brought over yesterday.'

'I shall,' nodded Mrs Hyne.

Brother Cook turned back to his charge. The old monk's face became increasingly taut with signs of pain, the old, leathery skin tightening, wrinkles losing some of their depth as his jaw clenched tightly and tendons flexed beneath.

Brother Elwin slipped from consciousness, the muscles in his thin face falling back from their tension, the monk's features softening into the semblance of deep sleep.

'May the Blessed Virgin Mary watch over you, Brother Elwin,' whispered Brother Cook as he brushed strands of white hair from the aged monk's forehead, where they had become caught in the moisture of mingled water and sweat.

11

B rother Cook walked beside Brother Elwin, who was
struggling to descend the stone steps despite the use
of wooden crutches. It was an unseasonably warm
day in late January and the sun shone in the clear sky above
as the old monk paused for rest.

'Are you sure you will not return to your cell and try
the full descent when fully healed?' asked Brother Cook,
both his tone and expression filled with concern as
Brother Elwin wiped his brow and took deep breaths.

'I know patience is a virtue, dear Brother, but I cannot
remain cooped up within those walls any longer. My patience
has grown thin and I feel like an animal in a cage. All I ask is
to be able to sit on my bench for a while within the joys of
nature.' Brother Elwin held the young monk's well-meaning
gaze. 'I do not think that is too much to ask.' He smiled at the
monk who had spent more time than any other at his bedside.

Brother Cook smiled faintly, though the concern was
still evident in his dark eyes. 'No, it is not too much to ask,'
he nodded, all the monks fully aware of Brother Elwin's
love of nature and his habit of spending his sparse free time
either wandering the gardens or finding tranquillity upon
his bench positioned on the high northern terrace.

The young monk looked down the steps as four pilgrims
came up towards them. 'We should wait for them to pass,'
he said with a nod ahead.

Brother Elwin looked at the men dressed in dark,
hooded tunics and stepped to the side, the rocks of the
Mount rising directly to his right.

The four men nodded their thanks as they drew near, their bare feet silent upon the carved rock. The tap of a walking stick marked their steady progress, borne by an elderly man with a long, grey beard, the edge of his hood casting a shadow over his downcast eyes. They made their ascent with a considered pace and passed with heads bowed slightly as they headed for the priory in order to give gifts and praise the Lord upon the summit of the Holy Isle.

'Let us continue,' said Brother Elwin, carefully descending to the next step and not moving on until both feet were firmly planted upon it.

The descent was slow and laborious, but the old monk was filled with a determination that the throbbing pain in his healing knees could not shake. He wanted more than anything to look out over the gardens and the ocean beyond, to feel the sea breeze upon his lined face as the swells of the waves rolled in with the tide.

'What of the stranger?' asked the elderly monk, wishing to turn his mind from the pain.

'There is little to tell,' replied Brother Cook. 'He is rarely seen and does not speak a word to anyone.'

Brother Elwin nodded thoughtfully. 'Is he really as tall as the image my mind conjures?'

'Yes,' nodded the young monk. 'Well over 7 feet,' he added.

They fell into silence and the minutes passed with drawn-out slowness as Brother Cook hovered at Brother Elwin's side, ready should the old monk slip or fall. He had not spent so many hours nursing his Brother only to see him break his body once more so soon after his recovery to walking health. For days he had fretted over the unconscious form lying in the cot beside him. Amidst the peaceful restfulness had been times of fearful flushes, of back-arching pain and terrifying convulsions. Many a time he had feared the loss of the priory's most treasured and most gentle Brother and he thanked the Lord for returning him to the land of the living despite the shadow of death having been gathered about the bed.

Brother Elwin tottered and released the crutch in his left hand, the thin wood clattering on the stone as he raised his hand to his forehead and closed his eyes.

Brother Cook rushed to his side, supporting him with an arm about his shoulders as the old monk swayed precariously.

He took deep, steadying breaths as the dizziness abated and he opened his blue eyes. Brother Elwin turned to his companion, his face pale. 'Maybe I overestimate my own recuperation,' he admitted with a pained expression, his legs weak.

'Let me guide you back to the priory after you have regained some strength,' responded Brother Cook.

Brother Elwin nodded weakly. 'It is wrong what they say about wisdom and age,' he said with a vague smile. 'You are wiser than I, Brother Cook, despite your apparent youthfulness. Next time you would do well to remind me of your insight and stop an old man from indulging his foolishness.'

'I see no fool beside me,' said Brother Cook, his arm still about the thin shoulders of his fellow monk. 'I see a beloved friend whom I would have restored to full health before attempting the descent to the gardens again.'

'Thank you for your kindness.' Brother Elwin looked into the young monk's eyes, his words and gaze expressing more than a mere gratefulness for his help on the steps, but a deep gratitude for all that Brother Cook had done.

The young monk smiled warmly. 'Maybe we could have the bench brought to you rather than you having to risk life and limb in attempting to reach its restfulness.'

Brother Elwin returned the smile, but shook his head. 'The thought of its welcoming peace upon my return to fitness is a motivation which I would not be without.' He paused a moment, glancing down the curved flight of steps upon which they had yet to reach half distance. 'Though a chair upon the southern bluffs would not be a kindness I should soon forget.'

'A chair it shall be,' said Brother Cook. 'I will see to it once you are returned to your cell in safety. You are my charge and I would ne'er hear the last of it should further harm come your way.'

Brother Elwin nodded his consent.

'Are you recovered from the spell of dizziness?'

'Yes,' said the old monk, his legs still weak and knees throbbing with incessant pain.

Brother Cook removed his arm from Brother Elwin's shoulders and crouched to retrieve the fallen crutch. He passed it to the elderly monk, who carefully turned to face the climb which seemed so forbidding now his strength had waned. He had not known his own limits and was glad for Brother Cook's company and greater understanding of his condition. His slow, crutch-aided wanderings about the priory had filled him with false confidence in his own abilities. When he was younger his recovery would have been speedier and more complete, but with age came a drawn-out convalescence and the possibility that a full recovery might never occur.

He began the ascent one careful step at a time, his jaw clenching as the weight of his small, thin frame became almost unbearable. Brother Cook lingered patiently at his side, intent upon Brother Elwin's face, fearful of another bout of dizziness as they rose to the heights of the Mount.

12

Brother Elwin descended the steps alone. The chill wind pulled at his brown cowl with invisible and insistent fingers, the ends of the cord tied about his waist gaining a life of their own, hood raised over his head. It had been a month since the attempted descent with Brother Cook at his side and he had often thought of this day, of being able to visit the gardens once more. He had been attending to his monastic duties for some weeks, despite Prior Vargas having let it be known that such was not expected of him so soon after his recovery. Upon his first appearance in the refectory there had been expressions of much gladness made by the eleven monks, who greeted his return to them with joy. Even the prior displayed a rare smile upon his tight lips as he watched the Brothers gather about the old man, their silence and contemplation temporarily forgotten and only regained after Prior Vargas loudly cleared his throat, the sound echoing around the simple granite hall with its two long tables set between wooden benches.

The aged monk breathed deep the winter air and smelt the ocean's scent as he had during the many hours sitting on the chair that Brother Cook had placed on the southern bluffs. During inclement weather he had been forced to retreat from high winds which brutally tore at the heights, sheets of stinging rain whipped with great fury at the exposed summit. There had been many times he had found himself sat on the edge of his cot listening to the wind and wishing he could go to his bench with its vista over the gardens. It had a degree of shelter from the elements as it rested against the north terrace's stone wall with the boughs of an evergreen draped overhead, nature's protective canopy.

Now, at last, he was fit and able. Though his knees still ached, the pain had lessened to such a degree as to be ignored, shut away in the recesses of his mind as he stepped gingerly down towards the gardens and could not help but feel a sense of excited anticipation.

He had been informed that the giant was in the gardens before the descent and had waited a long time to set eyes on the man once again. Though he had hoped to see him in the priory, Brother Elwin had only caught a couple of brief glimpses of the stranger, whose existence was akin to that of a ghost haunting the granite buildings clustered atop the Mount.

The monk's recollections of the stormy day when he had slipped upon the stone steps were vague, but he could recall the giant who had lifted him and borne him to safety. He had believed the man's size to be a conjuring trick of his mind until Brother Cook had informed him otherwise. He had also heard from young Brother Thomas that one of the local men from Marghas Byghan had seen a large creature upon the hill above the town about the time of the stranger's arrival and thought it likely the giant was the creature that had been sighted.

Brother Elwin could recall the feelings that had caused his careless flight from the gardens on the stormy November day. It was his own foolishness, his own lack of self-control and judgement which had caused the fateful accident. The blame did not lie with any other but himself.

He reached the bottom of the steps, the path leading to the harbour and its warehouses branching off to the left as he made for the gate a few yards ahead. Its hinges creaked with comforting familiarity as Brother Elwin entered the gardens, the sound of his footfalls softened by grass. His gaze immediately fell on the dark figure crouched below, bent over one of the vegetable patches as he tilled the rich earth with a trowel which seemed like a child's toy in his huge hands.

Brother Elwin paused as the gate swung shut with the gentle tap of wood upon wood. Moving to the right, he began to make his way along the north terrace path that would lead him to the bench. He cast intrigued glances towards the stranger, whose dark cloak was draped upon the ground about him, its hem dirtied with mud. The giant did not seem to have noticed he had company in the gardens, so intent was he on the task at hand. The lack of acknowledgement made the old monk feel at ease and without threat, the tension which had been rising in the pit of his stomach dissipating.

Brother Elwin arrived at the old bench. He smiled at it in fondness. It had been over thirty years since he had collected all the timber required to create the seat. Some he had discovered abandoned at the harbour and other planks had been surplus to the materials needed for a shed which had fallen prey to the elements during the intervening years, the only evidence of its prior existence a thick pile of ivy beside the eastern wall of the gardens. The arms of the bench had been made of driftwood found upon the Mount's shore and he felt glad of their use and the time spent whittling away the bark to reveal the knotted paleness beneath. They spoke of nature, adding a sense of connection between the rough seat and its surroundings.

Sitting with a slowness that allowed him to savour the moment for which he had so longed, the seat creaking a gentle greeting, Brother Elwin's smile grew. His creation had stood the test of time with little need of repair. Ever since its construction he had regularly sat upon its timbers and found peace within the embrace of its arms of yew. The life of a monk was a frugal one of structured repetition, but unlike the others who inhabited the priory, he had included this as one of his regular forms of worship, for where else was the Lord's bounty clearer than in the majesty and workings of nature?

He relaxed against the seat and rested his right arm on the twisted yew branch beside him, his bony fingers gently and absent-mindedly caressing the grain with soft strokes. A feeling of contentment filled him with a gladdening warmth of spirit as he looked out across the gardens to the rough ocean beyond. White peaks rose above troughs as the waves came in, spray torn from them by the blustery wind. A constant roar filled the air as rollers crashed upon the rocks.

His gaze turned to the giant who continued to work with obvious care, intent upon the earth before him. Brother Elwin wondered about this stranger, about his life and the reasons for his seeking sanctuary upon the island. He had heard tell of many priories and monasteries taking in those of misfortune, those cast out by society because of their difference. They were given shelter and sustenance in return for labour, but never had another come to seek such things on the Mount of St Michael in all his years of residence, and this gave the newcomer an added sense of mystery which set questions in the old monk's mind. What had he done prior to his arrival? Was he a heathen fallen on evil times or was the evil within him? Was he the perpetrator of some foul deed, a villain in hiding?

Brother Elwin shook his head to clear his mind of such pointless wonderings. He briefly entertained the thought of rising and approaching the man, but cast it aside when he felt tension begin to rise within him again. No, he would remain patient. Maybe he would never discover the truth, a truth that this man had so far kept hidden within the dark folds of the cloak with which he surrounded himself. As far as Brother Cook could discern, the stranger's only word had been that which he had spoken to Brother Elwin and so nothing was known of him, not even his name.

'Friend,' the monk whispered to himself, the sound quickly ushered away by the strengthening winds, the stranger remaining crouched beneath the leaden sky as the first drops of rain began to fall, the clouds washed with shades of grey and touched with the blue of winter's lingering chill.

13

It was over a week until Brother Elwin again made his way to the gardens and in that time he had seen neither hide nor hair of the giant, though he knew the enigmatic stranger watched the services which took place in the chapel on the summit of the Mount. The man had been granted sanctuary in an anteroom off the chapel, reached by a small, but steep flight of stone stairs, the doorway to the room affording him a view of Prior Vargas as he gave his sermons and thanks to the Lord through prayer. The room was used as a store for the priory's valuables in times of conflict, but was currently empty and so had been given over to the visitor. It was felt proper that the heathen be within earshot of holy worship so the grace of the Lord could fill his spirit and he could find forgiveness for sins he may have committed, sins which may have chased him to the Mount of St Michael and would always tarnish his soul until the Day of Judgement.

The westerly storms had finally broken during the previous evening and now, in the early hours of the morn before his Brothers awoke and rose in readiness for psalms, Brother Elwin made his way into the gardens beneath the full moon, not a cloud visible in the sky. The gardens were coated in soft quicksilver which drained colours from the landscape. The ocean was also monotone, the ever shifting waters with the look of tarnished steel as the moon shone its stolen light upon them from the eastern sky.

The monk made his way along the edge of the gardens. His sandalled feet were caressed by the dewy lips of laden grass as he descended the gentle slope to the southerly borders and the wind-sculpted evergreens that ran along the wall there.

The alarm call of a gull echoed off the distant cliffs below the town of Marghas Byghan. He paused and looked towards the mainland lying to his left. His blue eyes scanned for any evidence of disturbance as he raised his hand to cover his mouth and coughed lightly.

His gaze settled upon the figure walking along the pale sand and shingle of the eastern beach, stretches of dark rock marching to the cliffs at either end of the beach's gentle curve, their shadows mingled with swathes of dark seaweed revealed by low tide. The height of its shadowy form left him in no doubt as to the identity. The stranger slowly meandered between the dark silhouettes of scattered rocks which rose from the sands.

Brother Elwin watched in silence as the figure crouched for a moment, the old monk narrowing his eyes in order to retain sight of him in the silver-clad darkness. He could not discern the man's actions and felt his curiosity rise as the giant rose to his full height and once more began to stroll along the beach with dark cloak gathered about him.

A little further and he crouched again as if studying the sand at his feet in the moonlight. Brother Elwin could see him reach down before him and wondered at the purpose of the giant's actions. There were so many unanswered questions that he longed to ask, but it was not his way to intrude or pry, as was the case with all the Brothers who dwelt at the priory. The man had come for sanctuary, not an inquisition, and his reasons were his own to withhold or reveal as he saw fit. None would enquire of him as to his past or his affairs unless there was need.

Brother Elwin watched the man a while longer as he continued along the beach, moving further east and becoming increasingly indistinct as he regularly paused to crouch and examine the sands before him, the white-topped surf occasionally surrounding and washing up against him, though he apparently remained oblivious to the chill waters.

The old monk tore his gaze away and looked up to the priory. Candlelight spilled from the stained-glass windows of the chapel high above and he knew it was time to return. Glancing up at the dusted globe that hung in the dark firmament amidst a halo of paleness, Brother Elwin then began to make his way back to the gate, his mind turning to the day's duties as he pushed all curiosity from his mind.

14

He sat silently on his bench, the growing warmth of the sun upon his lined face. For two months he had seen the giant in passing either in the gardens or walking along the beach of Marghas Byghan in the early hours. The seeker of sanctuary remained a stranger to all, keeping himself to himself as he went about his tending within the gardens. The old monk had never witnessed him there during the times he and his Brothers had toiled either in the vegetable patches where the crops were now green with spring growth, or amidst the fruit trees on the western slopes beside the rocky crags that rose to the priory. Only when he spent precious moments of peaceful contemplation upon his old bench had Brother Elwin seen the man working in attentive silence.

Many had been the occasions when he had wished to approach the stranger, whose cloak became increasingly ragged and whose feet were always wrapped in threadbare cloth of dark grey, but the man's demeanour was one which forbade intrusion. He never looked up, keeping the secrets in his eyes hidden. He never made so much as a gesture to acknowledge Brother Elwin's presence. He also kept himself perpetually hidden when within the confines of the priory, though Prior Vargas had witnessed him watching many a sermon, apparently bearing an expression of sad wonder as the Latin words of worship echoed round the small chapel and light pierced its interior through stained glass; bright beams from heaven where eddies of dust glimmered in the hush. He had not been seen eating in the refectory and had at first been a subject of great curiosity, though this had diminished as the stranger's routines became commonplace.

Brother Elwin sighed as the white sails of a merchant ship became visible on the horizon. On this day the giant was not to be seen within the gardens and the old monk found himself missing the man's presence, the diligent tenderness evident in his work bringing with it an additional sense of calm and goodness.

He coughed as his gaze continued to rest on the ship which was ever drawing closer to the Mount. It was one of many that came with cargos from the warmer climes of the Mediterranean, cargos that had been traded for tin and copper taken from the deep mines which had been dug into the land and followed its lodes, the crude smelting chimneys of these mines rising all about the fair lands of the west. Soon the vessel would dock at the island's jetty and be emptied and its sailors would seek a place to spend their wages on the mainland, arriving there by rowboat at high tide and across the bar of sand and shingle at low.

Despite the closeness of the harbour and its accompanying warehouses there were rarely any intrusions of noise from the activities which took place there.

A large, dark form appeared in Brother Elwin's peripheral vision and disturbed his reverie. He turned in surprise to find the stranger standing to his left, his black curls straggly and unkempt. The giant towered over him and held his gaze a moment before nodding silently at the bench beside the old monk.

'You are welcome to join me, friend,' Brother Elwin said in answer to the unspoken enquiry.

The stranger gathered his cloak and sat beside the monk, the timbers creaking beneath his weight. His hands rested within the folds of cloth upon his lap and he stared out to sea, his dark eyes settling on the approaching ship as Brother Elwin studied his profile. The brow was large and protruding and he recalled the pools of shadow it had cast in the man's eye sockets when he had stood before him upon the steps in the rain and high winds. The dark hair upon his face was thick and bushy, his lips all but hidden by the moustache and beard which added to his dishevelled appearance. His height was substantial, but his frame thin beneath the rough clothes, almost emaciated from what the monk could deduce, the man's sunken cheeks confirming this estimation.

Realising that he was staring, Brother Elwin turned his attention back to the sea. He was filled with eager questions, but put voice to none as the man wrapped himself in an impenetrable silence. The old monk did not dare break it, could not bring himself to intrude into the privacy the stranger so clearly longed to retain.

At the edge of his vision he could see that the giant made no movements bar the almost imperceptible rise and fall of his chest beneath the cloak. The man remained motionless as they shared the seat that had so often been Brother Elwin's place of solitude and retreat. He could not recall another time when he had been accompanied upon its timbers and felt a little curious as to why he did not find the presence of the man disconcerting. He had allowed the stranger to sit where a Brother had never been seated.

Brother Elwin sought out the root behind this fact as he watched the merchant ship sail beyond sight around the western side of the Mount to his right, hidden by the rocky bluffs beneath the priory. The truth came to him in an instant of clarity. There were no demands put upon him by the stranger. There was no expectation to converse. With the stranger by his side the tranquillity he found while sitting upon the bench could remain greatly undisturbed and without the pressures of social intercourse.

He smiled to himself, lines about his eyes deepening. A familiar bell rang out three times across the gardens in a summons to dinner. Brother Elwin looked at the giant, who turned to him, his expression giving no clue as to his inner thoughts or emotions, though his eyes were filled with a peaceful sadness.

'I must go,' said the old monk.

The man nodded.

'Before I leave you there is one thing I must say, for I have a debt of gratitude.' He paused and allowed a faint smile to grace his thin lips. 'Thank you,' he stated simply, his words filled with conviction as he held the stranger's gaze.

The man nodded once more and Brother Elwin thought he saw a fleeting glimmer of happiness in his dark eyes.

The monk stood. 'Fare ye well, friend,' he said. 'And may the Lord watch over you,' he added, before walking away along the northern terrace path.

15

Summer was upon the land and the sun's warmth lay comfortingly on Brother Elwin's face as he sat upon the bench, his lined eyes narrowed against the glare from the glittering ocean. A feeling of meditative peace had settled upon him. Birdsong filled the branches of the evergreens and fruit trees, the latter in full leaf, the last spring blossoms fading on the ground beneath the boughs after falling with the softness of snowflakes. Crickets chirruped in their hiding places in the tall grasses beside the bench as bees visited the scattered wild flowers, butterflies fluttering on the gentle breeze that rose from the south.

The giant walked up to the seat without his cloak in the growing heat, garbed in a simple linen tunic of pale grey, stained by sweat and toil and ripped in numerous places. The man nodded towards the vacant space on the seat, as he had on numerous occasions, never a word passing his lips.

Brother Elwin nodded his consent, as was the habit. The stranger settled to his left, the sound of the timbers creaking now familiar and comforting as the giant entered his domain of peacefulness and partook of the natural beauty which had recovered full wakefulness after winter's sleep.

They sat in contented silence, but Brother Elwin detected a vague air of tension. He had felt such on their previous two meetings, the giant apparently struggling with some inner turmoil. The stranger had a tense stiffness not usually evident in his wide shoulders, something the monk gleaned with surreptitious glances.

The silence drew out and Brother Elwin felt the change in his companion more keenly with each passing moment as a blackbird called out in alarm and a buzzard passed casually over the gardens.

'What is your name?' the words were cumbersome, but clear, the giant's voice deep and surprisingly sonorous.

Brother Elwin turned to him in shock and found the man looking at him intently. 'My name is Arthur Elwin,' he replied after regaining his composure, feeling the pressure of the giant's expectant gaze. 'Though the other monks call me Brother Elwin.'

The giant nodded. 'Arthur Elwin,' he echoed, glancing out to sea. 'It is the name of a good man, I think.'

'Thank you,' said Arthur, noticing the loneliness within the stranger's eyes. 'May I enquire of your name?'

The man looked down at his lap, his hands clasped tightly together. 'I do not remember,' he replied, looking up at the old monk.

'You do not remember?' Arthur's brow was furrowed, lines deepening, their shadows pale in the sunlight.

He shook his head. 'I have not been called by my name since a young child.'

'What have you been known by?'

The giant turned to look at the sea, searching for the right words and his mind filled with tortuous images of the past as his gaze settled on two fishing boats rising and falling upon the swell. 'My father used lots of names,' he said, voice becoming quieter and thick with emotion, 'but I was most recently called "Beast".' Memories coupled with great sadness sparkled in his dark eyes.

Arthur looked at his miserable countenance and wondered whether he should pry further, but the giant continued without need of encouragement.

'My father was a drunkard and I took beatings at the lash of his belt every day and night. My birth had been the death of my mother and for that he could ne'er forgive,' said the giant as he continued to stare across the waves, his jaw tense and a faraway look in his eyes.

'He called me a murderer, a killer, a child born of great sin and marked by it through ugliness.' The giant's voice trembled slightly and he took a deep breath. 'He was punishing me for the sin I committed. Then he could bear sight of me no longer and I was left without a home, living on the streets of London with others of ill fortune.' His voice trembled and he took another deep breath by which to calm himself. The memories arising were painful, uncovering wounds that ran deeply and had yet to heal.

Arthur sat in silence. It was clear the giant needed to tell his tale of woe, to release all which had been pent up inside. He was finding release in the sharing of his sorry history. He was opening the door to the cage of his mind.

'I was taken to an orphanage and there found shelter, but little kindness. Soon my height was beyond all others and I found myself sold to a man who put me in chains, treating me like an animal as we went about towns and cities so people could stare in horror and wonder at my form.

'It was called a freak show and I was but one of the people to which he acted as master. A woman of very short stature was there also, as was a man with the arms and legs of a child, another with lower limbs missing who walked on his hands, and a bearded lady who was the only one of our number who was not bound by chains or kept under lock and key.

'Of that strange collection of unfortunates I was the Beast, as he called me and announced me to the crowds who gathered to look at us as creatures of entertainment. I would lift great weights and even my fellow unfortunates in displays of great strength, all the time harbouring dreams of freedom which I thought would ne'er bear fruit, but only act as a constant torment.'

The giant fell silent as Arthur studied his face. At last the barriers had fallen and he had revealed himself so unexpectedly. It was as if a dam had burst and the past which the man had held within had rushed out in a torrent of anguish.

'It saddens me to hear your tale, my friend,' said the old monk in a whisper. 'No one should have to endure such things or be treated in such a deplorable way.'

The giant looked into his eyes. 'I have ne'er before had a friend,' he said.

'Your friend I am, one who owes you his life.'

'Surely you owe me nothing. I am but a sinner.'

'Because your mother died in childbirth?'

The man nodded.

Arthur shook his head. 'That is no sin, a misfortune of the most terrible kind, but certainly no sin.'

The giant searched Arthur's gaze. 'Is that what you truly believe?'

Arthur reached out and gently placed his hand on the man's shoulder. 'I do. Your father was blinded by his loss and grief. He was mistaken.'

The giant's eyes sparkled with tears as a great weight was lifted, one which he had borne since his troubled childhood. It had been a crushingly heavy burden upon his shoulders, but was now lifted by the words of a man of God.

'Thank you,' he said quietly. 'Your debt of life is repaid, for you, dear friend, have just vanquished some of the darkness from mine.'

Arthur smiled, his hand remaining on the giant's shoulder as silence descended, the tension of earlier now lifted.

After a few moments the old monk removed his hand and turned to the vista afforded them as they sat on the seat. The trials of his life were trivial in comparison with those of the man beside him. Times of hardship had been few and he had been young when first joining the order, the span of his life having mostly been spent in service to the Lord.

'Arthur?'

The monk turned to his companion. 'Yes, friend.'

'You do not mind that I have broken the silence which has lingered between us so long?'

Arthur shook his head. 'No. I am glad you think me worthy as a confidant and hope we will talk more in times to come.'

There was the faintest trace of a smile upon the giant's lips.

The sound of the bell rang down from the priory.

Arthur stood. 'Until next time,' he said, holding out his right hand.

His companion looked at it for a moment as if not comprehending its meaning. He then stood and grasped the old monk's hand, his own nearly engulfing it, such was its size. The shake was firm as they looked at each other, a fondness reflected in their eyes.

'Goodbye, friend, and may the Lord be with you,' said Arthur before turning and making his way along the path above the vegetable patches where the crops were green and filled with vigorous growth.

'Goodbye,' said the giant as he stood and watched the old monk leave, a slight limp visible in his gait as he walked away beneath the early summer sun.

The giant settled on the seat once again and leant against its back. He felt freed by the man of God, released from the guilt and feelings of being a sinner which his father had imbued him with. There was a new hope for the future.

He stared at the vibrant gardens and the ocean visible over the southern wall and its widely spaced evergreens. Maybe, in that magical place, he could find happiness, that gift so rare. Amidst nature's bounty and beauty his life could begin anew without much of the burden he had carried to the Isle.

He glanced towards the garden gate to the left, but Arthur had passed from sight. A soft smile graced his lips. He had a friend, a companion with whom he enjoyed spending his time, whether it be in silence or the newly established art of conversation. The old monk emanated a sense of deep calm and his blue eyes were filled with a kindness and serenity which had quieted the giant's torments.

Though he did not believe Arthur to have noticed, the giant had watched him from time to time, either tending the gardens or upon the bench. He had noted his gentle, contemplative ways and spent much time considering whether to converse with him. None of the other Brothers had the same degree of calmness that Brother Elwin's demeanour showed and the giant had noted the old monk's appreciation of the natural world, one which he shared.

A rustling and fluttering in the branches of the evergreen above intruded upon his thoughts and he looked up to try and spy the source of the disturbance. Something small and brown fell to the long grass on the far side of the bench and he watched for movement which did not come.

Slowly rising, he stepped over and crouched beside the seat, his hands carefully reaching forward and brushing aside the grasses in search of that which had tumbled from the boughs. Revealed to him was a young, male sparrow not yet fully fledged, a cap of dark brown feathers upon its head. It rested still and silent in heart-racing fear.

The giant sucked air between his teeth and a soft sound issued forth as he looked upon the young bird. With his left hand he slowly cradled the creature and lifted it from the ground, its underdeveloped wings fluttering briefly as it stepped onto his large palm after a little coaxing with his other hand.

He studied its immature form, pale down still visible between its feathers. He made the soft sounds once again and looked into its dark eyes, ones filled with innocence and trepidation.

Turning his attention upward, he straightened to his full height and sought the location of the nest from which it had fallen. The giant spied it in the crux of branch and trunk way beyond even his reach. The young sparrow must have been attempting to fly, to depart its place of nurtured rearing only to fall with the futile flapping of inadequacy.

He stroked the creature's head with the tip of his index finger, the feathers like velvet to the touch. The bird remained motionless, a captive of its own fear. He was unsure as to what action to take. Either he could place the sparrow in the boughs above and let nature take its course, whether for good or ill, or he could take the bird into his care, try to sustain it until such a time as it could take flight and find independence.

He looked at the high nest. There was no way to place the sparrow back into the relative safety of the entwined twigs and leaves. He would have no choice but to balance the creature on a branch where it would be far more vulnerable to predation or another tumble to the grass.

His mind was made up as he turned his attention to the bird cupped in his hand. It looked so small upon his palm, the size of which lent the creature an increased sense of helplessness.

He began to make his way to the gate, holding the sparrow with attentive care in both hands, surrounding it and darkening its world so the movement about it was masked and would not cause undue alarm as they journeyed back to the priory.

16

He walked with care down the steep steps that led to the anteroom off the chapel. His hands were held before him with the young sparrow sheltered within as he tried to deaden the jolt of his footfalls so the creature's fear would not rise with the movement.

Entering the small room with a bow of his head, he stepped to the bed of straw which covered the stone floor to the left. A simple table marked with the drippings of candles and circular water stains from countless cups and bowls rested to the right, a solitary white candle upon its surface in the grip of a brass holder. He lowered himself to the musty straw and sat with legs crossed. His gaze was fixed upon his hands as he lowered them to his lap and daylight slanted into the room through the single, high window which was no more than a slit in the thick granite walls, a few bright shells placed upon the sill.

With a measured slowness, he removed his right hand, the bird revealed upon his left palm. He softly sucked air through his teeth and stroked its head with his finger. The bird blinked, but remained still, showing no desire to flee in the face of its terror.

The giant looked around for a suitable place of rest for the little creature and spied his cloak, which was balled into a pillow to his left. Turning, he reached for it and dragged it across the straw, the garment unravelling as he did so.

Setting the bird upon his knee, a slight flutter of its wings marking the transition, he then took the hood of his cloak and placed a handful of his bedding within its confines. He diligently pushed it to the hood's inner edge, creating a nest of sorts where the bird could rest until he found a home of greater permanence.

He picked up the sparrow, all the while making the noises which he hoped would calm and comfort the sorry creature. It was carefully placed within the makeshift nest as the cloak rested on the straw bed, the bird remaining still.

Putting his hands beneath the hood, the giant shuffled upon his knees across the small room and placed the nest under the wooden table. He looked down on his fragile charge and stroked the dark brown feathers upon its head for a few moments.

Moving back to his rough bed, he searched beneath the straw where he laid his head when sleeping. He produced a small sheet of yellowing paper and a simple brooch of pewter fashioned into the likeness of a rose, this having been both a possession and the name of his mother.

He studied the trinket as he held it between his fingers. It was the only item he had of his mother's, one taken without his father's knowledge as a keepsake and reminder. It had so recently been a symbol of his guilt and sin, but now the tarnish of such feelings had receded it became the symbol of love's lost potential, the love of a mother for the child she bore. How different his life may have been if only she had lived, he thought as his thumb caressed the rose which was forever cast in a state of closed petals, never to blossom, its potential never to be fulfilled.

He laid the folded and crumpled piece of paper beside him on the straw and got to his feet. Stepping over to the window with the brooch clasped in his right hand, he stared out at the view afforded him. With tearful eyes, he gazed at the ocean as a few cirrus clouds drifted high in the azure sky like pale ribs against the rich blue, the waters beneath vibrant and appealing in their calmness.

A ship sailed into view from the right, the sound of called instructions audible as the deckhands busied themselves at the start of the voyage, white sails capturing what breeze there was in order to propel the ship southward. He watched the vessel and the sailors upon its wooden deck. The horizon was their destination, a bank of cloud building where the sky and ocean met, its darkness filled with rain which blurred the caress of heaven and earth while casting a shadow upon the distant waves.

His eyes filled with a faraway look as he toyed with the brooch. His past would remain like his shadow, always a part of his existence and never to be evaded. For the rest of his natural life the painful memories would be trapped

64

within his mind, and he trapped with them. The petals were closed, never to open.

He sighed, the sound of the ship's captain barking orders to his crew still audible above the tide lapping the rocks far below his vista. His dark eyes turned to the brooch in his hand, to the rose trapped in perpetuity.

Shaking his head, he looked over to the cloak placed beneath the small table, just able to spy the young sparrow's head as it sat in the straw-lined hood. He stepped over and carefully laid the brooch upon the table amidst the water stains as tears welled in his eyes.

17

Darkness had settled on the priory by the time Arthur filed out of the chapel with Brother Cook by his side and the other monks behind them. He had looked to the doorway beyond which lay the giant's room as Prior Vargas had led the prayers given during the last hour of daylight. He could only see the top of the door towards the front of the chapel and it had remained shut, there being no sign of the man who had revealed himself so suddenly and surprisingly that day.

'Was I mistaken, or did I see you conversing with the stranger earlier?' asked Brother Cook quietly, leaning towards the old monk as they made their way to the entrance hall, descending a few stone steps as the breeze brushed against their faces.

'You were not mistaken,' replied Arthur with voice lowered as he looked to the mainland in the north, lights visible in Marghas Byghan and a few torches being borne across the sand and shingle bar which was revealed by low tide, those that carried them mere silhouettes in the darkness.

'Have you been given answers to any of the mysteries which surround him, Brother Elwin?' asked the young monk, looking at the man he had helped to nurse back to full strength.

'I have learned of a past which I would not wish upon any man. He has suffered greatly at the hands of others,' he replied as their pace remained slow and steady.

'And what of his reasons for sanctuary? Does he hide from a crime's consequence?' Curiosity was clear in the young man's eyes.

'This I do not know, but if a crime it be I cannot imagine there be any malice involved, for this man, this giant, is a gentle soul incapable of such in my estimation.'

Brother Cook nodded as he mulled over the old monk's words and they arrived at the rear door to the entrance hall.

'May I speak with you, Brother Elwin?'

Arthur turned to find the prior standing behind him and nodded his acquiescence. Brother Cook entered the single-storey granite building and the other ten monks filed in behind him as they made their way to the dining room. It was not until the door was shut that the prior spoke once more.

'You say there be no trace of malice, no evil you can discern in the manner and make-up of our guest?' Prior Vargas fixed Arthur with his cold gaze, his face long and thin, nose hawkish, skin pale as snow and pulled tight over high cheekbones.

Arthur nodded. 'I believe the man capable of nought but good.'

'It has not passed my notice that you sit with him day after day upon the seat on the north terrace of the gardens. Can you be certain it is not familiarity that clouds your judgement? Is it not pity for such a wretch that guides your thoughts in this matter?'

'I am certain. There is no lie in his eyes and no masking from the eyes the truth held within. In them I discern nothing but an honesty of spirit. As for pity, this I feel as of this day for he revealed his story unto me, but this feeling is secondary to our friendship, which lies as the foundation of what we share.'

'Friendship?' said the prior, unable to mask the surprise in his tone. 'Surely you misspeak, for how is friendship possible with such an ungodly wretch?'

'He is not a wretch in spirit, Prior Vargas, and it is in his spirit that the Lord lies,' answered Arthur, holding the prior's gaze. 'There is no mistake. We share a bond of friendship for which I am grateful.'

'We have known each other for many years, Brother Elwin.'

'Indeed,' the old monk nodded.

'Then let me leave you with a word of advice. Do not let your guard fall so low that you fall victim to this association. Even a master's faithful dog can turn upon him after years of service. Do you understand my warning, Brother Elwin?'

'I do, and it shall be heeded. Thank you, Prior Vargas,' Arthur nodded.

The prior turned and opened the back door to the entrance hall and then paused in the doorway. 'Heed my warning, Brother Elwin, for it is given in goodness for your own sake,' he said before entering the hall.

Arthur lingered a moment. He had seen no evidence that the man was capable of any deed other than those motivated by a gentleness of spirit. All malice, all evil deeds had been done to him, not by him. He had suffered and borne his suffering without recourse to violence or ill-temper as far as he could discern.

He shook his head to clear his mind and then entered the hall. His footsteps echoed about its emptiness as he walked to the door on the left. Passing through, he made his way along the corridor where the monk's cells were located, the prior ahead of him. Arthur stared down at the stone floor as his sandals marked his passage with soft sounds. He had known his friendship with the giant could cause consternation and even outrage amongst his Brothers, but he had never been one to shy away from what he believed, and he believed there was no harm in such a friendship, that it was nourishing for the giant and for himself.

Halfway along the corridor he passed through a door to the left, Prior Vargas holding it open for him. They entered a shorter corridor, passing the doorway to the library, simple wooden shelves upon its walls lined with musty parchments and a number of wooden chairs scattered in its hushed confines where Brothers often found rest as they studied the scriptures or read psalms and prayers. They exited the short corridor through a doorway at its far end and entered the refectory, a stone stairway descending to their left leading down to the kitchen and stores which lay beneath. The other monks were gathered about the two tables, one passing between them with a large jug of water, filling his Brothers' cups.

Arthur went to a seat and settled in contemplation He turned his thoughts away from the giant and tried to quiet his mind. Now was not the time to dwell on such things. He would not give up the friendship and that was all that was of importance.

Sighing, he picked up his tin cup and sipped at the cool water as the smell of vegetable soup and wood smoke rose from the kitchen below and his stomach grumbled gently.

18

The following day was as clear and warm as the last. Arthur sat on his seat and waited for his unusual friend to join him as the gardens hummed with the activity of insects, a pair of red admiral butterflies passing on the breeze as he watched their fluttering courtship dance. His sleep during the night had been disturbed by dreams no doubt triggered by the warning words of Prior Vargas and the old monk could feel a little tension in his shoulders as time passed.

In the dreams a shadow of huge proportions had hunted him. It had wanted to engulf him with a cloak of all-encompassing darkness. No matter how far or fast he ran it would always find him. There was a sense of calm assurance to the beast which sought him. At no time did it hurry. Its pace was steady and constant, filled with confidence, with the knowledge that it would find its prey, that there was no escape.

Arthur had woken suddenly, wide-eyed and in a cold sweat as the creature had finally cornered him in the chapel upon the Mount, opening its cloak to engulf him in the black void within.

He felt a shiver run the length of his spine and the hairs on the nape of his neck tingled in response to the recollections as he sat on the seat in the gardens. After the terrifying visions of sleep he had not been comforted by the light of his candle. The silence of the night had closed in about him with a palpable pressure as he lay staring at the door to his room, trying to push the vision of the incessant beast with hidden, shadowy features from his mind, for there was one characteristic about the demon which disturbed him. It was not the semblance of the giant that set a chill in his bones, it was the creature's eyes. There was no doubting they belonged to the man who had first spoken at length to him the previous day, but the light within them had turned from sad kindness to madness and malice.

Arthur took in the view before him, trying to shake the vision of the dark, glittering eyes from his mind. The sound of the gate creaking filled his shoulders with increased tension and he turned to see the giant walking towards him, thankfully without the cloak which would have been sure to reinforce the feelings left by his night terrors.

'Good afternoon, friend,' greeted the aged monk.

'Good afternoon, Arthur. May I join you?' asked the man, still finding a formal invitation to be seated a necessity.

'Of course. Please, sit down.'

The giant sat to Arthur's left as always and leant against the seat's creaking back, his gaze turning to the vista set out before them. His cheeks were no longer sunken and he had regained much of his former strength during the months since his arduous journey to the Mount.

Brother Elwin glanced at the man's eyes, seeking any trace of that which he had witnessed in his dreams, though in profile it was hard to tell what harboured there.

The giant turned to the old monk. 'Is everything as it should be, Arthur?' he asked when noting the unusual expression on the monk's face, which retained a tension he had not seen displayed during their previous meetings.

'All is well,' replied Arthur, trying to assure himself that his own words were true. Raising his hand before his mouth, he coughed before speaking further. 'I did not sleep well, is all, and feel in need of rest.'

'Then please do not remain on my account. I would have you rested and forego our meeting rather than have you suffer further.'

Arthur smiled, seeing the genuine concern and goodness within the man's eyes and feeling a sense of relief despite the fact he knew his nightmares to be but a fiction arising from the words of the prior. 'I thank you for your concern, but I will remain. I would not wish to miss this time and the sharing of nature's beauty.'

The giant held his gaze for a moment and noted that much of the old monk's tension quickly evaporated. He fell silent for a while and turned his eyes to the calm ocean and rich blueness of the sky above. Gulls flew close to the waters and bobbed upon the waves, a shoal of mackerel boiling the surface as they attempted to elude capture in the birds' beaks. The gulls' calls rang out, the sounds echoing off the rocky crags as the giant imagined the shimmering fish in their liquid domain darting this way and that in fear of being plucked from their world.

He turned back to the monk with a touch of nervousness. 'I have something I would ask you to read on my behalf,' he said, taking the folded and yellowing sheet of paper from where it had been tucked inside his grubby tunic. 'I have not the ability and know not what it says. All I know is that it relates to me, but how I cannot say.'

Arthur looked at the small sheet that was being held out and took it carefully into his hands. Unfolding it upon his lap, the old monk studied it a moment, having to raise it closer to his eyes, his sight slowly fading with age. 'This is a baptismal registration,' he said in surprise.

The giant's eyes widened as he looked at the old man expectantly.

'Was your mother's name Rose and your father's Alfred?'

The giant nodded his confirmation, unable to speak as he waited to hear more.

'Then we have your name at last.' Arthur smiled warmly as he looked up at his friend. 'Your name is William Tillbury,' he announced.

'William Tillbury,' echoed the giant in the merest whisper. There were vague stirrings of memory, the faintest recollections of his father calling him to supper when still but 4 or 5 years old, the name he used being that of "Will".

Arthur studied William's response, the giant's eyes filled with a distant look. He glanced down at the baptismal registration, which confirmed to him that at least some of what had been revealed the previous day was, indeed, true. William's mother had died during the birth and this had all transpired in the City of London. If these things were true then he could find no reason to doubt that everything else he had been told was also factual. There seemed no lie in William's story, but there remained a question unanswered.

'How did you come to arrive here, William?' asked Arthur quietly, putting voice to his desired enquiry.

William looked at the old monk a moment as his thoughts returned from their distant meandering. 'My master was displaying us at the City of Winchester. I heard speak of the Isle of Ictis and the priory upon its summit when two merchants lingered. As soon as I heard their words I knew that was where I must go if ever I found freedom from the chains which had held me so long. I felt the distinct pull of these western lands and the Isle in particular.'

'The Isle of Ictis. Yes, that is what merchants and those well travelled call this place. We monks call it the Mount of St Michael, a vision of that saint having appeared here. The locals still call it Carrack Looz en Cooz, which means "grey rock in the wood", this being a name which has survived since ancient times.' Arthur looked out to sea momentarily and coughed. 'That does not explain how you came to leave the service of your master, William. Though you will not find me offended if you do not wish to reveal this.'

The giant smiled, not because of the words he was about to speak, but due to the sound of his name being uttered by another. It filled him with a new-found joy and released him from the name of "Beast". 'I believe I mentioned the

bearded lady who was not kept in chains or captivity.'
Arthur nodded. 'She and my master shared his bed on
occasion, and that is why she had her freedom. Elsbeth was
her name, a kindly woman who would bring the rest of us
scraps of food when the master was away visiting an ale or
…' He lowered his voice, '…whore house.' He paused and
looked out to sea, the sails of ships dotted upon the waves
bright in the sunlight, the air golden and hazy above the
waters, lending a mystical air of shrouded beauty to the
sight which filled his eyes as dark thoughts filled his mind.

'One night he beat her terribly, her face bloodied and
bruised by his cane and fists. It was then she swore
vengeance upon him. On the next occasion of his
drunkenness, when he had passed out in the grip of
intoxication, she stole the keys to our bonds and in the
depth of night released all who were part of the freak show
by which the master made his living.' He turned back to
Arthur. 'This is how I found my liberty. I made my way on
foot for three weeks until I arrived here, at the Isle.
Travelling at night, I avoided detection by and large,
feeding off the land and sleeping in barns and hedgerows.'

'What happened to the others?' asked Arthur.

'We went our separate ways, believing this would
increase our chances of evading recapture. If this be the
case I do not know, but I pray the others who shared those
evil times have met with the same good fortune as I.'

'And Elsbeth, did she take flight?'

William's expression fell and he shook his head. 'She
did not.'

'Surely she would have faced a greater wrath than that
previously impressed upon her by your master,' said the old
monk in surprise.

'This I said to her. I pleaded for her to make good an
escape, but love be a stronger bond than any chains.'
William sighed. 'I fear she may not have lasted that night
for the master's temper knew no bounds. Upon his

wakefulness he would have discovered her treachery and her punishment would have been so severe I think her already battered body may not have endured.

'It is by his fist that my nose was broken and by his cane that I bear this scar upon my lip. It did not take much to awaken his anger.'

Arthur looked at the lingering signs of the wounds which had been inflicted upon the giant's face and thought how unfortunate William was. The crooked nose and scar upon his upper lip added to his unusual appearance, the latter lending an appearance of a slight sneer which had unsettled the old monk when first seeing the giant upon the stone steps. 'Did you not take revenge on your master upon your release?'

William shook his head. 'No.'

The old monk studied the giant's expression. 'You did not bite him?'

The giant looked at the monk in surprise, a hint of concern in his eyes and face draining of colour. 'What makes you ask such a question?'

'Brother Stewart heard that you had bitten your master, who passed through these parts late in the autumn of last year. At least, I presume him to have been your master. He was searching for a beast of large proportions.'

'It was not I that caused him to limp,' said William. 'He was bitten by a black mongrel which had suffered greatly under his ownership. One evening, after he had kicked at its side for stealing a meagre strip of pork from above the cooking fire, the dog, half starved and ribs like blades along its flanks, turned on him and sank its teeth into his leg. It was the last thing the hound ever did. The master beat it to death with his bare hands, yelps of pain filled with pitiful helplessness rising in the alley in which we were rested for the night.'

'Your master sounds to me like a truly wicked man,' said Arthur sadly. 'It fills me with sorrow to learn that people can act so abhorrently.'

'He knew no better,' said William. 'He was created by the world of men, and until it changes more shall rise like him.'

Arthur looked at the giant seated beside him, surprised by the calm insight of his words, but reprimanding himself for such feelings. There was no reason why such a man could not be wise and he was annoyed at having let the judgement of appearances cloud his mind as to what lay within William.

'Your words are true and hold compassion the likes of which I have rarely witnessed,' he said, having heard no trace of ill will within the giant's words. 'Had I borne such treatment from another I cannot swear I would be so understanding,' he admitted.

William looked into the old monk's blue eyes. 'Then I am thankful you have not come to such harm under the will of another, for ne'er a kinder or warmer spirit have I come across than that which you display. Our friendship is much valued, Arthur.' He smiled at his companion.

Arthur returned the gesture. 'I also value it greatly. I am very glad to have made your acquaintance, William, and have a proposition which may go some way to repaying the debt I owe you for saving my life. If you will allow it, I would be happy to teach you the skill of reading and writing.'

William looked at his friend fondly. 'You have already lifted a great burden from me by revealing my misfortune of birth was no sin. You have also revealed my name to me. Your debt is already repaid and more.'

Arthur's smile grew. 'Then let me teach you out of friendship.'

William thought for a moment and then nodded. 'Thank you, it would be a kindness I would not soon forget,' he replied.

'Then it is settled. When the days draw in at autumn's onset I will begin teaching you and can see by your intelligence that the lessons will go well.'

'I am honoured by your confidence in my ability and hope not to disappoint.'

'Here,' said Arthur, handing the baptismal registration back to William. 'Some day soon you will be able to read this for yourself.'

The giant took the yellowing sheet of paper in his large hands. Folding it, he tucked it back into his tunic. 'It took me some time to find the courage to speak with you,' admitted William, 'but I am glad to have done so.'

'I am glad also,' replied Arthur.

'First I had to feel comfortable in your presence, so used was I to feeling apprehensive with others, wary of their motives and actions. I needed to find the ability to trust another.'

'These things do not surprise me after all you have been through during your life. I only hope that now you can find peace and freedom from persecution.'

William nodded and his thoughts turned to his new home. Upon the island he was isolated from the rest of the world, secure and safe. He felt as if the Isle were removed from all he had known, set apart, not just in its separation from the mainland, but by a deeper partition of consciousness.

He had heard the legend of the Isle of Avalon and wondered if it could have arisen from the existence of the Mount, where nature was softened and yet heightened to the senses. The world of men intruded little and the parts of the island he inhabited were lent a sense of being removed from time itself. The waves and tidal movements marked time, but the island rose from the ocean defiant and unyielding, the waters dashed upon its rocks.

On days of mist or thick sea fog the Isle became a place of myth, the slopes ghostly and grey in the clinging damp. In those times William felt most removed, a wraith in a land existing beyond the death of his previous life.

He turned to the panorama visible from the seat on the northern terrace of the gardens and drank in the sun-hazed view. William was filled with a new-found contentment. His name had been discovered and he knew that beside him sat a true friend.

Arthur's tension had faded to nought and he felt secure in the knowledge that the man beside him was incapable of harm or misdeed. He was a truly gentle giant, a man of good spirit who had been mistreated, but had not let this tarnish his soul and turn him into a bitter and twisted creature.

With the heat of the summer sun upon their faces, the two companions were comfortable with the silence they shared as nature filled their senses and happiness filled their hearts.

19

William sat on the straw of his bed later that afternoon with a collection of twigs upon his lap, the cloth which usually covered his feet lying beside him. With a surprising dexterity, he was creating a nest by entwining the supple twigs about each other, his concentration bent upon this purpose. The young sparrow had survived the night and needed something more than the hood of his cloak in which to abide while its strength built in readiness for flight.

Finally he completed his task, setting the woven nest on the straw before him with a sense of satisfaction. It would be well suited for the sparrow until its time of release came to pass.

William crawled the short distance across the floor to the table. Reaching into the straw-lined hood, he removed the sparrow and gently placed it into the new nest he had constructed. Moving the cloak, he put his woven creation in its place, whistling to calm the sparrow after the handling and movement. It chirped in response and the giant smiled warmly as he stroked its tiny head.

After a few moments he withdrew his attentions and turned to his cloak. The inside of the hood bore the unsightly signs of the sparrow's residence and he lifted it from the stone floor after removing the straw lining. Rising to his feet, William stepped to the door, ducking as he vacated his room and took the short flight of steps up into the chapel.

There were no monks in attendance, their work duties taking them elsewhere, and so he lingered a few moments. Sunlight shone through the stained-glass windows, beams of coloured brightness soundlessly piercing the hush within the small building. Despite his many months of sanctuary within the priory, the holy chapel never ceased to fill him with tranquillity. The air was aglow in the light from the windows and there was a hallowed aura which hung in the stillness as if the Lord filled the chapel with His presence.

William glanced up at the eaves and then looked at the pulpit opposite him, set to the left of the chapel's nave. It, like the building itself, was carved of granite, and many times he had watched the prior give praise to the Lord from its confines. Even though he could not understand the foreign words, he could comprehend their sentiment and felt his heart filled with gladness as he stood at the door to his room or sat within and listened.

He took a deep breath and then walked down the nave between the rows of pews which filled the chapel's interior. Carrying his cloak, he exited with one last glance at the glowing interior and stepped into the windless day of bright sunshine from the chapel's rear door.

Turning left, he took the steps that led down to the rear door of the entrance hall. Skirting the hall, he walked alongside the building rather than entering, passing a tool shed used by the monks. He arrived at the front of the building and then took the path which led to the steps descending to the gardens. With large strides he took two at a time, his gaze continually turning to the view above the tops of the trees which were gathered on the slope below. He looked at the town of Marghas Byghan which clung to the mainland, the sound of a hammer upon an anvil peeling out across the bay as people walked across the bar of sand and shingle, the tide low. There were two ships at the island's jetty, visible through the trees, their holds being filled with copper and tin from the warehouses upon the wharf, the scene filled with activity as life beyond the priory continued at a pace from which William was glad to be removed. He did not wish any part of the world of men, was content and happy, grateful for the isolation afforded by his life amidst the Benedictine monks.

Soon the harbour and warehouses were obscured from view, as was any sight of the sand bar or Marghas Byghan beyond, only the brow of the hill upon which the town rested and the woods above the settlement visible above the treetops.

William entered the gardens and a few of the monks looked up as they tended the vegetables, which were thick with the growth of spring and summer. Despite knowing that Arthur would be engaged in other duties, he glanced over at the seat as he began to walk down the gentle slope to the southerly wall and its windswept evergreens.

He followed the wall westward, towards the crags of pale rocks which rose high above. Upon reaching the western fringe of the gardens, William clambered over the wall, glancing over his shoulder to see if any of the monks were noting his actions, but finding them busy with the tasks at hand.

He was soon at the shoreline on the southern reaches of the Isle and climbed down upon the rocks revealed by low tide. Selecting a rough stone the size of his fist, William then scrambled down to the water's edge as small waves lapped at the smoothed rock. A few yards ahead he could see the deep blue waters where the rocks fell away, the colour indicating great depth.

Crouching, he bathed the hood of his cloak in the salt water, rinsing away as much of the sparrow's droppings as he could. Then, using the stone he had chosen, he rubbed at the cloth to cleanse it of the last of the dirt. The sea air filled his lungs as he put down the stone and wrung out the hood, the water running over his thick fingers to fall back to the embrace of the sea.

Setting the cloak to one side, William stepped into the gentle surf and peered over the edge of the shelf of rock, feeling the cold caress of the water upon his toes. There he saw the vagaries of his reflection, the brightness of the sun above obscuring detail from his eyes. He could make out the mess of black curls and the large brow, the darkness of his facial hair and shadows of his eye sockets, but little else. The sunlight was like a halo about his head as the water undulated with each passing wave in a regular rhythm, as if the world were breathing softly.

He had spent many hours sat on and about the rocks listening to the sounds of the ocean, often with his eyes closed to the world, allowing the rhythmic pulse of the waves and smell of salt water and seaweed to fill him with calmness. William often caught small fish in the pools left by the receding tides by which to supplement his diet of vegetables which were given him for his work about the priory and its gardens.

The sound of children's voices and playful laughter distracted him from his reveries and he turned to see a young boy and girl making their way along the western shoreline, apparently unaware of his presence as yet.

Quickly gathering up his cloak, William made his way back to the grasses and wild flowers which marked the high boundary between shore and sea and strode to the wall beyond which the gardens found shelter. He turned to see if the children had noticed his departure, but could no longer see them, the base of the southern crags hiding them from view, though he could still hear the sounds of their voices and laughter.

He paused and continued to listen. The joy and excitement clear in their tones filled him with a sense of melancholy as his thoughts turned to his own childhood and the father who had left him with so many scars, both physical and mental. A deep sadness welled up within him and he sighed.

The children came into view, their attention caught by a bright butterfly which lifted into the air from pink thrift clinging to the overhanging shoreline beside them. William quickly made his way over the wall and dropped low on the other side to avoid any chance of detection.

Bent over, he made his way up the slope of the gardens to the northern terrace. He passed through the small orchard of apple and pear trees which Arthur regularly tended with great care, knowing the southern crags would again obscure him from the children's sight and put pay to any chance of his presence upon the Isle being discovered.

20

John Hadden staggered along the track with arms limp at his sides. The night was still, clouds veiling the moon and stars as crickets filled the hush with their shrill serenade. Head dizzy, the farmer stopped to catch his breath halfway up the length of the hill on the way home from the King's Arms.

Peering towards the sea, his gaze settled upon the vague shapes of cattle and sheep on the common land below, before the cliffs of the town's eastern beach. Then his sight was drawn by movement on the sand and shingle of the shoreline beyond as one of the cows lowed, the sound filling the night.

He blinked, trying to force his vision to focus on the shadowy apparition that wandered upon the sand before the pale surf. Its large silhouette was framed against the white caps of the waves rolling in and crashing upon the shore.

His pulse began to race as he watched the giant. Fear rose like trembling poison in his veins as the figure crouched upon the sands for a few moments and then continued westward, towards the rising darkness of Carrack Looz en Cooz.

Turning with fright in his heart, he made his way back in the direction he had come, stumbling on the rutted track as he tried to make haste. He fell, arms out before him as he braced himself against the fall. Grit dug into his palms, but the pain was masked from his mind by the brandy he had consumed.

With a grunt of effort, he got back to his feet, the world about him moving in and out of focus as his head swam and his heart thundered. Taking greater care, he again began the descent into the lower reaches of Marghas Byghan.

Out of breath and after another tumble on the dirt track, John almost fell through the front door of the tavern, only two regular customers present at that late hour, along with three sailors seated at the table beside the fire, their skin browned by the Mediterranean sun. The men of the sea were all settled in drunken stupors, their heads resting upon their arms on the tabletop, one opening his eyes briefly at the sound of John's entry.

'Could ye not find your way home, John?' asked Pete the Hand, called such on account of having his right hand cut off for smuggling five years previous, his stump wrapped in a brown rag as he grinned, his two front teeth noticeable in their absence.

John fought for breath as he tottered over to the bar, his face drained of blood.

'What be wrong with you?' asked Richard, his cheeks flushed with alcohol consumption as usual.

'I saw ...' John gasped and clutched at his chest, closing his eyes as the room spun, the flickering candlelight adding to the chaos of the images about him. 'I saw a giant upon the eastern beach,' he wheezed.

Pete the Hand slapped him on the back and chuckled. 'Aye, brandy will do that to a man,' he said in amusement. 'Only last night I saw a green-skinned boekka creeping amongst the trees beside my home.'

Jebbit stared at the farmer. 'A giant,' he said with measured words, 'upon the town beach?'

John nodded as he leant against the rickety bar, eyes remaining closed as he tried to gain some semblance of composure. 'Aye.'

'Richard, I think ye better not serve any more brandy to him tonight,' said Pete. 'Not unless ye be happy for him to sleep upon the floor.' He kicked at the sawdust before his leather boots and Tinker looked up from where she rested beside Jebbit's feet.

'It was not the drink,' said John. 'I saw a giant, I tell ye. It were a terrifying sight. Its shadow was so big as to engulf a man.'

'Are ye sure it was no rock and your mind be mistaken?' asked Richard as Tinker sneezed.

John slowly shook his throbbing head and tried to open his eyes, finding the madness of the room had abated. 'It were no rock I spied. Rocks do not walk nor crouch upon the sands.'

'Not unless ye has had far too much liquor before setting eyes on them. I have known rocks to sing and dance on occasion.' Pete the Hand raised his cup and swigged his drink. 'And if luck be with me, they will do so tonight,' he added as he wiped his lips with his stump, the rag which wound about it stained with dirt and alcohol.

'I tell no lie, Pete,' insisted John as he turned to the shorter man and fixed him with his bloodshot eyes. 'This were a creature of unnatural size walking along the beach beside the surf. The sea's froth afforded me its outline. It wore a long cloak and its stride was twice that of any ordinary man. The sight of the creature filled me with sobering horror.'

'Sobering,' mocked Pete. 'Not if I be any judge of your condition.'

Jebbit remained silent, his thoughts returning to the night in late autumn when he had spied the shadowy beast atop the hill behind Marghas Byghan.

'My very soul was chilled, I tell ye.' There was something about John's expression and his tone that caused the smile to fade from Pete's face. There was a genuine fear which filled the farmer's drunken gaze.

'Where was it headed?' asked Richard as one of the sailors mumbled indistinctly, voice thick with phlegm, head remaining on his arms, right hand clutching a cup which was still half full.

'Westward,' replied the farmer, 'towards Carrack Looz en Cooz.'

There were a few moments of thoughtful silence.

'I need a drink to calm my nerves.'

'Are ye sure ye want another? It looks as if ye has already had your fill judging by your hands,' replied the innkeeper, nodding towards John's palms.

The farmer lifted them and stared at the bloodied injuries sustained in his haste. He could not recall how he came to bear such wounds, had no recollection of falling upon the track during his descent, his brow furrowing as he picked at the embedded grit.

'Ye should work those out and watch for infection,' said Pete the Hand.

'Do you think this creature ye saw could be the same as I witnessed late last year?' asked Jebbit, the others turning to him without comprehension, the drink slowing their minds.

'Ye remember, we went hunting for it upon the hill and found traces of its passing.'

The looks on Richard and John's faces changed to ones of recollection and the farmer nodded. 'It may well be the same creature, for it filled me with the same dread as ye expressed upon your telling of its discovery.'

Jebbit swallowed hard, the memories as clear as if from the previous day. 'What should we do?'

'I say we not get carried away. This may still be a tall tale of intoxication's creation and nothing more,' said Pete the Hand.

'I tell ye it is not so,' said John forcefully, the sailor who had previously stirred looking up with bloodshot eyes, his skin leathery, nose wide and nostrils flaring as he fought a wave of nausea which washed over him.

'This creature was as real as I standing before ye,' continued John, his voice filled with conviction as he straightened, trying to stand without the need of the bar's assistance, but only successful for the briefest moment as the sailor vomited upon the floor beside the table at which he sat.

Richard stared at the patch of warm liquid soaking into the sawdust with an expression of tired resignation and then turned back to the local men. 'There be only four of us, so what do ye propose we do? There are too few to seek this thing out and the hour is late to go a-knocking on the doors of others.'

The men fell silent, Pete the Hand drinking the last of his brandy and setting his cup upon the bar. Richard refilled it and topped up his own, his hands a little shaky and some of the brandy spilling onto the already stained wood.

'We must stay watchful and keep alert to the creature's presence,' said Jebbit eventually, Tinker sniffing the air as she rested beside him.

'Is this the first time it has been seen since autumn?' asked Pete.

Jebbit nodded.

'Then surely it does not dwell here for it would have been noted with greater frequency.'

'Not if it only roams by night.'

'There are those who are afoot during the hours of darkness and no others have witnessed a dark giant,' stated Pete before having a drink. 'Maybe it only passes through, living its life in some other quarter at a safe distance from the town.'

Richard nodded. 'What Pete has said must be the truth. It would have been spied before this night if dwelling nearby. What do ye say, John?'

All eyes turned to the farmer, the colour having returned to his cheeks and the pain in his palms beginning to penetrate the inebriation of his mind. He thought for a while and then nodded. 'Aye, what has been said makes much sense. If the creature dwelt near it would have been seen often. It must be passing through only. At least, let us pray this is so.'

Pete the Hand and Richard nodded their concurrence, but Jebbit turned his gaze downward, looked at Tinker with an expression of doubt upon his lined and weathered face as another of the sailors stirred.

The heavily built seaman raised his head from the table slightly, a string of saliva hanging from his lips as he burped. His lacklustre eyes tried to comprehend where he was and then he slumped back into place with a low groan.

21

William crouched before one of the vegetable patches in his grey tunic. His gaze was fixed on a globe of water which had gathered at the centre of one of the cabbage leaves before him, its shape held by surface tension. It shone like a smooth, liquid diamond.

He peered closer and saw that it reflected the pale clouds and the green of its resting place. His distorted face could be seen in miniature in its bright surface, the shadows cast by his brow the most striking feature which could be discerned. It was a wonder to him that such a simple thing could, in essence, contain the entire world about it and in this simplicity of nature he found intense fascination.

Slowly reaching forward, he dipped his fingertip into the globe and raised it carefully, a single drop clinging to the ridges of his skin. It hung there sparkling with the light of the day. His finger trembled slightly and the drop fell to rejoin the rest of the rainwater, its form vanishing into the greater whole.

There was a gentle clearing of a throat on the other side of the vegetable patch and he raised his head to discover the two children he had seen three days previous watching him intently. So concentrated had he been on the water remaining from the night's rain that he had not heard their barefooted approach. They stood in simple clothes woven of cheap cloth, a boy and girl both with golden hair and hands behind their backs. The boy wore a deep blue tunic and the girl, who rocked back and forth on the balls of her feet, wore a dress of sun-bleached yellow.

'Are ye the giant?' asked the girl with a look of curiosity. William nodded.

'Ye do not look very giant to me,' stated the boy doubtfully.

William slowly rose to his full height, the children's blue eyes following every move, heads craning back. 'Better?' he asked with a soft smile.

'Much,' said the boy.

'Do ye eat children and grind their bones to make bread?' enquired the girl, her eyes sparkling with youthful light.

William could not help but chuckle at the suggestion. 'No, I do not,' he replied as he crouched again so they would not have to strain their necks.

'What are ye doing?' asked the boy.

'I am weeding and seeking out worms.'

'Worms?'

'They are food for a young bird I discovered in these gardens,' responded William.

'Are ye going to eat the bird?' asked the girl.

'Why would I do such a thing?'

'Our father gives the pigs lots of food and then we eat them,' she said matter-of-factly.

'Well, little one, I will do no such thing. I shall set the bird free once it is able to fly of its own accord.'

'Can we see it?' asked the boy.

'Maybe another time.'

'Tomorrow?'

William smiled. 'We shall see. You can help me in my search for worms if you wish.'

The children looked at each other briefly and then knelt on the grass beside the vegetable patch.

'My name is William,' he said, a degree of pride in his tone now that he had come to know his own identity.

'I am Jacob and this is my sister, Rachel.'

'Glad to meet you, Jacob.' William held his hand out over the cabbages which separated him from the children.

Jacob looked at it with caution and turned to his sister with a questioning look. She nodded in response to his silent communication and the boy leant forward and took hold of the giant's hand, his own swallowed by its enormity as they shook.

'I am glad to meet you too, Rachel,' said William, the girl taking his offered hand without hesitation.

'We have ne'er met a giant before. Not a real one anyway,' said the girl with a smile. 'Have you ever seen a unicorn?' she asked hopefully.

'No, I cannot say that I have.'

'Do not be so silly, Rachel,' scolded her brother.

'That is not to say they do not exist,' added William. 'If giants are real then unicorns may be also.'

Rachel smiled, turned to her brother and stuck out her tongue. 'I told ye.'

'He did not say they do exist,' replied Jacob with a frown.

'This is not a place for argument,' said William with a kindly expression. 'This is a place of beauty and I will have no frowns here.'

Jacob huffed and crossed his arms over his small chest.

'We must find worms for my young sparrow so that it may grow strong and fly to freedom.'

Rachel began to dig into the soft earth with her bare hands. Noticing her brother's inaction, she nudged him in the side with her elbow.

'Be careful of the cabbage plants, they are food for the monks and I,' said William as Jacob begrudgingly bent forward and began to hunt for the sparrow's foodstuff.

They dug in the vegetable patch in silence for a few moments.

'I have one!' Jacob called excitedly, holding up a large worm in triumph and watching it wriggle between his fingers.

'Well done, it is a big one and the bird will be well fed by it.' William picked up a tin bowl which had been resting beside him on the grass and held it out to the boy.

'Drop the creature in and we shall see how many more we can find.'

Jacob did as instructed, the worm's moist body making a faint sound as it hit the interior of the dented bowl which William had borrowed from the kitchen stores.

Rachel dug with additional vigour, not to be outdone by her older brother. Fingernails black with earth, she clawed at the ground until she caught sight of her quarry. 'I see one,' she shrilled, her fingers trying to gain purchase on its slippery form as the worm attempted to evade her and find escape in its hole, finding success after a brief struggle.

Rachel looked at the hole she had dug in annoyance. 'It got away,' she stated with a pout.

'Ne'er mind, there will be others,' said William.

The children continued to dig, seeking out any sign of a worm. William also moved the damp earth with his hands, but could not refrain from glancing up at the children. The look of concentration upon Rachel's elfin features was mingled with mud she had accidentally wiped across her forehead when brushing back stray locks of her long hair, and the sight brought a warm smile to the giant's face.

After a while there were a good deal of worms writhing in the bowl and as Jacob dropped another in, William's gaze was caught by the sight of Arthur entering the gardens at the gate above. He lifted his right hand and waved at the old monk, the greeting returned as Arthur made his way along the north terrace to the seat they so often shared.

The children, having followed William's gaze, turned back to the giant. 'Is he your friend?' asked Rachel.

'Yes, and a very good one.'

'Are ye here to visit with him?'

William thought for a moment. 'Yes,' he lied, deciding it better not to reveal the truth. He had no wish to reveal that the Isle was his home. Neither had he any intention of subjecting their childhood innocence to the dark story of his life prior to his arrival, and they would be sure to ask countless questions were the subject raised.

'How long are ye going to stay?' asked Jacob.

'I cannot say. It may be a few more days or a few more weeks.'

'Can ye at least stay until the bird is released?' Rachel looked at him, her blue eyes pleading for him to respond in the affirmative.

William nodded and smiled at the children.

'Do ye promise?'

'I promise, and I will not release it unless you are both with me.'

Jacob and Rachel looked at each other with excitement and then got to their feet.

'We must get back or father will wonder where we are,' said Jacob.

William rose to his full height, the bowl of worms held in his right hand. 'Are you both good at keeping secrets?' he whispered, bending down towards them.

'Yes,' said Jacob quietly, his sister nodding as they looked up at the giant with wide eyes.

'You must not tell anyone that you have seen me, do you understand?'

'Why?' Jacob looked at him curiously.

William thought quickly. 'Because adults cannot see me and they will think you both mad.'

'But our father saw ye a few nights ago,' replied Rachel.

'He did?'

The children both nodded.

'He saw ye walking along the beach in the darkness,' said Jacob.

William frowned. 'Then please tell no one simply because I ask it of you. Will you do that for me?'

The children both nodded solemnly.

'When can we meet ye and see the bird?' asked Rachel.

'This time next week, but only if you promise not to tell a soul that I am here.'

'We promise,' said Rachel.

William smiled thinly, fearing the children would be unable to keep his existence a secret.

They turned and began to skip arm in arm up the gentle slope to the gate. William straightened as he watched their departure, hoping they would be able to contain themselves and not reveal the story of meeting a giant upon the Mount.

Jacob and Rachel paused at the gate to the gardens.

'Bye, Will,' called Rachel.

'See ye next week,' shouted Jacob as they both waved their farewells.

William raised his hand as they left and vanished from sight, taking the path which branched off to the warehouses and harbour beyond. He looked at the bowl full of worms which they had helped collect and a sad smile curled his lips. He sighed and looked over to the bench, Arthur seated and staring out over the gardens.

Taking a deep breath, he strode up the terraces between the vegetable patches to his friend, the sun trying to burn through the white clouds above and its warmth briefly settling upon his face.

'May I sit with you?' he asked as he came to a halt before his friend.

'Please,' replied Arthur with a nod.

William sat and rested the bowl upon his lap.

'An interesting collection you have there,' said the monk as he looked at the glistening, squirming bodies within the tin vessel.

'They are food for a young sparrow I found here. I hope to nurture it until it can find the power of flight and freedom.'

Arthur studied the giant's expression. 'You value freedom highly.'

'I do.' William looked down at the pink bodies smeared with earth as they continued to wriggle.

'Then a warning I must give to you as a friend. Should the local inhabitants learn of your presence on the Mount there could be trouble for you. It is not for certain, but I guess their reaction would not be a good one.'

William turned to Arthur. 'Surely my safety is assured while I have sanctuary at the priory?'

The old monk nodded. 'That is so unless people demand your expulsion.'

'Can they do such a thing?'

'We rely on them for many things and should these be withheld there would be little choice left open to Prior Vargas.'

William sighed, a sense of frustration welling within. No matter how hard he tried, there seemed no escaping the cruelties of the world. Even when he thought himself beyond its grasp it found a way to reach in and clutch him with a hand of ignorant animosity.

'What am I to do?' he asked in a hushed voice. 'There is nowhere left for me to go.'

'It is only a warning I give to you and by no means a certainty,' said Arthur, seeing William's distress. 'My intent was not to cause you undue alarm, only to forewarn.'

'Must I always be hounded by those who see only what I am and not who I am?' William shook his head miserably.

'Please, friend, do not let my words unsettle you so,' said Arthur in an attempt to calm his companion.

William put his head in his hands and began to sob, the sight of the forlorn giant making Arthur's heart ache. He put a hand upon his friend's shoulder and wished for words which would bring an end to such sadness, but could think of none. The tears that flowed, that dampened William's fingers as they hid his face, were those of an outcast. He had always been so and had suffered at others' hands due to this misfortune, this twist of fate which was beyond his undoing.

The old monk took a deep breath and looked out to sea as time passed slowly. William's tears subsided, but his face remained hidden, hands sodden with the salt waters of deep sadness and a sense of inescapable doom.

Three chimes rang out high above.

'I must go, William,' said Arthur in a soft voice.

The giant lowered his hands and turned to the monk, his dark eyes like the depths of the ocean, touched with a lasting chill. 'What am I to do?'

Arthur sighed. 'Try not to worry yourself. As yet there is no question as to your continuing residency here.'

'And if the children tell?'

Arthur held his friend's gaze. 'That is a bridge we may ne'er have to cross. Let your mind be free of such thoughts, dear friend,' he said. 'For my part, I am sorry, I should not have mentioned such things to you.'

'No, you did well to warn me. I count you as a valued friend as much for your honesty as your company and constant kindness.'

The old monk smiled thinly. 'Then I tell you, dear friend, what I have spoken of will probably not come to pass and fretting will not change what the future holds within the folds of its cloak. So do not burden yourself with worry, but arm yourself with knowledge. Do not let a new darkness descend upon you, but find contentment in these moments which were ne'er meant to last.'

'You speak much wisdom, and for that I am eternally grateful. I shall try to banish such worries and enjoy the life I have found here for as long as I am able.' William placed his hand on Arthur's as it continued to rest on his shoulder. 'Thank you, friend.'

'There is naught to thank me for, I assure you,' responded the old monk, feeling guilt at having woken such feelings.

'Until our next meeting.' William forced a smile.

Arthur nodded as the giant withdrew his hand. The monk stood and glanced out to sea before turning back to William. 'The world does not judge you, only men, and men are blind to what lies within,' he said and then began to walk towards the gate.

The giant watched him depart, hearing the faint creak of the gate as it opened and closed. He turned his gaze seaward and sat back against the bench, the bowl of worms still upon his lap. With a deep breath he took in the fragrances of the summer and sea air. They filled him with a growing sense of calm as his despair faded, his friend's words chasing it away upon the soft breeze.

22

Arthur struggled up the last few steps, a little out of breath and his knees giving him pain. He feared a time when disability or old age would keep him confined to the priory, imprison him atop the Mount of St Michael, and hoped that time would never come.

Reaching the top, he paused for breath, head bowed and lungs burning as he coughed a little. Looking up, he spied Prior Vargas standing outside the door to the entrance hall 20 yards away, up a slight incline into which no steps had been cut. The prior was watching him with some concern and so Arthur straightened and tried to don the appearance of full health and normality. He slowly made his way over to his superior, whose grey eyes regarded him closely.

'Are you sure you are still able to make the ascent from the gardens, Brother Elwin?'

Arthur came to a halt before the gaunt-faced prior and nodded. 'Yes, Prior Vargas, it is just today that I find it a little hard. My knees give me pain from time to time, but it is not a constant ailment and should be paid no heed.'

Prior Vargas noted the glistening sheen of perspiration on the old monk's brow, but decided not to pursue the matter further, there were more pressing concerns he had been waiting to discuss. 'I saw your friend with the children below. Do you think it wise that his presence be known to the inhabitants of Marghas Byghan?'

'No, I do not, and I told William so after the children had departed the gardens.'

'William?'

'William Tillbury is his name.'

'Why have you not spoken of this before?' Prior Vargas looked at him with disapproval. 'We have known each other a long time, Arthur, and I would hope that you would keep me informed of such matters.'

'It was only revealed unto me a few days ago and I had not yet thought to speak with you about it.'

'What else has the creature revealed to you? Do you know what deeds brought him to this place?'

Arthur nodded. 'I do.'

'Be they as I fear, touched by the hand of the fallen one himself?'

'Not in the sense that you believe, for the hand of the fallen one did not guide William's actions, but the actions of those about him. He has suffered great injustice in the world of men.'

'This is what he told you?' The prior looked doubtful.

'Yes, and I have no reason to doubt its truth.'

'You would take the word of one so wretched? Do you have so little judgement?'

Arthur tensed at the prior's rebuke. 'If his story were filled with crimes and evil deeds committed by his own hands I fear you would have believed every word without doubt, Prior Vargas.'

The prior's cold eyes narrowed and his expression hardened. 'What were the tales he told you?'

'His childhood was filled with beatings at the hands of his father, his adulthood with a life chained for amusement in a show of people seen as no more than animals and called "freaks".'

Prior Vargas looked towards the mainland on the other side of the wide bay. 'That, in truth, I can believe, but how did he come to the Mount of St Michael if so imprisoned?'

'A kindly soul and kindred spirit released him and others who found themselves similarly chained. William then undertook the journey from Winchester on foot.'

'What of his master?'

Arthur looked at the prior in puzzlement as a pair of gulls flew overhead, calling out as they swooped down towards the harbour.

'Surely you do not think he left without exacting revenge once his bonds were released?'

Arthur stared at Prior Vargas in shock. 'I do, and if you were to know his gentle nature there would be no question in your heart as to this fact. William would have no part in such actions.'

'That is what he tells you?'

'No, that is what I discern in his manner, and more, it is what I know from the depths of his eyes, which are filled with a goodness rarely seen and the rarer still after the suffering he has endured.'

The prior's frown deepened. 'Are you sure you do not allow a supposed friendship to cloud your judgement? Much time you have shared together and he saved you from peril. It may be that this has blinded you to some darkness on his part, or some deception in his tales of the past.'

'There is no sense of deception and any darkness could only be imagined by those who do not know him and judge by appearance, so different is he from the average man.' Arthur could feel his tension rising. To his surprise the prior seemed intent upon harbouring suspicion in regard to William's past deeds and motivations. Yes, he had become close to the giant and a bond had been created on that first fateful meeting, but he felt sure he had not misjudged the man, that there was no evil or darkness within him.

'You must be on your guard, Brother Elwin, for I fear you may be mistaken. His stories of the past may be a clever fiction intended to deceive, and until we can confirm his words there must be an element of caution and doubt. Not lightly do people seek sanctuary, and light are not the deeds which often cause them to do so.' Prior Vargas fixed Arthur with his gaze. 'I warn you as I did before, Brother Elwin, and I hope you will return to the sense of good judgement I know you to be capable of.' He paused and glanced towards the mainland to the north. 'Now, I must go and prepare to greet pilgrims who have arrived from distant lands in order to visit us here.'

The prior turned away from the old monk and opened the door to the entrance hall, stepping inside the granite building. Arthur watched him, feeling anger at the man's words, though he tried to cast it aside in the knowledge that William was as he judged him to be and had no trace of the sin which seemed to be expected of his character by Prior Vargas.

Arthur sighed and tried to release the tension in his shoulders as he stepped through the doorway and entered the hall, beginning to understand the hardships the giant had faced, not least in overcoming the quick judgement of others.

23

The light sea breeze made the leaves of the fruit trees whisper as Arthur walked amidst them checking for any sign of fungal or insect infestation. He was thankful for the dappled shade the boughs gave him from the warm summer sun as he moved slowly, examining the occasional leaf or branch with great care. The anger he had felt four days previous after hearing the words of Prior Vargas had long since passed and been replaced by the inner certainty of William's honesty and goodness. He had not a single doubt about the giant's character. The man's words were no lie and his actions spoke greatly of his gentleness. They had sat together on the seat the day before, sharing a few scattered words and enjoying the silences between as they took in the glories of nature beneath a hazy sun which was softened by high cloud. Arthur did not care that others may deem him foolish, his friendship with the giant was stronger than any he had with a Brother.

He raised his right hand and turned a leaf above his head, finding the darkness upon its veined greenness to be merely a shadow cast by a high branch. He smiled and stepped a little further around the apple tree as the soft sound of footsteps could be heard approaching.

Turning, Arthur saw Brother Cook walking up to him. 'Brother Cook, how are you this fine day?' he asked with a smile, the young man's face covered in sweat after toiling at the vegetable patches.

The other monk did not smile in return, but bore an expression of grave seriousness. 'Brother Elwin, I must speak with you on a matter I know is close to your heart.'

Arthur's smile faded as he noted the look upon the Brother's face and the touch of sadness in his tone. 'Is all not well, Brother Cook? Tell me your problem so I may offer counsel and give help should it be within my power.'

'This matter is not with regard to myself nor any quandary I find myself in.'

Arthur's pulse increased. The young monk before him was clearly concerned and upset by some circumstance of importance. 'Brother Cook, I would have you tell me of what you speak.'

'Prior Vargas, he has been talking with each of us in turn about the residence of your friend. From his words, his purpose is clear. He wishes rid of the giant.'

Arthur's eyes widened. 'What reasons has he given?'

'He suspects a great, ungodly evil to reside within the wretch and that his flight to this place was forced by some great sin committed by his hands.' Brother Cook heard the faint sound of footsteps and paused to glance over his shoulder, spying two of his Brothers walking gently up the incline of the gardens with cut herbs bundled in their arms ready to be sun dried and then hung in the kitchen stores. They soon passed out of hearing distance and he turned back to Arthur. 'He seeks support in expelling the creature from the priory.'

'Expulsion!' exclaimed Arthur in horror. 'By what proof does he make such claims about William's character and his past?'

'None but that of argument and reasoning. Brother Elwin, can you be sure Prior Vargas is mistaken?' The young monk searched Arthur's gaze.

Arthur nodded. 'I am certain of William's goodness. He is a kind man who has been badly treated and I will not have that treatment continued in a place of our Lord such as this.'

'What will you do?'

'There is only one thing to do. I must take William to Prior Vargas. They must meet and converse. Prior Vargas can question him and discover for himself the truth which lies behind his unusual appearance.'

'Then you must hurry for Prior Vargas seeks the giant's departure in haste.'

Arthur nodded again and lay his right hand upon the young monk's shoulder. 'I am thankful, Brother Cook, that you came to speak with me about this matter.'

'How could I not, Brother Elwin? I count you as a friend amongst the Brothers and one who has helped me on many an occasion. Your advice has seen me through times of doubt and kept me upon the path of our Lord.'

'I am glad of it, and should you ever have need again I shall always be willing to give you aid in whatever way I can, especially after your attentiveness in bringing me back to health after my accident on the steps.'

Brother Cook forced a smile, the dimples in his cheeks deepening. 'Thank you, Brother Elwin. I am sorry to be the harbinger of such news.'

Arthur squeezed the young monk's shoulder. 'It is I that must thank you for informing me of Prior Vargas' intentions. After dinner I shall fetch William to his quarters and act as witness to their meeting.'

'I pray it goes well for you.'

'Your prayers should not be for me, Brother Cook, but for William, for he is in need.'

The young monk nodded as Arthur withdrew his hand.

'Now, return to your duties and worry not, for this matter is now out of your hands.' Arthur smiled.

Brother Cook looked into the old monk's blue eyes and found solace in their firmness of conviction. Turning, he departed in order to tend the vegetable patches once more, leaving Arthur to the whispering of the fruit trees.

24

After a dinner of thick, turnip soup and fresh bread purchased from the mainland, Arthur left the refectory. He walked past the library and into the corridor where the monks' cells were located. Entering the entrance hall at the end, he went to the back door to his right. Exiting into the shadow cast by the chapel, he ascended the few stone steps which led to the high building. He stood a moment and looked to the north. The beaches below Marghas Byghan curved gently to the east and west away from Top Tieb harbour, which was built in a small promontory of rocks midway along the town's length. Small boats came and went, ferrying people and goods between the Mount and the mainland while the tide was high.

Arthur watched the boats upon the blue waters for a moment, the sand beneath the waves lending them a turquoise richness as the wakes of the vessels marked their passage to and from the Mount. He was glad to be away from the hustle and bustle of the hurried world beyond the priory and hoped that he could soon ensure that William's residence upon the island would continue.

He turned to the chapel and entered through the rear door. His sandalled footsteps echoed hauntingly in the eaves as he walked along the nave to the front of the building and descended the steps which led to the giant's door. It was closed and he paused momentarily to listen for sounds of activity beyond, hearing none and fearing William may be out.

He knocked and waited for a response, feeling a little tense as he anticipated the meeting with prior Vargas and hoped all would go well.

'Who is it?' came William's muffled enquiry from within.

'It is Brother Elwin. I would speak with you on a matter of some importance.'

There were sounds of movement from within and the door swung open. 'Arthur, it is good to see you,' greeted the giant with a smile, the expression falling when he noted the serious expression on his friend's face. 'Please, come in,' he said, stepping back.

The smell of mouldy straw and body odour struck Arthur as he entered the small room. He noted that the entire left-hand side was devoted to a rough bed of straw laid upon the flagstones and saw a male sparrow sitting on the edge of a battered and stained table to the right.

'Please forgive the humbleness of my surroundings.'

'There is nothing to forgive, William. Humbleness is a virtue.'

The giant nodded as he closed the door.

Arthur looked around for a place to sit. He decided upon the straw bed despite its damp smell, fearing the cold stones of the floor would cause him considerable discomfort. He settled upon the bed with legs crossed and William followed suit.

'What is this matter you have come to see me about?'

'I wish you to accompany me on a visit to Prior Vargas.'

'Have I done something wrong?' asked William with concern.

Arthur shook his head. 'No, dear friend. I only wish for the two of you to meet and converse a while. To this day I am the only member of the priory with whom you have spoken, and though this is a valued honour, I feel it only right that you reveal yourself to the head of the priory.'

William looked into the monk's blue eyes. 'Have I need for alarm, Arthur? Has something been said or done of which I should be informed?' he asked, detecting something more within the depth of his friend's gaze, something which was being left unsaid.

Arthur sighed. 'There is a feeling afoot that you are not as you seem. I would have Prior Vargas discover for himself the truth of your person and the goodness within.'

'What have I done to warrant such feeling? Surely none of my actions upon the Isle have caused any need for concern.'

'Though I am loath to say it, I fear it is your appearance that sets these feelings within the minds of men, and your silence and secrecy have aided in this.'

William looked at the floor. 'So it is my doing.'

'In part, but I believe it is the minds of men which are at fault here, men who have grown used to a world that judges without knowledge, without discovering the underlying truth. If you will but accompany me to see the prior I am sure all will be righted, for he cannot fail to see what I see.'

The giant was silent and then turned to his friend. 'When would you have me accompany you?'

'Now would be the best time for this visit, for it is our time of rest and contemplation. Prior Vargas will be in his rooms and we can have an audience which is not likely to be disturbed.'

William nodded and stood up. 'So be it.' He held out his hand and helped Arthur to his feet.

'I see you have another friend amongst the residents of the Mount,' said the old monk, hoping to lighten the mood a little as he looked at the sparrow which watched every movement the men made with its head cocked to one side. It teetered precariously upon the edge of the table, its wings fluttering a little.

'It is the bird I found in the gardens beside our seat.'

'How goes it with his development?'

'His strength increases daily and in truth he could probably take flight upon this day if I were inclined to release him, but I promised the children they could watch his time of liberty and do not relish the ending of his companionship.'

The sparrow chirped and looked up at William expectantly, hoping to be fed.

'It has been a comfort to have his company and he shall be sorely missed.'

Arthur nodded. 'I once had a hound to which I became greatly attached. When she departed this life I suffered from the loss a great deal.' He reached up and patted William on the shoulder. 'Come, we must go and visit Prior Vargas.'

The old monk led the way from the small anteroom and they walked up the chapel's nave as gulls called loudly from the roof above, breaking the silence which gathered itself within the hallowed building.

Soon they passed through the entrance hall and were in the corridor where the monks' cells were located, doors lining the right-hand wall. Arthur stopped before the first of these and William lingered behind him, a little tension creeping into his muscles. There rested much of importance upon the coming meeting. If it went well then all would go well with regard to his continued residence. He dared not think of the consequences if it were to go ill.

Arthur knocked and they waited for a reply.

'Enter.' The word was both loud and firm.

The old monk grasped the brass handle which was tarnished by years of sweat and grime. Entering, he immediately spied Prior Vargas sitting behind his desk opposite the door, a quill held between the fingers of his right hand. The prior stared past him as William ducked low and entered the small study, the prior's sleeping chamber visible through a doorway to the right.

'What is the meaning of this disturbance?' asked Prior Vargas with a tone of annoyance, his pale brow furrowed as he turned his cold gaze to Arthur.

'I thought it timely for William to speak with you,' replied the old monk with his eyes narrowed against the sunlight pouring into the room from the window behind the prior.

'On what subject, Brother Elwin?'

'Any you should choose with regard to my life before arriving here,' replied William, straightening to his full height and studying the prior's long face, his cheeks hollow and nose hawkish.

'I have not the time. There are important matters to attend to.' The prior continued to address Arthur rather than the giant standing beside the old monk.

'Surely this matter is itself of great importance, Prior Vargas?' Arthur held his superior's gaze without faltering.

The prior lowered his quill. 'I will have a private word with you when this is done, Brother Elwin,' he stated before finally turning his attention to William, whose fearful countenance was brightly lit by the sunlight. 'Please sit,' he said, indicating a simple, wooden chair before his desk.

William stepped over and did as Prior Vargas had instructed, the seat complaining under his substantial weight. 'Thank you.'

'Now,' said the prior with a glance at Arthur, who stood with his hands clasped before him to the giant's right. 'You say your name is William Tillbury, is that correct?' he asked, a slowness to his words as if talking to a child.

William nodded. 'It is.'

'You were granted temporary sanctuary here because of the aid you gave to Brother Elwin, do you understand?'

William nodded again.

'However, I am concerned about your reasons for being here. Why did you come to the Mount of St Michael?' Prior Vargas stared across the table at the giant, his fingers steepled and elbows resting on the table as he studied the man of unfortunate appearance.

'I came to seek a peaceful life,' replied William.

The prior shook his head. 'That is not what I meant,' he said with a hint of irritation, his words still spoken with exaggerated clarity and slowness. 'What did you do that caused you to flee from the world beyond this holy place?'

'It was not I, but another who caused me to flee. A woman freed me from the chains in which I was held captive. Once free, I made good my escape and journeyed here in order to find a new life.'

The Prior frowned at William. 'You committed no crime?' he asked.

'No. I escaped from a master who treated me as a beast and exhibited me as an abnormality to be used for his financial gain. There has been no wrongdoing on my part.'

'If this is the truth, then why have you kept your own counsel during your stay here until only recently?' asked Prior Vargas, the condescending manner of his speech gone now the giant had displayed that he was not slow of mind.

'At first I feared to approach another. The world of men had made me wary and fearful of others. Then, in time, I learnt to trust Brother Elwin. It was only recently that I finally found the courage to bring words to our companionship. Believing Brother Elwin to be a man of great kindness, I decided it was time to trust in another and this has been rewarded.' William glanced up at Arthur and smiled briefly.

'Am I truly to believe you have not committed some terrible act, the consequences of which have caused you to seek refuge amongst us?'

'Yes. My only crime is that of a man fleeing a master who mistreated me. There is no other tarnish upon my soul,' he said with sincerity. 'As a man of God I ask you, look into my eyes and you will find no lie there, only the suffering which I have endured at the hands of others.'

William held the prior's gaze and the two men stared across the table at each other. The air of the simple study was thick with expectancy. Prior Vargas studied the giant's striking features, but tried not to let their ghastly nature influence his thoughts.

'I believe your words are true,' conceded the prior after a few moments of consideration. He leant back against his chair. 'You are due an apology, for I judged you from afar and did so incorrectly. There was great error on my part, and for both this and my misjudgement I hope you can forgive me.'

'There is nothing to forgive, Prior Vargas. You have allowed me the opportunity to show my true self and that is enough. I am mindful of my appearance and understand how it influences the thoughts of those who witness my abnormality.'

'Then you have an understanding few can possess.' The prior looked at William with a soft smile. He stood and held his hand out over the desk. 'You are welcome here and your stay need know no limits.'

William stood and took the offered hand, the two men shaking firmly.

'Thank you for your generosity.'

'I hope you find the peace you desire and that you will find the time to speak with me again sometime.'

William nodded and turned to the door.

'Do you still wish to have a word with me, Prior Vargas?' asked Arthur.

'Yes, but it is not of the kind that was originally intended, Brother Elwin.'

'If you wait for me in the entrance hall I shall not be long, William,' said the old monk over his shoulder.

The giant nodded again and opened the door. Ducking, he stepped into the gloomy corridor beyond and shut it behind him, his footsteps faint as he walked to the door which led to the entrance hall.

Prior Vargas looked at Arthur as he continued to stand behind his desk, silhouetted against the brightness of the window. 'I cannot say I am pleased that you imposed such a visit upon me without warning, but am thankful at its outcome. Had it not been for your intervention I may have committed my own crime in casting William from among us.'

Arthur dipped his head, keeping his hands clasped before him.

'I am glad to have met him and now I see why you share a bond of friendship. His gentleness and intelligence are clear in his eyes and in his words were no lies.' He paused for thought momentarily, glancing down at the desktop. 'Though I detect a great sadness residing within him which fills me with pity.'

'I have witnessed this sadness and indeed it is great, but in time it will depart if peace he can find here.'

'Thank you, old friend, for saving me from foolishness.'

Arthur smiled warmly. 'There was no foolishness on your part. You looked, but you did not see, and that is an easy mistake for any man to make. I cannot claim innocence when it comes to such things.'

'Then maybe we are both fools, Brother Elwin,' responded Prior Vargas with a regretful smile. 'As fools together we shall say a prayer for William with our Brothers on this day and let it be known that he is to stay and be welcomed into our hearts. Now, I must return to the duties with which I was busied upon your arrival.'

'May the Lord be with you, Prior Vargas,' said Arthur with a bow of his head.

'May the Lord be with you, Brother Elwin, and I thank you once again,' replied Prior Vargas.

Arthur turned and left the simple study, the corridor beyond noticeably cooler, no sunlight penetrating its confines. He walked a short distance to the left and entered the entrance hall, William waiting, pacing back and forth.

'Is all well?' asked the giant.

Arthur smiled. 'All is well and you are welcome to continue abiding here among us, my friend,' he replied, glad his intuition had served him well. He had been sure Prior Vargas would be able to discern the truth of William's goodness and this surety had been borne out. 'Shall we go sit awhile in the gardens?'

William nodded and returned Arthur's smile.

The two companions left the hall through the main door and headed for their favourite place of restfulness, the warm sun lighting their expressions of renewed calm and tranquillity as they descended the stone steps where they had first met in the stormy throes of autumn.

25

William crouched on the rocks on the south side of the Isle, the expanse of the ocean before him. It was low tide and no ships would be using the harbour on the other side of the island, there was no chance of being seen by passing vessels and he felt secure in this knowledge as he gazed into a rock pool.

Beside his bare feet was one of the grubby pieces of cloth in which they were usually wrapped. Contained in its folds were a number of small fish he had caught with his hands, some of which would become his supper, the others his breakfast, along with some bread he had been given by Brother Cook. The young monk had come to his room, forcing an apprehensive smile as he had left the piece of bread on the table before bowing in silent departure, not wishing to linger and unable to find the power of speech, such were his nerves.

The giant watched a hermit crab scuttle back beneath a stone he had just moved in order to search for any fish that may have been using it as a hiding place, the creature's shell a vivid orange. He smiled as the light breeze rippled the surface of the pool and then picked a pale whelk from a rock beside the shimmering waters, placing it upon the cloth amidst the fish, one of which flicked its tail in response to the disturbance, its life not yet departed.

Looking up, he spied a larger pool closer to the point where the rocks fell away to the deep waters. He stood and walked over to it, the rocks warm beneath his feet after a day of bright sunshine.

As he approached there was a sudden ripple in the pool which indicated the presence of a fish and his smile grew. During the winter months this had been a hard task sometimes made impossible by the violence of the weather, but in the heat of summer he found great pleasure in being upon the shore. He enjoyed the solitude and the uninterrupted view across the ocean, its tidal caress soft and soothing.

He crouched beside the new pool and saw the crevice on the far side which was the only place of hiding for the fish. Vibrant green seaweed covered the right-hand side of the pool and glistened on the rocks beyond, winkles moving slowly amidst its tendrils. On another day both would have served as adequate food, but not on this. When autumn came William knew he would have to make do with such, but while the fish were plentiful and the waters calm and warm he would enjoy their succulence and nourishment.

With great care he leant forward, hands before him. His movements were slow and considered as he placed them into the water and moved them to either side of where he knew the fish to be concealed. Then, steadily, he brought his hands closer together.

There. He saw the fish peek from the crevice. His hands came together with surprising speed, but the fish evaded them and darted to the edge of the seaweed, the water becoming too shallow for it to hide in the green tangles.

William sidled to the right, his hands dripping as he continued to hold them out before him. Repeating his previous actions, the giant tried to limit the chances of escape, his huge hands slowly closing in on the fish as it remained motionless.

His hands rushed together, the disturbance in the water creating large ripples upon its surface. William smiled victoriously as he felt the creature in his grasp and rose to his feet. He took his catch over to the cloth and dropped it amongst the others. It tossed and writhed in the sunlight for a few moments, its movements soon losing their vigour.

The sound of children's laughter made William look up and he spied Jacob and Rachel clambering over the rocks towards him.

'Will,' called Jacob, waving at the giant enthusiastically and wearing a short, grey tunic.

With a hint of regret that his solitude had been short-lived mingled with joy at the sight of the children, William raised his hand and waved in return.

They quickly scrambled across the rocks towards him, William watching worriedly as Rachel briefly tottered in her haste, sure she would fall, but the young girl regained her balance and advanced as if nothing untoward had occurred. Soon they drew up in front of him breathlessly, his large shadow falling across them.

'Good day to you both,' greeted the giant as he crouched and the sun shone in their eyes, Jacob and Rachel raising their hands to act as shades as they squinted.

'Hello, Will. What are ye doing?' asked Rachel, her pale green summer dress rippling slightly in the breeze.

'Have ye caught all these?' asked Jacob, noticing the cloth upon which the fish lay with a scattering of whelks.

'Yes, I have caught every last one.'

'What are ye going to do with them?'

'They will all find a home in here.' William patted his stomach and Rachel wrinkled her slightly upturned nose. 'Do you not like to eat fish?' he asked the girl.

'Not when they still have heads on. I feel as though they are staring at me from my plate,' she replied.

William smiled. 'What about with their heads removed?'

'Our father brings home much larger fish than these,' stated Jacob as he bent down beside the catches.

'I am sure he does, but your father probably does not catch them in rock pools with his hands.'

'Ye used your hands to catch them?' asked Rachel in surprise.

William nodded. 'Have you ne'er done such a thing?'

She shook her head.

'What about you, Jacob?'

The boy shrugged and prodded at the largest fish, which was not much bigger than one of the giant's fingers.

'Then I must teach you both, if you wish to learn, that is.'

'I do,' said Rachel, putting her hand up as if in a classroom.

'I am the eldest, so Will should show me first,' said Jacob as he stood up.

'I can show you both and so it matters little who is first.'

The young boy frowned, but voiced no disagreement.

'First, we must find a rock pool with at least one fish in it,' said William, rising to his full height.

The children looked about them.

'The best ones are often the closest to the sea,' added the giant, having already spied what appeared to be a suitable location and using subtlety to guide the children's gazes in the right direction.

'There!' called Jacob, pointing to a pool near the water's edge, the surf still occasionally washing into it when a larger wave than most broke upon the rocks.

The three of them made their way over, the children rushing ahead despite William's large stride. They crouched at the pool's edge and the giant's gaze fell upon an anemone of deep red with tentacles reaching out before it, swaying back and forth as the waters of a wave rushed into the pool before receding gently.

'Do you see that?' William pointed at it.

'It is a sea anemone,' said Rachel.

'You have taught me something new today,' said the giant. 'Until now I did not know the proper name for that creature.'

'I knew it too,' said Jacob with a tinge of disappointment.

'Then I must thank you both for contributing to my growing knowledge of the seashore.'

The children beamed.

'Do you spy any fish in the pool?'

Their young, innocent eyes scanned the waters.

'I see one,' stated Jacob excitedly, pointing to the far side where a pale brown fish of small proportions lingered beside the rock, hoping to go unnoticed.

'That is not big enough to eat,' said Rachel.

'I did not say it was,' responded Jacob.

'Its size matters not as long as I can use it in order to teach you both to catch fish with your hands. I must admit, I am surprised you do not already have such a skill.'

Rachel turned to the giant. 'We usually use a net,' she stated in a matter-of-fact manner. 'It is much easier.'

'I am sure it is, but I am also sure it is not as much fun nor as satisfying.'

She looked at him dubiously.

'Will ye show me what to do?' asked Jacob, leaning out over the water.

'First, you must put your hands into the water some distance from the fish, so as not to disturb it,' instructed William.

Jacob put his hands into the water, which remained cool after so recently being left behind by the receding tide. 'Now what should I do, Will?'

'Ever so slowly, move your left hand to the rear of the fish and your right in front of it, but still keep them as far away from the creature as possible.'

Jacob leant further out over the water, dropping to his bare knees, which slipped a little and entered the edge of the pool. The fish remained motionless despite the slight disturbance and the boy's gaze was unblinking as he stared at his prey.

'Now, bring your hands together very slowly,' said William, 'and when I say the word "go", quickly snap them shut about the fish.'

Rachel watched her brother, wide eyes filled with fascination, almost holding her breath, such was her tension. Jacob did as the giant had said, his hands moving slowly through the water towards the fish from front and rear, all his concentration upon the task.

'GO!' called William.

Jacob's hands quickly clasped shut.

'Did ye catch it? Did ye catch it?' asked Rachel breathlessly.

Jacob opened his hands and peered within. With a frown, he revealed the emptiness. 'It got away,' he said with a glance towards the waters before him.

'Do not worry, Jacob. It took me many attempts before I caught my first fish. They are extremely quick and sometimes, even when you think they are captured, they wriggle free between your fingers.'

'Can I try now?' asked Rachel, looking eagerly up at William.

He nodded. 'Though we first have to discover where the fish has hidden itself this time.'

The children's attention again turned to the rock pool and they sought the fish.

'There, do you see it?' asked William with a nod downward, spying the creature before him hiding amidst some strands of brown seaweed.

'Can ye help me, Will?' asked Rachel, looking up at him as he moved aside so she could gain better access.

He nodded and manoeuvred himself so that he knelt behind her. Taking her small hands in his and looking at her thin fingers, William was reminded of delicate porcelain as he guided them beneath the clear waters of the pool. The contrast between the fragility of her hands and the largeness of his was very apparent, causing a strong protectiveness to rise within him with regard to the children.

The fish gently flicked its tail, but did not leave the meagre shelter of the seaweed. Guiding her hands closer, William kept his gaze on the creature as he looked over the girl's golden hair and the trap closed in about the quarry.

'Now,' he whispered, moving her hands to ensnare the fish in a sudden wash of movement.

'I've got it. I've got it,' she called out as William released her hands and she held them high in the air, water dripping from her fingers like glittering diamonds capturing the sunlight in their descent back to the pool.

'Have ye really got it, Rachel?' asked Jacob, feeling excitement at his sister's aided success rather than bitterness that she was able to capture that which had eluded him.

With an animated, joyful expression, Rachel looked at her brother. 'I can feel it wriggling,' she said, shrieking with delight in response to the slightly ticklish sensations against her palms.

'Well done, Rachel,' said William with a large smile.

She looked over her shoulder at the giant. 'I did it,' she stated with a triumphant grin, her eyes sparkling.

'Let me see,' said Jacob, craning his neck to see into her hands as she held them out before her and William moved to her side.

Rachel carefully opened her hands and jumped in surprise as the fish suddenly leapt out, Jacob falling back upon his heels as it dropped back into the waters. 'See,' she said, 'I caught it.'

William nodded and smiled. 'Indeed you did. Would you like to have another try, Jacob?'

The boy shook his head, blond locks bright in the sunshine.

'Is there anything else you would like to do?'

'Can you give me a piggyback ride?' he asked.

'And me,' said Rachel quickly, putting her hand up again, her recent achievement quickly forgotten as she got to her feet.

'Do you think I could carry both of you at the same time?' asked William, his smile warm.

Jacob nodded. 'I do.'

Rachel regarded him with her head cocked to one side. 'Probably,' she replied after a moment's thought.

'Come on then,' said William as he reached down and picked Rachel up, swinging her onto his left shoulder as she giggled. Then he took hold of Jacob and bore him up onto his right shoulder, the children's legs dangling to either side of his face. He wrapped his arms up and over their laps to hold them in place and slowly stood, turning to the rocky crags that rose 50 yards ahead of them, the shoreline a little way from their base and rich with green grasses.

Testing his balance with a couple of tentative steps, he then set off across the rocks, which were relatively smooth until closer to the shoreline. William took great care as he conveyed the children towards the Isle, their weight growing with each step. Rachel put her hand in his mop of black curls and gripped tightly as he briefly lost his balance and had to take a quick sideways step in adjustment, wincing at the slight pain caused by her actions.

They reached the rough, rocky climb to the shoreline and the going became much slower as he bent over a little and began to make his way up to the grass and thrift. Then, before the ridge which marked the point of high tide and border between earth and rocks, William stood as the children disembarked onto the Isle.

'Ye did it,' said Rachel happily as the giant climbed up to join them below the southern bluffs.

'Can ye carry us to the harbour?' asked Jacob.

William wiped perspiration from his brow and chuckled as he shook his head. 'I am afraid not. I fear it would be the death of me in such warm weather.'

'Can we still meet ye in two days to watch the release of the bird?' asked Rachel.

'Of course.'

'We should be getting home, Rachel,' said Jacob with a glance towards the sun, which was hanging in the western sky, gathering clouds threatening to mask its presence, its rays piercing through gaps in the greyness and moving slowly across the land like beams of hazy gold descending from heaven.

'Goodbye, Will,' said the little girl, stepping forward and hugging the giant's leg.

'Goodbye, Rachel. I will see you soon.' He patted her head affectionately.

Jacob stepped forward and hugged William's other leg, a large smile on his face. 'Thank ye for the ride, horsey.'

William ruffled his hair. 'My pleasure.'

The children released him and turned to make their way around the western side of the Mount. They skipped and bound over the grasses, looking over their shoulders and waving their final farewell before being hidden from view by the rising rocks.

William stood and stared at the point where they had disappeared from his sight. A warm smile graced his face as a group of gulls flew overhead towards the ocean, calling as they went. He sighed with contentment and then began to make his way back down to the rocks to collect his catch and the cloth in which the fish rested.

26

They sat together in silence upon the seat and stared out over the gardens and the sea beyond, where a weather front of thick clouds obscured the horizon with grey rainfall. Above them the sky remained clear and the sun beat down upon the companions as they shared moments of contemplative peace.

'I saw the children again today,' said William without turning.

'Were they in the gardens?' asked Arthur, also continuing to gaze at the panoramic view before them.

'No, I met them on the southern rocks revealed by low tide.'

'Your residence upon the Mount has remained a secret thus far, but my confidence does not lie in the loose tongues of children.'

'I have faith that they can keep my presence secret. They have succeeded so far and I see no reason why they should fail.'

Arthur turned to his friend. 'I hope you are correct in your estimation, William.' He studied the giant's profile. 'Was your childhood truly only filled with the hardship you have described to me?' he enquired, his words soft, a yellow brimstone fluttering about his head and then taking wing to the terraces below.

There was a brief hesitation before William replied. 'In relation to my father, yes. When he was not in attendance I recall playing at a nearby stream. I would build dams of piled stones held together with thick mud to hold back or divert the waters. Beneath the stones fish were revealed on occasion, bullheads and sticklebacks which I would catch with my hands and then contain within pools dug beside the running waters. By chance, that is the activity in which I was engaged when meeting the children this very day.'

'Did you not have any friends?'

William sighed and shook his head as the reflections in his eyes were filled with the rain clouds passing on the horizon. 'No, I preferred solitude even then. The cause may have been the treatment I suffered at my father's hands, but of this I cannot be sure.' He paused a moment, looking at his friend. 'And you, Arthur, did you have many friends with which to find adventure?'

'A sister only. I grew up a farmer's son in the wilds of rural England. She was three years my senior and we would play in the fields, fighting with sticks for swords or climbing trees. They were happy times indeed,' he said with a melancholy smile.

'Do you still have contact with your sister?'

Arthur shook his head. 'She died six years past and I did not hear tell of it until she was long since buried.'

'I am sorry,' said William, hearing the sorrow and regret in his friend's tone.

'We are all touched by such things as life goes on.'

William turned back to the view and his thoughts returned to Jacob and Rachel. The children were like a couple of joyful faerie folk who had come dancing into his life, magic glittering in their eyes. As far as he could discern, they were still untouched by the harshness that life could bring, were removed from the realities of the adult world to a great degree. Their youthful innocence was a gift which he had never experienced and he was thankful to be able to share it, even if only briefly. Their purity made him glad of heart and he was happy to have made their acquaintance.

27

Three shadowy figures waited on the beach beneath the red-brown cliffs of Marghas Byghan as a small rowboat approached in the darkness. The southerly wind that had risen during the evening had swelled the tide, the waves crashing upon the shingle and rocks, the surf angry and filled with white froth.

The wooden hull of the vessel scraped on the shingle as it beached before the waiting men, one of its two passengers leaping into the waters and making his way to those upon the shore.

Pete the Hand stepped forward as the sailor came towards him from amidst the boiling surf. 'It is good to see ye, Adam. How was your voyage?' he greeted, holding out his left hand.

'It be good to be back upon these shores, I can tell ye,' replied the muscular man, dressed in a grey sarong and a pale shirt laced with cord. 'A merciless storm consumed us in howling winds and mountainous waves, the air thick with spray and rain, the deck awash and the day turned to night beneath black clouds. It unleashed itself upon us during the return and for a time we thought ourselves lost to the depths, such was its fury,' he said as they shook hands.

'I am glad such thoughts came to naught,' said Pete before turning to the Tupp twins, who remained a little way up the shingle in silence. 'Come on boys, lets get this boat unloaded before any chance of discovery. I have no wish to lose my other hand.'

The four men waded into the rough waters, the waves buffeting their thighs as they moved alongside the rowing boat. Adam climbed aboard and, with his crewmate, lifted a barrel which was passed to the twins. They took it back to shore and carried it well out of reach of the waters as Adam and Pete the Hand shared the burden of another.

They removed two further barrels and then Adam gave a black bag to Pete, its metal contents chinking with the movement. 'See what ye can get for these,' said the sailor as he stood in the boat. 'It should be a goodly sum if I guess their value correctly.'

Pete the Hand stood in the waves and let the bag rest against the bottom of the boat. Undoing the drawstring, he peered inside to find a selection of pewter plates and goblets, along with silver cutlery and candle holders which glinted in the gloom. With eyes bright, he looked up at the other man, whose face was clean-shaven and defined by strength. 'Where did ye get these?' he asked, a piece of seaweed wrapping itself about his leg, the smuggler reaching into the waters and taking its slimy fingers from about his thigh, throwing the glistening brown mass out into the rough waters.

'When the storm which had nearly overwhelmed us abated we happened upon a small boat. There was but one man within its waterlogged confines, a man so battered and bruised that his life was stowed away deep within. Accompanying him on that boat were these treasures and more.'

'He was just drifting upon the ocean?'

'Aye. From the pieces of debris we came upon soon after we guessed his ship had not found the same fortune as ours and had gone down in the maw of the storm.'

'Will your captain not miss these things?' Pete the Hand held Adam's gaze in the darkness, his eyes sparkling.

Adam shook his head. 'They were ne'er counted as part of the haul, for me and Robert were set to the task of logging all that was found with the sailor,' he said with a nod towards his young companion.

'And what of the sailor?'

'He still lies upon his sickbed with no sign of life other than the rise and fall of his chest. At low tide on the morrow he will be taken to the mainland across the bar as we again take on cargo in readiness to depart in three days.'

'So he is the only man who could tell these things have gone astray?'

Adam nodded. 'Aye. That is so.'

The hoot of an owl could be heard above the sounds of the surf and Pete the Hand stiffened, quickly turning to look back at the shore. Another hoot sounded and he could just about discern that Jack Tupp had his hands to his mouth.

'It is the warning signal,' Pete said to Adam, pulling the drawstring of the bag tightly shut and looking along the beach in both directions, seeing no sign of any others beneath the cloudy sky.

His gaze turned to the rolling waters, eyes narrowing as he scanned the waves, searching for the cause of Jack's alarm call. Still he saw nothing.

Looking towards Carrack Looz en Cooz, he first peered at the harbour, which was no more than a deep shadow at the foot of the island. Then his gaze was attracted by movement on the eastern shoreline of the Isle and his eyes widened. There, standing atop the dark outline of rocks before the waves, was a tall shadow, a giant whose cloak billowed in the wind.

'Do ye see it?' he asked the sailors without turning his gaze from the unsettling sight.

'Aye,' replied Adam, he and Robert watching the giant intently.

'Is it watching us or does it face the ocean to the south?' asked Pete the Hand, his voice quivering with trepidation.

Adam shook his head, the wind tossing his brown hair as a large wave hit the stern of the boat, rocking it and twisting it so that its port side ran parallel to the shore. 'I cannot tell,' he said before jumping into the waves and manhandling the vessel so that the stern again faced the incoming waves, not wishing the boat to be capsized by the force of the rollers.

Adam stood in the surf beside Pete, the two men staring at the alarming silhouette upon the island rocks. It began to move, heading inland with large strides beyond those of a normal man. Within moments it was gone, hidden in the pitch gathered upon the northern side of the island.

'Do ye think it lingers hidden in the darkness and notes our activities?' Pete turned to the sailor.

'There is naught we can do if that be the case,' replied Adam, turning to the one-handed smuggler. 'It is time for us to return to our ship, though I do not relish the thought of being moored at the harbour now I have seen what dwells upon the Holy Isle.'

'Should we warn the captain?' asked Robert as he sat within the rowboat.

'Nay, we cannot give any clue as to our whereabouts this night. We must stay alert and watch for this beast, but tell no other. The risk is too high that we be caught and I have no liking of the hangman's noose.' He turned to Pete. 'Do ye have our share of the monies from our last visit?'

Pete the Hand reached to the leather belt about the waist of his dark tunic and untied a black pouch. The coins inside chinked as he passed it to the sailor, who tested its weight upon his palm. He then passed the purse to Robert, who set it down in the boat.

'Now help me launch into this unruly sea so we may return undetected.'

Leaving the bag of booty on the rowboat, Pete grappled with the bow of the vessel beside the sailor, his cloth-wrapped stump slipping against the wood. They pushed the hull off the shingle, the scraping sound making him wince with its volume, gaze quickly moving to the shadows of the island to search for any sign of the creature which he felt sure lay hidden in the darkness, feeling its malicious gaze upon him and shivering.

The two men moved to the port side and manoeuvred the vessel in the jarring waves until it was clear of the shore and beyond the breakers, both waist-deep in the water and thankful the slope of the beach was a gentle one. The swells of the waves rose about them, one so high as to cover their shoulders, spray upon their cheeks and hair, Pete spitting salt water from his mouth.

Adam pulled himself aboard. 'Here,' he called, passing out the black bag before he and Robert picked up their oars and slid them into the sea. 'Until next time. We shall return in a month if all goes well, so keep watchful for our sails.'

'That I will,' replied Pete, feeling uneasy and wishing to be hidden from prying eyes.

The sailors began to row, their muscles straining as the boat was tossed and battered. Pete turned from them and waded towards the shore, the sack thrown over his shoulder. The Tupp brothers waited in the shadows of the cliffs as he made his way from the surf and across the shingle, the faint sounds of the sack's contents audible as he tramped up the beach, the wind setting a chill upon his skin as his wet clothes clung to his thin frame.

'What was that?' asked Jack in a hushed voice, the brothers looking at Pete with fearful expressions.

Pete the Hand looked over his shoulder, seeing the struggling sailors rising and falling upon the waves, his gaze then fixing upon the rocks where the giant had stood. 'I do not know,' he replied as he turned back to them.

'Were it the giant of which John Hadden spoke?'

The smuggler looked at the elder twin. 'Maybe it was, but let us not speak of it now. We must get these barrels to the King's Arms in haste. The longer our time here the greater the chance we will be found out.'

The twins stared at him wordlessly, fear still apparent in their shadowy expressions.

'Do ye hear me?' hissed Pete in urgency.

They stepped forward as one and made for the barrels which were 10 yards down the incline of the beach. Pete watched them, lowering the sack onto the mix of sand and shingle. A shiver ran the length of his spine and he trembled from the chill which was digging deeper by the moment. It was a chill not only of the wind and water's doing, but one he felt sure had been set within his bones by the unnatural creature they had spied upon the Isle. He was certain it had been watching them and its evil he could sense in the pit of his stomach.

The Tupp twins came towards him bearing the first of the four barrels. When they drew alongside, he fell in step beside them as they made their way to the hidden tunnel entrance which would mask them from the gaze he felt sure was still upon them, filled with malice and the devil's dark light.

28

James Tupp opened the cellar door as he stood on the stone steps leading down into the musty room. To his right a group of sailors lounged at tables dressed in cord-laced shirts of linen and pale blue sarongs. Mary sat with her arms about one of the men and a woman with red hair was seated opposite, face alive with laughter as she joined in with the jollity. The sailors clapped and cheered as one of their number played a fiddle, doing a jig around them, much to their amusement. The playing stopped and tin cups were lifted in salute.

'More. More,' they cried boisterously, their cheeks flushed with consumption as the merrymaking continued, the fiddler striking up another lively tune.

Mary and her companion rose, linking arms and twirling in a vibrant dance made unsteady by the sailors' inebriation.

James peered round at the bar to the left. None of the local men gathered there had noticed him and so he loudly cleared his throat to attract attention.

Richard spied the younger Tupp and nodded, walking around the bar towards the twin. 'I shall be back shortly,' he said, the other men turning back to their drinks and conversations, all fully aware of the activities in which the landlord was involved, but happy to turn a blind eye while the drinks continued to flow.

James led the way down into the low-ceilinged cellar with its rough stone walls and earth floor, Richard following close on his heels after making sure to shut the door atop the stairs, the sounds of the raucous sailors drifting down into the gloom.

Below, in the light of a single lamp hung upon a wooden beam to the left, the landlord found Jack Tupp and Pete the Hand, four barrels of contraband placed beside the wall beneath the sickly, yellow light, the small door to the tunnel hidden behind them. There were rickety shelves upon the right-hand wall made of planks which had bent beneath the weight of the jugs and bottles they had borne during the years. The smell of earth and mould hung thick in the air, a large, dark patch of rising damp creeping up the back wall like a disease.

'It looks as if ye have been for a swim this night,' commented Richard, eyeing Pete's dripping clothes and noting the sack slung over his shoulder.

'The sea be rough, the south winds whipping the waves to a greater height than I had expected,' replied the smuggler, his dark hair glistening with moisture.

'Are ye going to tell him?' asked Jack, looking at Pete.

Richard glanced at the more vocal of the brothers and then turned his attention back to Pete the Hand. 'What is it that ye has to tell me?'

Pete breathed deeply and felt as if the walls and low beams of the ceiling were closing in about him. 'Do ye remember what John Hadden said he saw upon the beach when making the journey home one night?' he asked as cheers rose from above and the fiddle-playing came to a temporary end.

Richard nodded. 'Aye, a giant of sorts.'

'I did not believe his ravings to be true. I thought the drink was playing tricks on his mind.'

'As did I,' concurred Richard with another nod, scratching his beard briefly as another tune drifted from above, the sound dulled by its passage into the murky room.

'On this very night I have learned the truth of his words. It was no illusion John saw, but a giant of fearful appearance, for we saw it on the rocks of Carrack Looz en Cooz.'

Richard's bloodshot eyes widened momentarily and then narrowed as his expression changed from surprise to one of doubt. 'Ye be pulling my leg, I warrant.'

Pete shook his head. 'I wish it were so. The sight filled me with dread and I still feel its vile hand upon me.'

'Could ye have been mistaken in the darkness?' asked Richard after studying the other man's expression and finding no deception, his pulse quickening in response to the haunted look in the smuggler's eyes.

'No, there be no mistake,' he replied with a shake of his head, a drop of water snaking down his forehead. 'Its shape and size were without doubt as it stood upon the eastern rocks. Both of the brothers Tupp witnessed its presence also, as did the sailors with whom we met.'

'What did it do?'

'It watched us and then vanished into the darkness of the island.'

Richard thought for a moment. 'What do ye think we should do? How should we act upon this matter?'

'I do not know, for to alert the authorities will raise questions as to our activity upon the beach.'

'Then we should tell only those who are drinking above our heads,' said Richard. 'They must be warned that there is a beast afoot.'

Pete the Hand nodded. 'Aye, but they must swear to keep this only to those they trust.'

'Should we not seek it out as we did after Jebbit's sighting?' asked Jack, his brother standing silently beside him with a fretful look upon his face.

Pete and Richard turned to him, but gave no answer to his question. They stood in silence for a few moments, the muffled sounds of conversation apparent from above as the playing again came to a halt and the local men spoke loudly at the bar so as to be heard above the din arising from the group of drunken sailors as they banged their cups upon the table and called for another tune. The flame of the lamp flickered in a draught and the shadows upon the stone walls moved as if suddenly given the breath of life.

'We must hope the beast is not in residence in these here parts,' said Richard.

'I wish I could be confident of such, but fear it abides nearby.' Pete the Hand wiped away a drop of water which hung from the end of his nose. 'We must be watchful. If my fears are borne out it will not be long until it is seen again and this will be our confirmation.'

'Then let us keep your sighting a secret that only we four will share,' said Richard, the fiddler beginning a shanty in the room above.

'Are we not going to tell the others?' asked Jack with an upward glance.

Pete looked at the elder twin thoughtfully. 'That was my intent, but I believe it best to wait. If there be another sighting then we have our proof that the beast has made his home not far distant from the town.'

Richard looked at Pete, knowing the smuggler's sense of self-preservation had moulded his thoughts on the matter. Even to tell those who drank at the bar would be a great risk to his neck, for who could hold such a dark secret in silence, who could not let it be told to those they held dear for the sake of warning? Those in the tavern knew of the smuggling with which the establishment was connected and did not speak of it, but a tale of a giant on Carrack Looz en Cooz was a different matter. Richard was sure it would take little time for it to spread around the town, especially when brandy and mead had loosened tongues and with the previous sightings already having paved the way.

'Ye be right, Pete. This must be kept to us alone,' said the landlord, knowing that his own neck risked the noose if the authorities got wind of his shady dealings. He turned to Jack. 'Ye must swear an oath not to tell another living soul.'

The elder Tupp looked from Richard to Pete, who nodded his confirmation with a look of utmost seriousness.

'None of us wish to face the punishment of a creaking rope and dangling feet, and that be what ye bring upon us all should ye tell of the giant we saw this night,' said Pete the Hand to the twin, whose face became ashen at the thought, the consequences of his actions rarely perceived.

'I swear,' he whispered. 'I will not tell of this night and its terrifying sight.'

'Good.' Richard forced a thin smile. 'It is the only course of action truly open to us. We must watch and listen to discover if the beast is living nearby.'

'What then?' Jack looked at Richard and Pete, a worried expression upon his weathered face.

'The town will rally to rid us of its presence and it shall flee or die,' said Pete with confidence.

Richard nodded. 'Now, come and join the others for a drink and to dry yourselves before the fire.'

Pete put his sack upon the dirt floor beside the wall, the contents chinking lightly and the sound arousing Richard's curiosity, though he did not put voice to it. Instead, he took the lamp down from the nail on which it hung and led the way up the stairs to the warm interior of the King's Arms, the Tupp twins close behind as Pete lingered a moment in the growing darkness and stared at the barrels against the wall, the entrance to the tunnel leading to the beach firmly bolted behind them. A pang of fear came upon him as he imagined the giant creeping along the blackness of the smuggling tunnel with its head low, having spied their departure into the cliffs.

He shivered and quickly turned to follow the others as the sounds of the shanty and the sailors grew in volume, washing down the stone stairs as the door at the top was opened. He tried to convince himself that the bolt could hold should the giant find its way, though he was overcome by the feeling that the beast was already lurking on the other side of the small and low oak door in readiness to enter the cellar, its dark cloak gathered about it and filled with evil intent.

29

The day was overcast, gulls wheeling and turning over the steel grey sea south of the Isle, the winds perfect for the release of the sparrow. William sat alone on the seat on the north terrace. He glanced at the emptiness to his right where Arthur was usually seated. The nest he had woven for the bird rested there topped with a piece of deep blue cloth so the creature could not escape.

Resisting the temptation to peek within and check on the sparrow, William looked at the rough sea, a mist of spray rising from its turmoil. White crests crowned the swells as the waves rolled towards the shore. Ever changing, the waters held his gaze and filled him with a sense of calm.

There, upon the old wooden bench, he felt part of the world about him. Without separation, he was one with creation, his mind empty of distracting thoughts as he awaited the children's arrival.

Time grew meaningless as he absent-mindedly pulled his cloak tighter about his frame, the wind tossing his black curls with lithe fingers. The touch of a raindrop upon his cheek caused him to glance up, his eyes filling with thick clouds which laboured slowly across the sky.

'Will!' came a cry which shattered the calm and announced the children's arrival at the gardens.

He turned and greeted their presence with a warm smile as the gate creaked shut behind them and they ran along the path towards him, coat-tails flapping in their wake.

'Good afternoon, my friends,' he greeted, his deep voice filled with gladness. 'I am happy to see you could make it.'

'I would have come even if a gale were blowing,' said Rachel as both children tried to get their breath back, dark, hooded coats over their plain clothes.

'And I,' said Jacob.

'Then you would have not found me here, for I have more sense and would have stayed indoors,' he said with a grin.

The children chuckled and Jacob's gaze fell upon the cloth-covered nest. 'Is the bird in there?' he asked, his sister looking over, both their expressions filled with excitement and intrigue.

'Yes,' replied William.

'Can we see it?' Rachel looked up at the giant hopefully, her long, blonde hair blowing across her face.

'I see no reason why not,' he said, carefully picking up the nest and setting it upon his lap, taking the edges of the cloth from beneath it. 'Gather close,' he instructed.

The children stepped closer, their eyes intent upon the cloth which hid the bird from their sight.

'Do not make a noise, for you may frighten him.'

They both nodded without glancing up.

With slow deliberation, William pulled the cloth back from the nest slightly. 'Can you see him?' he asked in a whisper.

Rachel shook her head as her brother bent closer and peered into the gloom.

William pulled the cloth back a little further.

'There!' said Jacob in hushed exhilaration, glancing up at the giant with eyes alight.

William's smile grew as he watched the children, their expressions ones of wonder as they regarded the sparrow sitting motionless in the nest.

'It does not move,' whispered Rachel. 'Is it still alive?' Her gaze rose and she stared into the dark eyes of the man seated before her.

William nodded. 'It is most likely just fearful of the strange faces staring down at it. The sparrow is not moving because it hopes you will not detect its presence.'

'Are ye going to let it go now?' asked Jacob.

'Can I do it?' said Rachel, putting her hand in the air.

'What do you think, Jacob? Should your sister be allowed to release it?'

The boy looked at his sister for a moment as she gave him a pleading look filled with hopefulness. 'Aye,' he said with a nod.

'Yay!' exclaimed the girl, jumping in the air.

'Shh,' said William with a finger to his lips. 'You must try not to frighten the bird.'

Rachel's cheeks flushed with mild embarrassment and she put her hands behind her back. 'Sorry,' she said quietly.

'Carefully put your hands into the nest and cradle the bird in them,' said William. 'Do you remember how I taught you to catch fish?'

'Of course, it was only a few days ago,' she replied, her embarrassment forgotten.

'Good. Place your hands into the nest as you did into the water, making sure to keep them to the edges and as distant from the sparrow as possible.'

Rachel stood in front of William and slowly lowered her hands into the nest.

'Very good. Now, slowly move your hands to cradle the bird. Do not hold it too tightly or it will begin to struggle and become alarmed.'

William and Jacob watched as Rachel drew her hands closer together, her thin fingers trembling a little.

'I have it,' she said in a hushed voice. 'Its feathers are so soft and its body so small. I can feel its heart beating really fast.' She glanced up at William, her eyes glittering with delight as she raised her hands from the nest, Jacob's gaze fixed upon them in anticipation of the bird's release.

William balled the cloth which had been used as a cover and placed it inside the nest, which he then lay beside him on the seat.

'What should I do now?' Rachel waited, hands held out before her.

Standing, William moved round behind her and then lifted the girl onto the bench. She turned to face her brother and the giant who towered beside him, still substantially taller than Rachel despite her elevation.

'Open your hands ever so slowly,' said William in a whisper which heightened the children's feelings of expectant tension.

Rachel parted her hands the merest crack and peered in at the bird a moment. She then opened the cradle she had formed and the small, brown bird was revealed upon her tiny palms. It blinked and cocked its head, studying the two figures standing before the bench. Then it cocked its head to the other side and looked at Rachel.

'Why is it not flying away?' asked Jacob, standing on tiptoes in order to gain a better view of the bird.

With a sudden flutter which made Rachel give out an involuntary yelp of surprise, the sparrow took to the sky. It flew into the air and then dived towards the fruit trees on the western side of the gardens, vanishing into the branches of an apple tree.

Rachel giggled and leapt down from the seat. 'Let us go see if we can find it,' she said to her brother, the two of them setting off at a sprint.

William smiled, choosing to remain at the bench, feeling a tinge of sadness now that his charge had been given its freedom. Its soft chirping within his room would be sorely missed. The sparrow had been a welcome companion, but he could no longer keep it in captivity without feeling like its master. It had been caged against its nature, for birds were meant to fly and fly free.

'There it is!' came Jacob's cry of discovery from the far side of the gardens, the children all but hidden amidst the trees.

William chuckled to himself and shook his head as he sat down and glanced at the nest beside him. Taking out the balled cloth which Arthur had kindly lent to him for the purpose of transporting the bird, he then began to deconstruct the woven nest.

By the time the children returned to him, William had taken the nest apart and deposited the twigs over the stone wall behind the bench, beside the evergreen whose branches afforded a little shelter to the seat. He smiled at them as they came to a halt before him, their hair ruffled and a few stray leaves caught in Rachel's long locks.

'We saw it a few times,' she stated with a grin. 'All those worms we found for it must have given the sparrow lots of strength because it is a very good flier.'

'I am pleased to hear it.'

'Ye should have seen it dart between the branches,' said Jacob.

'I am sure it was a sight to behold.'

Rachel reached out and took hold of William's left hand, surprising him with her unexpected actions. 'Do not be sad. He is with all his friends now.' She smiled up at the giant, having detected the sadness in his eyes.

William was filled with feelings of warmth and gladness as he wondered at the children's ability to notice such things when many a man would not. 'And I am with friends also,' he replied.

Jacob nudged his sister and gave her a conspiratorial look. She let go of William's hand and delved into a pocket sewn into the front of the blue dress worn beneath her coat.

'This is for ye,' she said, holding out her open palm to reveal a silver chain with a crucifix on it glinting in the soft daylight.

'It is from both of us,' added Jacob as William stared at the gift which was being offered.

'You are both very kind, but I cannot take such a beautiful gift from you.'

'Please,' insisted Rachel, stretching her hand out further. 'We really want you to have it.'

William hesitated and then plucked the chain from Rachel's palm, the girl withdrawing her hand quickly as if fearful he would try to set it down again.

'How did you come by such a wonderful trinket?'

'It was our mother's, but we would like ye to have it now,' said Jacob.

'Your mother's? Will she not miss it?'

'She passed away a few years ago.' Rachel looked up at him with a sorrowful smile upon her delicate face. 'She was giving birth to our brother, but neither survived.'

'Then I truly cannot take something of such value to your hearts.' He held it out to Rachel upon the palm of his right hand.

The girl reached forward, but rather than taking it back into her possession, she closed William's fingers about the chain. 'It is yours now,' she said softly.

William looked at the angelic faces of the children standing before him, his eyes glistening with tears. 'I am grateful for your immeasurable kindness and shall take good care of this gift, but for me to take it you must both promise me something.' He held their gaze. 'If ever either of you should desire its return you need but ask and I will relinquish it. Do we have an agreement?'

The children looked at each other momentarily and then nodded. 'Yes,' they said in unison, smiles broad upon their faces.

William looked at the chain and silver crucifix in his hand and then tucked it into his tatty, grey tunic, taking a deep breath to fight back the tears which still threatened to issue forth.

'Can ye give us a piggyback ride now?' asked Rachel with a grin.

William chuckled. 'So it was bribery all along. I should have known.' He quickly reached forward and gathered the children up in his arms, tickling them as they wriggled and laughed with joy.

30

William sat on his straw bed. The light was grey and dull as clouds continued to block out the sun beyond the thin window to his left. He stared across the room at the faint scuff marks left upon the table's edge by the sparrow's small claws and smiled thinly. Caring for the bird had given him tasks beyond those of duty to the priory and he had found much satisfaction in bringing it to the fullness of health in order for it to fly. Without his charge the giant felt a little lonely and there was a restlessness within.

Looking up at the collection of bright shells visible on the window sill, William then rose and collected a handful from their resting place. He returned to the musty straw and rested his cloak upon his lap, leaning back against the harshness of the stone wall. The shells were tipped onto the cloak and he idly brushed them this way and that with his fingertips.

A loose thread which had snagged on the straw caught his eye, its origin the hem of his cloak. It was then that an idea came to him, his lack of purpose vanishing in an upward curl of his lips as he smiled.

William removed the garment from his lap, careful not to spill any of the shells, and rose to his feet once again. He was about to step to the door when he heard footsteps approaching beyond, descending the stone steps which led from the chapel to his room. He was surprised to find the muscles in his neck becoming knotted as three knocks sounded upon the door.

'Who is it?' he asked, hoping to hear Arthur's familiar voice emanate from the other side.

'It is Prior Vargas. May I speak with you awhile?'

'Please come in,' he replied, fearing that the prior had changed his mind and wished to relinquish the sanctuary which had been granted.

The door swung open and Prior Vargas' long, pale face was revealed beneath the hood of his cowl, a soft smile disarming William's fears to a degree. 'I am sorry to disturb you, William, but there is a matter about which I must speak with you.'

'Come in. My apologies for the odour, but I have yet to change the straw of my bedding this week and until earlier today had been nursing a young bird in this room.'

Prior Vargas stepped in and glanced around at the humble surroundings as he lowered his hood. 'The odour is of no concern. I have been without a sense of smell for many years due to a medical condition.'

'What is the matter that you wish to discuss? Have I done something wrong?'

'Well …' The prior glanced down at the stone floor a moment as he searched for words and then looked back up at the giant rising before him. 'It concerns the children whom you have befriended.'

'Are they ...?' began William in alarm.

Prior Vargas held up his hand to silence him. 'They are in full health, I am sure. It is their presence in the gardens of the priory which is of concern to me. I saw you with them on this day after hearing their voices from within the chapel walls.'

'I am truly sorry if they disturbed your meditations,' said William earnestly.

'William, I do not think the priory and its gardens are a place for children. Even when the Brothers work the land it is done in contemplation of the Lord and these children will only act as a distraction from this.'

'Surely the Lord welcomes all, whatever their age may be?'

Prior Vargas nodded. 'So He does, but this is a sanctified place where men come to leave such things behind. It is a retreat where we can live a life of devotion to our Lord. This you must understand.'

'I understand, Prior Vargas, and I am sorry to have caused any unwanted disturbance. I will not allow the children into the gardens again.' William looked at his cloth-wrapped feet guiltily.

The prior sighed. 'I do not ask that you cease contact with these children, only that you consider where you are. The Brothers have sacrificed much for the good of their souls and this sacrifice deserves respect and consideration.'

William nodded.

'The peacefulness of this holy place aids in our closeness to our Lord.'

'This I can bear witness to,' replied the giant without looking up.

'Do you claim to experience a closeness to our Lord?' There was incredulity in the prior's tone.

'I feel his touch upon and within me.'

Prior Vargas studied the giant with his head bowed before him for a moment, his eyes narrowed. The man seemed still a wretch to him, a heathen cast out of society and cursed in appearance. 'Indeed,' he said finally, turning back to the door.

'Heed my words with regard to these children, for I do not wish to speak with you again on this matter,' said the prior as he paused in the doorway and raised his hood. 'Tonight I will say a prayer for your soul.' With that he shut the door and left William standing alone in the centre of his small room.

William raised his head and stared at the door. 'I am not in need of your prayers,' he muttered as the prior's steps faded along the nave of the chapel. 'For I have found salvation in friendship and feel the spirit of the Lord within.'

31

Brother Cook stood before a workbench in the shed which was constructed against the lea of the entrance hall. The door was open to allow the fresh wind entry, the day warm despite its dullness. In front of him rested one of the tables that each monk had in their cell. One of its legs had broken off and Brother Cook sought nails of correct length with which to reattach it from amongst a selection in a square tin with a hinged lid and patches of deep rust. Other tins were lined up beneath tools hung neatly from hooks above the workbench. The larger, more unwieldy implements hung on the wall behind him, two of the scythes clinking together softly as the wind reached into the small, wooden enclosure.

His dirtied fingers delved into the contents of the tin, his mind fully engaged on the task, eager to get the table mended for Brother Stewart before it was time to attend to his holier duties. Many of the nails were rusty and weakened by this affliction, others were too short to be of use or bent out of shape to such a degree that he doubted they could ever be restored and put back into the service for which they had been made.

The sudden darkness of a large shadow falling upon him gave Brother Cook a start and he turned in fright to the towering silhouette framed against the view of the sea and the hills which curved round the western side of the bay. There was no disguising the fear in his eyes as he regarded the giant. Despite Brother Elwin's words and the prior's acceptance of his sanctuary amongst them, the look of the man still set a chill within him.

'I am sorry to have scared you, Brother Cook,' said William. 'I was hoping you may be able to lend me some assistance.'

The young monk took an involuntary step backwards as the giant leant forward and glanced about the interior of the shed. 'What is it you seek?' he asked in a hushed voice.

William studied the Brother's expression closely. 'You have no need to be fearful of me, Brother Cook. I mean you no harm.'

The monk took a few deep breaths, his pulse racing and perspiration glistening on his forehead and upper lip. 'I am sorry. You startled me is all.'

'If you are busy I can come back another time,' said William, knowing full well that the monk's reaction was related to more than just his sudden arrival.

'No. There is no need for that. If I can help I will,' replied Brother Cook, regaining some composure and trying to push his fear to the back of his mind.

'I seek a tool with a small point which can be used to pierce things.'

The monk glanced along the row of tools hanging above the workbench, but there was nothing which matched the giant's requirements. 'Let me see what is contained within the drawers,' he said, opening the top drawer of three beneath the bench to his right.

William watched from the doorway, purposely not stepping inside the shed in case he unsettled Brother Cook further. The sound of metal upon metal lifted into the air as the monk searched through each drawer in turn, still finding nothing of use to the man whose proximity he felt so keenly.

'I am afraid there seems to be nothing I can offer you,' he said, pulse almost returned to normal.

William's gaze settled on the open tin resting upon the workbench. 'One of those nails may be well suited to the task I have in mind,' he stated, forgetting himself momentarily and stepping into the shed, head bowed low and black curls brushing against the door frame.

Brother Cook stiffened and stared at the giant with worried eyes. He swallowed hard as he tried to control himself. He knew there was no foundation for his trepidation bar the size and look of the man before him, but despite this could not vanquish his fear.

Without taking a nail from the tin, William retreated back beyond the doorway.

Brother Cook took a calming breath and shook his head. 'I am sorry. I know not what comes over me. Your name is William, is it not?'

The giant nodded. 'Yes.'

'Brother Elwin has spoken with me on several occasions about your goodness, about your gentleness and kindness of spirit. Because of this I find myself perplexed. I do not understand why I still take fright at your presence, and no matter how sternly I reprimand myself these feelings I cannot shake.'

'I think, Brother Cook, that the fact you do not know me is the reason for such feelings. We fear the unknown, especially when the unknown has a strange appearance, such as I.' William's tone was soft and conciliatory.

'You have great understanding, William, and in it I see why Brother Elwin counts you as a friend. Please excuse my behaviour and I hope there has been no offence caused.'

'I take no offence, Brother Cook.' He smiled disarmingly at the monk.

'Please, feel free to select any of these that you may need.' The monk stepped over and picked up the tin of nails. He held it out to the giant and was ashamed to see that his hand was shaking as he did so.

'Thank you,' said William as he took the tin, noting the trembling hand which quickly withdrew. 'What task are you busy with at present?' he asked conversationally, already having divined what Brother Cook was working on from the sight of the broken table upon the workbench.

Thankful for the distraction from his disturbing feelings, Brother Cook turned to the table resting upon its side next to him. 'Brother Stewart's table is broken and I must fix its leg back into place. I was searching for suitable nails when you arrived,' he said as William looked through the tin's contents, finding nothing which suited his purpose.

'I hope you have better luck than I. There is naught here of use to me, though I thank you for allowing me to look.' He stretched forward and set the tin on the workbench inside the door so Brother Cook would not have to reach towards him, but could collect it once he had made his departure.

'Think nothing of it,' responded the monk, feeling more at ease with the giant's presence as each moment passed. 'Is there anything else which might be of use?'

William pondered awhile. 'It may be that a sturdy pin of sorts would suffice.'

Brother Cook turned back to the workbench and eyed the selection of other tins resting beneath the hanging tools. He selected one and opened its lid, finding screws and shaking his head as he put it back in its place. Picking up another, he peered inside and a faint smile dawned upon his rounded, youthful face, the vague dimples in his cheeks deepening.

'Here, there may be something of use in this one.' He held out the tin, the shaking of his hands having subsided considerably.

The giant took the offered tin and looked inside, shifting the contents with his index finger. Within was a selection of metal fastenings, most brown with rust. There were hinges, tacks, bolts and even a couple of keys towards the bottom, the use of which had long since been forgotten. Beneath the collection of fastenings and other oddities was what appeared to be a large hatpin. It was flecked with rust, but looked strong enough for what he intended.

William plucked it from amidst the other items and held it up for the monk to see. 'May I take this? I will return it once my task is done.'

Brother Cook nodded. 'Of course, and feel free to keep it should you so wish. I very much doubt I shall ever find use for it.'

William smiled at the monk. 'I am very grateful.' He placed the tin on the workbench beside the one containing nails. 'Thank you for your time and assistance, Brother Cook.'

The monk regarded the giant, his expression softened by the time they had shared together. 'You were right, William. We truly are afraid of the unknown, of the different, and I must thank you for making yourself known to me, even if only for a short while. If the chance arises I should like to speak with you again.' He smiled.

William returned the gesture and then turned from the door in order to make his way back to his room.

Brother Cook stood for a moment, his gaze fixed on the doorway. His sight did not take in the view, his thoughts distant as he listened to the giant's steps pass softly alongside the shed and fade away, the sound of the ocean a constant exhalation in the background, one rarely noticed due to its familiarity. Now he could truly understand why Brother Elwin spent so much time in the giant's company. There was a sense of calm about him and he had a surprising degree of insight.

The young monk shook his head and cleared his mind. He picked up the two tins from the workbench, setting the one filled with fastenings back beside the others collected beneath the tools. Then he once more began to search through the nails in the hope of finding those of a suitable size with which to fix Brother Stewart's table.

32

The following day there were only a few clouds in the sky and the sea shone brightly, though the wind remained brisk as it blew in from the south. William made his way down the stone steps which led from the priory to the gardens and recalled the time he and Arthur had first met, the fateful autumn day when he had carried the aged monk to shelter after having watched him from the crags. That stormy day seemed so distant and yet so close, a strange paradox which he often found arising in relation to his memories.

He glanced to his left, the tide out and the bar of sand and shingle busy with comings and goings. Chapel Rock rose darkly from the western beach of Marghas Byghan at the bar's far end and he recalled sheltering there on the night of his arrival. From his position halfway down the steps, William could spy the masts of ships above the tops of the trees nestled against the Isle's rising height, the harbour jetty and warehouses hidden from view.

'Good afternoon, William,' came the familiar voice of his dear friend.

William turned his gaze back to the steps to find the monk ascending towards him. 'Good afternoon, Arthur.'

'This is a happy coincidence, for I was coming to seek you out.' Arthur smiled as he stopped a few steps beneath the giant.

'You were?'

'Indeed. I have something for you, but I am afraid you will have to carry it to the priory, for my strength is not what it used to be and even in my youth I suspect I would not have been able to lift this item.'

'What is it?' enquired William as Arthur began to lead the way down the steps as they curved about the steep slope of the Mount.

'To tell would be to ruin the surprise,' replied the monk with a wry grin. 'You will find out soon enough, dear friend.'

William smiled. It was clear that the old monk was enjoying the secrecy.

'Did the release of your bird go well?' Arthur asked with a sideways glance, the giant a step behind him.

'Yes. I allowed the girl, Rachel, to release the sparrow and it found flight to be an easy task now that it had gained in strength.'

'Easy!' Arthur raised his eyebrows. 'Flight is not something I could achieve in a lifetime,' he commented with a warm smile.

William chuckled. 'Watching you try would be a sight to behold.'

'Find me some wings and it may be that I leap from the southern bluffs and glide over the waters like an aged albatross.'

'Or tumble into them like Icarus flown too close to the sun.'

146

Arthur laughed and turned to William, a bright sparkle in his blue eyes. 'Quite so, but …' He raised his hands to cover his mouth as he coughed. The sound was raw and the old monk's eyes shut tightly as the coughing continued to grip him and he stopped upon the steps.

William halted and looked at his friend with concern as the old monk's thin body convulsed. 'Do you wish to rest awhile?'

Arthur shook his head, the coughing slowly subsiding, eyes glistening with tears as he looked at the giant and blinked them away. 'No,' he said hoarsely. 'I shall be fine.'

'We could fetch your gift later, I am sure no one will remove it.'

Arthur coughed again as he stifled a laugh. 'As am I, dear friend, as am I.'

William looked at him, his curiosity aroused as to the identity of the item which rested somewhere below.

'Come, I can rest aplenty later.' Arthur led the way down the steps once again, William walking beside him and aware of the old monk's limp, a sign of the injury sustained to his knees which would remain with him for the rest of his days.

When they reached the bottom of the stone steps Arthur's breathing was laboured. He stopped and wiped his brow as he tried to calm his rapidly beating heart. He coughed again briefly and looked up at William. 'It is but a little way along the path to the warehouses,' he stated, nodding to the steps which descended to the track on the left. 'You go and fetch it while I await your return.'

'What is it that I should look for?'

'You will know when you see it.' The old monk smiled.

William studied his drawn face a moment longer and then turned and began to walk down the steps through the veiling trees, soon stepping onto the path alongside which the mystery item supposedly lay in wait for his discovery. Taking short steps, he looked to both sides in turn, seeking the gift within the grasses and wild flowers beyond the treeline, but spying nothing upon the open ground.

Then he saw it lying in the greenery and a wide smile spread upon his face. He shook his head and chuckled, glancing back at Arthur, who was watching from the cobbled path at the top of the short flight of steps.

William stepped over to the large piece of slate, which was fully 2 yards from top to bottom and left to right, and the thickness of his thumb in depth. Its use he could not fathom, but he understood his friend's amusement at the thought of someone removing such a cumbersome object.

Bending over, he grasped its sides and tested its weight. It was indeed extremely heavy and he doubted his ability to carry it all the way up the steps without pause. Bracing himself, William then lifted the slate, leaning it against his chest so his body bore some of the weight.

He walked with laboured steps back to where Arthur waited. His ascent up the small flight of carved stone steps leading back to the cobbled path gave him a hint as to how gruelling the passage to the Mount's summit would be, the slate's weight growing with every step as if it became more dense with each movement.

'What do you think?' the monk asked with a gleam in his eyes.

'I cannot say as yet. There is no doubt it is a fine piece of slate, but what am I to do with it?'

Arthur smiled at him. 'You will see soon enough. How do you think you will fare in carrying it up the steps?'

'I can do so, but will need to rest from time to time.'

'Then let us get started, for I will soon be called back to my duties.'

Arthur began to climb the long, stone stairway with William following behind, taking each step with great care as his hands tightly gripped the large slate against his chest. His breath soon became laboured and the muscles of his arms ached with the growing fire of strain.

They were but a third of the way up the side of the Mount when William felt his grip begin to fade. 'I must rest,' he said as he came to a halt and quickly lowered the slate to the ground, fearful of dropping it if he did not set it down in haste.

Arthur looked at him, the two men of equal height as the monk stood five steps further up the climb. 'Are you sure the ascent will not be too much for you?' he asked with concern, noting the redness of William's face and the perspiration upon it.

'I can take it up to the priory, but I fear it will take considerably longer than anticipated.'

Arthur thought, his gaze turning to the slate as it rested against one of the stone steps. 'Would it be unkind of me to leave you to the task? I must go and join my Brothers at prayer and may already be a little late.'

William nodded. 'I am happy for you to attend to your duties and without your watchful eye will take my time at the task.' He grinned at the old monk, who smiled in return. 'Only, I do not know where you wish me to place it upon my successful ascent.'

'Take it to your room and I shall meet you there on the morrow when no other duties call. If you wish to see me sooner I am assigned to the gardens in the early morning,' he said, a hopeful expression upon his lined face. 'I will not have the opportunity to sit with you, but we could work at each other's side tending the fruit trees. Your height would be an advantage in checking the health of the ripening fruit.'

'So, it is not my company you desire, but my height.' William's smile grew.

'Tis true, but should you wish to lend me your height advantage I will gladly accept your company with it.'

The two friends laughed.

The sound of the bell chiming up at the priory carried on the wind and the old monk glanced upward. 'I must be on my way.'

'I shall see you on the morrow, dear friend,' said William as Arthur began the ascent.

'Do not strain yourself in carrying the slate and rest well when it is needed,' said Arthur over his thin shoulder. 'May the Lord be with you, William.'

The giant smiled as he watched the monk limp up the steps, seeing that he was finding it quite a struggle. He sighed and turned his attention to the slate by his feet, his arms still aching a little, but ready to continue the climb towards the priory.

He bent down and picked up the unusual gift which Arthur had procured for him and wondered at its purpose. The old monk had been evasive, joyfully keeping his reasons to himself. No doubt they would be revealed the next day, and until then he could not even guess as to what use such an item could be put to.

With a slow but steady pace, he began the climb, glancing up and seeing the figure of his friend disappear to the left around the curve of the steps.

33

They stood together beside the most ancient apple tree in the gardens, "The Old Man" as Arthur called it, its trunk gnarled and covered in patches of green moss and grey lichen which looked almost beard-like in places. A few bees and wasps flew about them as Arthur and William checked for signs of illness or attack, having found none on the trees they had already examined in wordless silence.

William reached for a young apple that grew on the branch before him and turned it between his large fingers.

It was green and healthy. His gaze moved to the next and his hand followed as the sound of gulls rang out from Marghas Byghan's eastern beach, the day still and their calls carrying across the calm waters.

'The prior came and spoke with me yesterday,' said William as the sun peered out from behind high, white clouds.

Arthur stared up into the branches above him with a puzzled look upon his lined face. He was now on the far side of the tree from his friend, a side which had not borne fruit for nigh on a decade, a strange occurrence for which he had yet to find reason. 'Why did he visit you?' he asked, keeping his voice low, not wishing to disturb the other monks who busied themselves in the gardens nor to have them overhear talk of Prior Vargas.

'He has requested that the children do not enter the gardens.' William studied a young apple as he turned it. There was a growth of white fungus upon it, like fine hair that glistened with moisture. He touched his thumb against the growth and it left a permanent impression, flattening the fragile fungus against the unripe fruit.

'I hope you will not think ill of me, but Prior Vargas has cause to do so.' Arthur's attention turned to the base of the tree. Each year he had investigated the cause of the tree's failure to fruit upon its eastern side and each year had found nothing of consequence, but remained determined that the cause would one day be discovered and to that end knelt upon the grass and looked at the earth beside the trunk, seeking any sign of toxins.

William did not speak for a few moments, his gaze upon two more apples that had been infected with the white fungus as he pondered whether they should be removed for fear it would spread further afield. Eventually moving to pluck them from the branch before him, he took the three apples and put them into an otherwise empty cloth bag hanging from the cord securing his tunic at the waist. 'I understand his reasons, but thought the innocence of children would be welcomed in a place of God.'

Arthur looked up at his friend as he continued to kneel beside the tree as if in prayer. 'On my part, I found their interruption most welcome, though I understand Prior Vargas' motives.'

'No grievance do I hold against him.' William spied another infected apple and noted others along the same bough. His brow furrowed and he looked down at Arthur as the monk's withered hands brushed the soil about the trunk, their skin like dried leaves and the veins rising from beneath. 'There is infection here, but I do not know its seriousness.' He took one of the apples he had already plucked from the tree and held it out to his friend.

Arthur reached up and took it for closer examination. 'How much has this spread through the tree?'

'Only a few branches as far as I can discern, though there may be more. Is it serious?'

'Not overly. If I am not mistaken, this is merely mildew and can be halted without recourse to anything more than a treatment of powder,' he replied.

'Powder?'

Arthur nodded. 'It is what we use in the treatment of any such fungi. It kills many which grow amidst the fruit trees.'

William nodded.

'Do not pluck any more from the branches, but seek out others that may be similarly infected. Once the scale of the problem has been ascertained we can inform Brother Thomas and he will administer the cure.'

William turned his gaze back to the branches and looked for further growths of mildew.

'Have you discerned the reason for my gift to you?' enquired Arthur as he rose to his feet and the sun was temporarily covered by one of the clouds that drifted lethargically in the blue like white tufts of wool.

'No,' replied William as he ducked under a branch in order to continue his search farther around the tree. 'I am at a complete loss as to its purpose.'

'Good.' Arthur smiled, the crow's feet deepening about his blue eyes. 'I would have it so until this afternoon, then all shall be revealed.'

The giant looked up and saw more apples with the white growth upon their tough skin. As he reached for one a movement to the right caught his eye and he glanced over to discover a young, male sparrow watching him, its head cocked to one side and tilted towards him. He studied the creature, but could discover no sign as to whether it had been the one in his charge. Many of the birds on the island were more daring than most, would come closer than those on the mainland, and its proximity was no clue as to its identity.

Softly, and with his gaze fixed upon the bird, he drew air through his teeth. When it heard the sound, the bird's head cocked to the other side and it hopped closer along the branch upon which it sat. William smiled and held out his hand to the bird, which did not flinch. With due care, his hand approached the sparrow, which watched it at all times. As it drew close the bird sidled back along the branch and then fell still.

William whistled gently and continued the movement of his hand. The sparrow remained still. With his smile deepening, the giant began to stroke the bird's head with his index finger, its feathers soft to the touch. The bird gripped the thin bough as it closed its eyes.

The sound of Arthur's coughing brought the contact to a sudden end. The sparrow quickly flew from the apple tree and out of sight as William's hand hovered in the air above the space it had occupied.

He sighed, though his smile remained. Seeing his feathered companion had brought with it a lightness of spirit and he was grateful for the contact, however brief it may have been.

Withdrawing his hand, he glanced down at the old monk, whose coughing had abated. Holding his silence, he decided to keep the sparrow's visitation to himself, something shared only by him and the bird, something made more sacred by its personal nature, and turned his attention back to the immature apples hanging about him.

34

There was a knock at the door and William knew who was standing on the other side thanks, in part, to the old monk struggling on the short flight of steep steps outside his room.

'Come in, Arthur,' he said, rising from the straw as the door swung open to reveal his friend's smiling face. 'How goes it?'

'Good. You?' replied the monk as he glanced around the room and spied the slate leaning against the wall beside the table to the right.

'I have done little since being in the gardens this morning.'

'Then we should begin, for the sooner we do the sooner you will have something with which to occupy your spare time.'

William looked at him curiously. There was a grin on the old man's face. 'Am I soon to discover what the gift is for?'

'You still do not know?' Arthur raised his right eyebrow as he looked up at the giant, his eyes sparkling with mischief.

William glanced at the slate. 'Am I to learn to shape it so it may be used upon the roofs of the priory?' he asked.

The monk shook his head. 'How many guesses should I allow you?'

'It would not matter, for I fear I would never guess its purpose.'

'In which case I had better show you and not waste any more time in a game which could go on for an eternity,' he chuckled. 'Or maybe you would have the answer if I were to give you a clue.' He opened his left hand and held it out to reveal a piece of chalk resting upon his palm.

William looked at the white chalk and then the slate. 'Do you want me to draw?' he asked, his words filled with uncertainty.

'Of sorts. I am here to begin your reading and writing lessons.'

The giant stared at the monk in surprise, having forgotten his friend's offer to teach him the skills.

'I happened upon the slate and its purpose was clear immediately. I took this as a sign to begin our lessons in earnest and hope that soon you will be able to spend your idle hours occupied in the joys of reading and writing. We have a few parchments in our library which you will be able to read, though most are written in French or Latin. One day I will accompany you there and we will choose a suitable document from which you can read to me. Until that time you must be taught the basic foundations of our language in its written form.'

'Do you think it will take me long to learn?'

Arthur looked William in the eye. 'Judging from the intelligence of your speech and that which I detect within you, I do not believe you will be in need of too much tutelage. You will not be slow in your mastery of this talent if I am any judge.'

William smiled. 'I thank you for your confidence and only hope I have the ability which you attest to.'

'You do,' said Arthur without any doubt as he stepped over to stand beside the slate. 'Do not think me rude, but may I use your cloak on which to sit? The cold stone gives me pains that I would rather not endure.'

Plucking the cloak from where it lay balled as a pillow upon the straw, William then handed it to his friend. Arthur carefully folded the cloak and set it on the floor like a padded mat. He lowered himself onto it with a little difficulty, pain flaring temporarily in his knees and causing him to wince.

'Would you prefer me to go and find a chair on which you can sit?' asked William, the look of pain not having escaped his notice.

'Thank you, but this will suffice for today's lesson, though I would be happy for you to have found one by the time we next meet in these circumstances,' replied Arthur as he sat with the slate resting against the wall to his right. 'Now,' he said as he began writing, the chalk gripped between his thin fingers and William recognising some of the symbols that were being drawn. 'We must start at the beginning, with the alphabet.'

35

William walked along Marghas Byghan's eastern beach at a leisurely pace, heading back towards the bar which was revealed by low tide, the night warm and only a gentle breeze stirring in the wave-caressed hush. The moon had yet to rise and the stars were bright in the clear sky as he wandered along the sand and shingle, passing the dark shapes of rocks jutting into the gloom.

It had been a few weeks since he had last walked upon the beach, fearful that he would be spied by the local inhabitants, but the hour was early and he felt secure in the knowledge that the people of the town would be asleep and tucked within the land of dreams.

He paused and looked out to sea, the vague silhouette of a fishing boat visible amidst the gentle waves, a lantern hanging above the cabin like a firefly in the distance. His mind was filled with Arthur's teachings. They had met every day for the past week, each time spending nearly an hour concentrated upon the lesson at hand. William had sought out a chair, one of simple comfort, but which served the old monk far better than the cloak laid upon the cold stone. As far as he could ascertain he was making good progress, something which his friend had expected of him.

The giant crouched in the gloom and looked for shells about his feet. He spied one, soft yellow in the night and delicate in its hollowness. He carefully picked it up and rose to his full height. Examining the shell briefly, he then dropped it into a cloth pouch hanging from the frayed cord tied about his waist and heard the gentle sound as it tapped against others he had already collected.

William began to walk along the beach again, moving to the edge of the surf, his bare feet washed by the waters as they sank into the sand and his thoughts turned to his past. His expression grew saddened as he wondered as to the whereabouts of the others who had found freedom that fateful night after his master had taken his fists to Elsbeth. Was liberty still theirs or did they find themselves in the man's service once more, chained before an endless procession of gawkers who knew no better? What of Elsbeth? It was her actions which had given him his freedom, but she had chosen to stay behind as the others took flight. How would the master have reacted to the discovery of his livelihood vanished in the darkness? It would have been clear to him the manner of their escape and William feared the worst for Elsbeth. The master's temper was fast and his fury always accompanied by violence. He would have beaten her and she would have been lucky to have escaped with her life.

He sighed and hoped that the woman who had found love to be stronger than any chain of iron still lived and breathed, that she had found a way to be free of the man who did not share in her love, only her body. There was little he could do for her or the other freaks bar remember them. By keeping them in memory he gained perspective on the good fortune he had come upon. Not only did he have sanctuary in a place beautified by nature, but he had friends who treated him with dignity and respect, who did not recoil or stare at him in horrified wonder.

William paused again, the waves washing against his legs, cool against his skin. An owl called out in the darkness, though he could not see it as he glanced over his shoulder towards the rising cliffs, which were as a wall of pitch beneath the town.

Turning back to the ocean view, the Isle of Ictis rising to the right, he saw a diminutive figure crossing the bar. They were hurrying and if he was not mistaken they were dressed in a cowl. William's eyebrows rose in surprise, for the monks should have all been abed at that time of the night. He watched as the monk moved towards the island with head bowed slightly, the figure's haste soon taking them beyond his sight as they vanished into the shadows at the harbour-side.

William stared at the dim warehouses and jetty for a moment and then looked back along the beach to the east, noting the moon beginning to rise over the Lizard Peninsula. She was a gentle orange as her crescent slowly rose into the sky with a ghostly haze of moisture encircling her, the colours of the spectrum vaguely visible in pastel softness.

In silence, William watched her rise, soon passing beyond the mist which had lent her a ghostly glow. In clarity she now shone as the waves washed softly upon the sands and the night was filled with thoughtful calm.

36

'That is very good, William. Can you tell me what a noun is?' Arthur looked at his friend as they sat on the seat in the gardens, the breeze toying with his white hair.

'A noun is a word which represents an object or creature. It is a name given to something.'

'Correct. One thing you must always remember is that these words are not the things themselves, merely representative.'

'Yes,' said William with a smile. 'The word dog is not hairy and does not try to lick your face after jumping up with muddy paws,' he continued, recalling what his friend and tutor had told him during the last lesson word for word.

Arthur smiled. 'You have a very good memory, my friend.'

'And you an aversion to dogs with muddy paws,' replied William.

The monk laughed. 'I must say, I am pleasantly surprised by the speed of learning you display. I knew you to be intelligent and thought the lessons would go well, but ne'er would have guessed you would make such quick progress.'

'I am glad to be able to surprise you still.' William grinned at Arthur, the sun upon the old man's face, his eyes a little sunken and surrounded by yellow shadow.

'It will not be long before you can read simple passages without my assistance.'

'A pupil is only as good as their teacher, and in this case I do not suffer from a bad teacher, but gain greatly from one who is both patient and kind.'

'Thank you.' Arthur nodded and turned his gaze seaward as a wagtail flitted through the gardens before them. He coughed a little and then settled against the back of the bench, his hands clasped upon his lap. 'I shall miss this world,' he stated dreamily, moving his right hand and softly stroking the arm of the bench beside him, following the twisted contours of the yew branch.

William studied the monk's face. 'Why do you speak in such a way? Is there something you do not tell me?'

Arthur shook his head without turning from the view. 'No, merely thoughts of my own mortality. When you reach my great age you will know for yourself how such meanderings of the mind can easily come about.'

'Many more years can you live and there is no need to entertain such thoughts at this time.'

'It is the beauty surrounding us which brings such feelings to the fore.' He ran his tongue along his thin, dry lips. 'I long to linger for many years to come, to continue savouring this natural wonder.' He opened his arms to the view and sighed. 'But this cannot be.'

'How can you know this?' William sat forward and tried to look into Arthur's eyes. 'I ask you again, is there something that you keep hidden from me? Are you ill of health?'

'My health has been declining for a long time, dear friend,' replied the old monk, turning to William. 'The march of time is not just to be seen on the outside, but it is felt within also.' He smiled softly. 'And time's boots become heavy upon me.'

'Surely you are mistaken, for time's feet are bare and light of touch.'

Arthur's smile grew. 'Would that it were so.'

The creak of the gate drifted with the breeze and William turned to see Rachel and Jacob entering the gardens. He looked back to his friend after raising his hand in greeting and studied Arthur's expression. 'I must go for

160

the children are here and Prior Vargas will not be happy should I allow them to remain. I ask that you try to banish such thoughts, dear friend, for there are no certainties in life and yours may last a good deal longer yet.' William patted the monk's hands and then rose.

Arthur nodded. 'I will contemplate our next lesson instead.' He smiled up at the giant, whose shadow fell across him.

'I am glad to hear it and hope it is so.' William hesitated, his gaze lingering on the drawn, tight features of his friend. Then he turned and strode off to meet the children who were skipping towards him.

'Hello, Will,' said Rachel brightly as she stopped before him and craned her neck to look up at his face.

'Good afternoon, Will,' said Jacob as he halted beside his sister.

'Greetings to you both,' responded William with a smile as he crouched before them. 'How are you this fine day?'

'We were wondering if ye could take us fishing in the rock pools again,' replied Jacob, who wore a leather tunic which hung open, his chest and feet bare. 'Last time I did not catch a fish.'

'And I would dearly like to catch another,' added Rachel, her lime green dress fluttering in the breeze.

'I would be only too happy to take you fishing again,' said William, thankful he was not going to have to broach the subject of their unwanted presence in the gardens. 'I think we should go straight away and begin our hunt for a suitable pool.'

The children nodded their approval as he stood. Then, to his amused surprise, Rachel stepped forward and took hold of his left hand, her brother taking hold of the right after witnessing his sister's actions. They strolled together back towards the gate and the little girl swung his arm back and forth merrily.

'It has been some time since last I saw you,' commented the giant, his height accentuated by the small children to either side of him.

'We have been helping father on the farm. Tis a busy season and he needs all the assistance he can get,' replied Jacob. 'We have fed and cared for the pigs while he busies himself in harvesting.'

'I collected the eggs as well,' said Rachel, raising her hand in the air.

'And managed to crack a good deal of them as ye did so.'

'That was not my fault. I tripped and the bucket fell from my hands,' she replied to her brother, bending forward to glare at him past the giant's legs.

'It sounds as if you have both been kept very busy.'

'Can ye come and work for our father?' asked Jacob. 'I am sure ye could do the work of at least three men.'

'Then you have more faith in my stamina than I.' William smiled down at the boy. 'I may be big, but that does not mean my strength is so proportioned.'

'We know ye are strong,' said Rachel, the giant turning to look upon her.

'How do you know that?'

'From the piggyback rides,' she replied with a knowing grin. 'No one else has been able to carry us for such a distance.'

'We tried to get father to do so, but he could only carry us from the pig trough to the wall of their sty,' said Jacob.

'I guess that is not such a great distance.'

Jacob shook his head. 'No, 10 yards at most.'

William nodded as they arrived at the gate and Rachel opened it without releasing his hand. Allowing Jacob to file through first, they exited the gardens and the children began to guide him towards the path which led to the warehouses and island harbour.

He stopped them and stared down the track at the granite buildings that lined the seafront no more than 60 yards away.

'What is wrong?' asked Rachel, looking up at him curiously.

'We should go a different way,' he stated.

'Why?'

William tried to think of a reason. The children clearly did not comprehend the need to keep his presence hidden from those beyond the priory, could not conceive of the consequences should it become widely known that a man such as he was abiding on the Mount.

'It is more fun to cut across country,' he replied after a moment. 'Look, we can follow the wall of the gardens until we arrive at the south of the island.'

The children turned their attention to the wall beside the gate into the gardens, undergrowth thick at its base and trees beside it.

'There are nettles there,' said Jacob. 'We will both get stung.' He glanced at his bare legs.

'Then I shall have to carry you beyond them,' said William, knowing the children would not be able to resist the chance to ride upon his shoulders once again.

They looked up at him with bright expressions.

'Will ye carry us all the way down to the rocks?' Rachel's eyes were wide.

'We shall see. I fear that is too great a distance even for me.'

'I think ye could do it,' said Jacob.

'Thank you for your confidence in my ability.' William smiled and picked Rachel up, swinging her onto his left shoulder, her brother then placed upon the other side of his head, both held in place by his arms, raised and placed across their laps.

'Be careful of tree branches,' he stated, noting the boughs they would need to duck beneath before the treeline was cleared and they reached open ground.

'We will,' responded Jacob.

William stepped back towards the gate to the gardens and then veered left to follow the outside edge of the eastern wall. He and the children were able to spy the vegetable patches and fruit trees over the top of the stone wall to the right, the height of which barely reached his chest. He also spied his friend slowly rising from the seat, noticing for the first time that Arthur's back was becoming bent with age.

'Ouch!' exclaimed Rachel as a small branch whipped her cheek.

'Will told us to watch out,' scolded Jacob.

'I was looking into the gardens,' she said, rubbing at the red line which marked her face.

'Do not worry, we will soon be free of the trees,' said William as he waded through the lush undergrowth of grasses, nettles and ferns.

As they neared the island's south-eastern shoreline they broke free of the thick vegetation and trees which found shelter from the winds in the lea of the garden wall. William's cloth-wrapped feet stepped upon the coastal grasses and thick bracken, the pain from numerous nettle stings only a minor irritation, his feet numbed to such sensations after so long with only scant protection.

They reached the point were the wall ran westward, marking the southern boundary of the gardens, and William soon covered the final 20 yards to the shoreline, the rocks beyond stretching out to sea. He crouched and the children disembarked by sliding down his chest.

'Thanks, Will. I knew ye would make it all the way,' said Rachel before looking for a place to clamber down onto the rocks.

'Thanks.' Jacob followed after his sister, eager to find a suitable pool in which to catch a fish.

William smiled and flexed his shoulders while watching them for a moment. He wiped his brow and followed them onto the rocks, making his way towards the waves that washed upon them so relentlessly.

'Here is a good pool,' called Jacob, pointing in front of him.

Rachel moved quickly to join her brother beside the clear water gathered in a cleft in the rocks. 'Do you see any fish?' William heard the girl ask as he approached, the children kneeling and intent upon the pool.

Crouching beside them, he peered in, the surface covered with small ripples raised by the breeze. 'Have either of you spotted any fish yet?'

'No.' Rachel shook her head, but did not look at the giant, her gaze scanning for any sign of movement.

'There!' Jacob pointed towards the centre of the pool.

At its deepest point, more than 2 feet down, a pair of small grey-brown fish rested side by side. Their tails flitted and they swam a little way forward, hunkering against the sharply rising rock on the far side.

'I think this pool is too deep for either of you. I am not sure it would be safe to fish here,' said William with concern.

'But it would be easier than before,' moaned Jacob, realising that the cleft created a natural trap with its steep sides, knowing he could put his hands to either end and the fish would have few ways by which to evade capture.

'If you insist on fishing here you must let me hold onto you so there is no chance of falling in.'

'Even if Jacob fell in, the water is not deep enough to be dangerous,' commented Rachel with a sideways glance at the giant.

'What if he were to crack his head upon the rock?'

Rachel gazed thoughtfully into the pool. 'Ye are here to pull him back out.'

'That could be too late. Who knows the damage such a knock could do?' Without waiting for the boy to voice protest or agreement, William positioned himself behind him and put his arm around Jacob's waist, holding him securely.

'Will you let me try and catch them now?' asked the boy with a hint of indignant irritation.

'Them? Do you intend to outdo us all and catch both fish in one foul swoop?' responded William, trying to lighten the mood.

'Yes.'

'I bet ye cannot do it,' said Rachel with a sense of excitement.

'Ye just watch,' replied Jacob confidently, hoping the crevice would work in his favour as he believed it would.

He gently put his hands into the water as far apart as he could while leaning over the pool, William keeping him secure. His sister watched as Jacob bent low, his hands going ever deeper to either end of the crevice until they finally reached the bottom where small stones were gathered, his face barely above the pool's surface, breath creating ripples upon it as Jacob stared intently past his reflection.

His hands began to close on the pair of fish, which remained motionless close to the far slope of the crevice in the hope it would afford them concealment. William watched over the boy's shoulder and Rachel held her breath in anticipation, her eyes wide, heart fluttering like the wings of a butterfly against her ribcage.

'Now!' whispered William.

Jacob's hands drew together in a rush of motion. He raised them out of the water, drops glistening as they fell to the pool and ran down his arms. 'I have them,' he shouted victoriously as William lifted him to his feet and then released him to allow his movements freedom.

'Ye caught both?' Rachel glanced at her brother's joyous expression and then stared at his hands as they remained clasped.

Jacob nodded as he turned to his sister, holding his cupped hands between them. They both watched with great interest as he began to reveal what was held within, the boy having to fight the urge to open them with great speed, so eager was he to witness his apparent success.

Within a moment the contents were revealed and there, upon his palms, was a solitary fish.

'Where is the other one?' asked Rachel.

'I was sure I had them both. There was no way the second could have escaped.' Jacob's brow furrowed as his sister turned back to the pool and tried to locate the second fish, the first writhing in fits upon the boys hands.

'You had better return it to the water, Jacob.'

He looked up at the giant with a deep frown. 'I was sure I had captured both of them,' he said with obvious disappointment.

'At least you managed to ensnare one. That is better than the first time you attempted to catch a fish with your hands.'

'But I should have caught both.'

'You should be happy at your success and not treat it as a failure.' William gave the boy a conciliatory smile. 'Now return it to the water so it may live on.'

Jacob dejectedly tipped his hands to the side and the fish dropped into the pool, quickly swimming to the bottom and settling upon the stones which lay there. He stared at it a moment and then sought out the second fish, seeing it lurking to the far right of the pool, in the shallows nearest the waves which were slowly getting closer as the tide came in.

'I see the other fish,' he stated as he slowly moved along the edge of the pool towards its resting place.

William watched as the boy knelt and dipped his hands back into the water, secure in the knowledge that there was little danger now he was kneeling before the shallows. Rachel began to move towards her brother and he quickly looked up, his expression clearly communicating that she should remain still and silent in order not to frighten his prey.

With concentrated deliberation, he drew his hands closer together, watching the fish for any sign that it detected the trap which was closing about it. Its tail moved gently and it swam forward a short distance, the boy ceasing the movements of his hands as it settled back upon the rock.

In an instant his hands came together and were lifted from the waters. 'I caught it,' he called triumphantly, his expression once more of happiness.

'Your hands moved so fast,' stated Rachel with an admiring look at her brother.

'That was indeed a very impressive catch,' added William.

Jacob beamed and briefly looked at the fish held within his hands before gently releasing it into the rock pool, satisfied that he had not been outdone by the creature.

'We should probably go back home now,' said Jacob after a few moments of basking in his success, rising to his feet and glancing at the incoming tide. 'The bar will be covered in a short while.'

Rachel got to her feet and looked at William, who crouched before them. 'Will ye carry us across the rocks so we do not hurt our feet?'

He nodded. 'I would happily carry you over them even if you were wearing shoes,' he replied.

William put them upon his shoulders and once they were safely held in his grasp he began to carefully make his way to the grasses beyond the rocks. When he reached them he turned his back so the children could sit upon the shelf of overhanging earth and disembark, then climbed up to join them.

'Before you go I have a special gift for each of you which I hope you will like,' said William as he crouched before the children.

They looked at him curiously.

'What is it?' asked Rachel.

'If you wait just a moment you will find out.'

She stuck her hand in the air. 'Can I have mine first?'

'I will give you your gifts at the same time, that is the only way to be fair.'

Rachel frowned momentarily and then her smile returned as William reached into his grubby tunic. He was careful to conceal what it was that he withdrew in his right hand, amused to see the children's eyes following every movement.

Holding his hand out before him, he looked from Jacob's face to his sister's. 'Are you both ready?'

Jacob nodded.

'Yes,' whispered Rachel, shifting on her feet excitedly.

William unfurled his fingers to reveal two necklaces of bright shells. The children looked upon the vibrant, delicate colours with wide eyes. 'I made them especially for you,' he said as Rachel slowly reached out and picked one up, her brother then doing the same.

'It is lovely,' she stated, holding it before her eyes and entwining it about her tiny fingers, taking in the colours and shapes of the shells strung upon the thread.

'Thank you,' said Jacob, glancing at William before turning back to the necklace upon his palm.

'I know it is more of a gift for a girl, but I thought you might appreciate one as well, Jacob,' he said, worried that the boy was disappointed with the token of friendship.

Jacob looked up and smiled at him warmly. 'I like it very much,' he said, stepping forward and reaching up to put his arms about William's neck, hugging him tightly as the giant continued to crouch before the children.

Rachel tied the necklace about her neck and then put her arms around him after her brother had stepped back.

William looked at the children's sweet faces and was filled with joy. 'I am glad you like the gifts, they took a great deal of time and a good deal of effort to make.'

Jacob nodded as he glanced at the necklace held in his right hand. 'It must have been hard not to smash the shells when making the holes in them.'

'Indeed it was.'

'Thank you, Will.' Rachel grinned as she touched the shells hanging about her neck with an appreciative gentleness.

'We really should be going,' said Jacob regretfully. 'The bar will soon be covered and we will end up wading back. Besides, father will be wondering where we have got to and we should attend to the pigs.'

'I will see you soon, I hope.'

Rachel nodded. 'As soon as we can come again.'

'I am glad to hear it.'

'Goodbye, Will, and thank ye once more for your present,' said Jacob as he began to walk away along the coastal grasses.

'Bye,' said Rachel before turning to follow her brother.

William rose to his full height, his knees aching a little. He watched them follow the edge of the island where they could be sure of avoiding nettles or any other thick foliage that might otherwise block their way. He looked forward to their next meeting and the brightness they brought with them as he turned away and started to walk towards the wall of the priory gardens.

37

William waited in his room. He stared out of the window at the blue sky and wondered what had detained Arthur. Time dragged as the shadows of the table's legs opposite him moved upon the granite wall, marking the passage of the sun in the heavens. The old monk was long overdue and the giant was worried some ill may have befallen him, especially after his melancholic words a few days before.

He glanced at the door and wished to hear the approach of sandalled footsteps, but the stairs and chapel beyond remained silent.

Rising from the straw, he began to pace around the small room like a caged animal. His gaze settled on the slate resting against the wall and the chalk markings that had been left for him to learn, the chalk itself resting upon the tabletop. He could not help but feel agitated by the monk's failure to arrive.

Then a thought struck him, maybe he was mistaken and he was supposed to have met Arthur in the gardens. William imagined him upon the seat on the north terrace, his eyes fixed upon the gate as he waited for the giant's belated arrival.

He stepped to the door and made a quick exit with head bowed low. He quickly ascended the steep steps and then hurried along the chapel's nave, soon finding himself in the shade of the northern side of the building which faced the mainland. William then made haste to the entrance hall, walking around its exterior and passing the tool shed where he had approached Brother Cook before arriving at the front of the priory. Striding across the uneven rocks and grasses, he made for the stone steps which descended to the gardens.

Taking three at a time, he hurried down, heart thundering in his chest. He was as eager to let the old monk know there was no cause for concern as he was to discover that Arthur was seated upon the bench, and these motivations made his descent all the more urgent.

William arrived at the foot of the steps and leapt down upon the cobbled path, walking briskly to the gate ahead, passing the path to the warehouses and harbour. He walked hurriedly into the gardens and began along the terrace beside the northern wall.

Halting abruptly, the giant's heart sank. The monk was not present upon the seat beneath the overhanging boughs of the evergreen.

William raised his eyes to the priory high above, only the chapel visible at the summit of the rocky crags, the sound of rushing blood filling his ears as adrenalin pumped through his veins. There was clearly something amiss and he felt a sense of cold dread.

Turning, he started to walk back to the gate.

Five local men walked hurriedly into the gardens. William became still and stared at them in apprehensive surprise, his pulse quickening as they turned to him.

'There is the beast,' stated the lead man, his face thin and eyes filled with fury as he pointed at the giant accusingly.

The group of men approached with purposeful strides, though their pace slowed as they drew nearer to the large creature before them. Their faces bore expressions of anger mingled with waning determination, their eyes displaying a hint of fear at the sight of one so unnatural. A couple of them bore weapons which glinted threateningly in the sunlight, one a cleaver darkly stained with animal blood and another a smith's hammer.

The lead man, his jaw clenched, face weathered and marked with deep lines, drew closest to William as the others remained at a safe distance. He looked the giant in the eyes, rising on the balls of his feet slightly. 'Stay away from my children,' he hissed venomously. 'Do ye understand, beast?' The last word was stated with scornful disgust.

William stared at him as if not comprehending his words.

'I said, do ye understand?' His gaze burned into the giant and he mistook the scarred curl of the beast's upper lip as a sneer of response.

There was a moment of tense stillness.

The man's fist suddenly crashed into William's crooked nose with great force, one weighted by his fury. The giant tottered and fell back upon the grass like a drunkard. He raised his right hand to his nose and felt warm blood upon his fingers, eyes watering and having to blink away tears as he looked up at the man.

John Hadden leant over the giant and spat in his face. He reached into the pocket of his jerkin and pulled out the necklaces made of shells, holding them up so the foul beast could clearly see what they were.

'Ye recognise these, do ye not?' he said, noting the look in William's eyes.

Grasping them in his right hand, he crushed them with his fingers, bright pieces of shell falling to the soft grass. He threw the remains upon the giant and glared at him a moment, hatred simmering in his eyes.

John turned and stalked away, the men who had accompanied him parting to allow him passage as their eyes remained on the giant. The reality of his presence on Carrack Looz en Cooz came as a shock, for even after the children had been made to explain where the necklaces had come from, the men thought their imaginations to have clouded their judgement, that what they had seen was in truth no giant. But the children's words and the rumours had been proven true, there really was a beast living close at hand, a fearful and horrifying creature of abnormality.

The men turned from the beast and began walking back to the gate, glancing over their shoulders to check that it was not rising to chase after them as blood dripped down its face. Each was filled with the conviction that such a cursed creature could not be allowed to remain, that it must be expelled or destroyed. They would not rest until this was done, until the darkness of its shadow no longer fell on Carrack Looz en Cooz or Marghas Byghan.

William watched the men disappear from view, the gate creaking shut behind them. His breathing was heavy and pain throbbed in his nose.

Leaning to the right, he removed his hand from his nose and allowed the thick blood to drop onto the grass beside him. William looked at the remains of the necklaces lying scattered upon his lap and then his gaze moved to the bright shards of shells lying in the grass about his feet. Like the shells, his feelings of safety on the Mount lay broken about him. The sanctuary he had found had been invaded.

He felt violated, not just physically, but mentally, the sense of separation from the world of men vanishing like warm breath on winter winds.

He breathed deeply and tried to calm the beating of his heart. The whole incident appeared as if a dream, so unexpected and out of the ordinary it had been.

He glanced at the blood upon his right hand as if to confirm the reality of what had just transpired and then scolded himself for being so reckless with his gifts to the children. His thoughts turned to them and he hoped Jacob and Rachel had not suffered unduly on his behalf. He knew them well enough to know they would not have revealed the secret of his presence easily, and prayed there had been no need of physical harm on their father's part.

William sighed and shook his head sadly, a stray drop of blood falling upon his stained tunic to mingle with the sweat caused by his rapid descent from the priory. How could he have been so foolish? Surely he should have guessed at the consequences of giving such things to the children and in the least devised some fiction as to how they came to possess such things, some story which they could have told their father in order to keep his existence a secret?

The sound of the gate creaking caused him to look up in alarm, worried that the men of Marghas Byghan had returned to take his life despite the holiness of his sanctuary. Arthur and Brother Cook stood wide-eyed as they stared at the fallen giant, temporarily held motionless by the sight which greeted their entry into the gardens.

The monks broke the bonds of the jarring shock, hurrying over and kneeling to either side of William, Arthur putting a hand upon his shoulder as he rested to his left.

'What happened?' he asked, glancing at the broken necklaces.

'Men from Marghas Byghan came to see me,' replied William, wiping his nose with his already bloodied hand.

'What was their reason?'

'My foolishness. I gave to the children the gifts you see shattered about me. It was these gifts which led the men to me and which have revealed my presence on the Isle.'

Arthur shook his head. 'This does not bode well. The town's representatives are sure to come and talk with Prior Vargas.'

Brother Cook nodded his agreement. 'They will demand that we give you sanctuary no longer.'

'This I know, and it is all the doing of my own hands.' William fought back tears.

'You could not have foreseen the results of your actions,' said Arthur.

'I could and should have, dear friend. I am solely to blame.'

The old monk shook his head sagely. 'No, in this you are wrong. These gifts were given from the heart, but to see the consequences you would have needed to use reason, which is from the head. The love by which you gave these gifts was blind to reason, did not need reason save itself.'

William looked into Arthur's blue eyes for a moment. 'I confess there is truth in what you say, but I still feel the weight of responsibility upon my shoulders.'

'For which part of these unfortunate events? For the actions of the men? They were of their own doing and they could have chosen a different course if they were not guided by fear.'

William sniffed, the coppery taste of blood at the back of his throat.

'May I check to see if it is broken?' asked Brother Cook with a glance towards the giant's nose.

William nodded.

The young monk reached up. With delicacy he touched the bridge of William's nose, making the giant wince slightly. The monk then held it between his thumb and index finger, testing its flexibility and finding there was none.

'I think it is bruised only,' he announced as he lowered his hand.

'Thank you,' said William quietly.

'Can you rise?' asked Arthur.

'I think so,' replied William as the monks got to their feet and stepped back to allow him room.

He placed his hands on the ground and tried to get to his feet, his legs surprisingly weak.

'Here.' Arthur moved forward and put an arm about his friend's waist, Brother Cook taking a firm hold of William's right arm.

The monks helped the giant to his feet and he felt a little dizziness. His sight shifted out of focus and he blinked in order to restore his vision. The weight of his body caused his legs to almost buckle and the two men of God strained to keep him on his feet.

'We must get you back to the priory,' said Arthur. 'I do not think it will be long before people from the mainland return with their demands.' He turned to Brother Cook. 'You should go and tell Prior Vargas what has occurred and ready him for our arrival and that of the townspeople.'

'Will you be able to make the ascent without my assistance?'

Arthur looked up at the giant. 'How are you feeling now, William?'

'The strength is returning to my legs. In a short while I will be able to walk unaided, I am certain of it.'

'Good.' The old monk smiled thinly, turning back to his Brother. 'Go ahead, Brother Cook. We will meet you at the priory.'

Brother Cook hesitated, looking up at the giant's face, his nose red and sore, a little bruising already starting to darken the skin about his eyes, dry blood amidst the hair on his upper lip and perspiration on his protruding brow. He nodded and then walked away, exiting the gardens with a quickness to his pace.

'Are you ready to walk unaided as yet or would you like my continued support?'

'Your support would be much appreciated, dear friend. I fear I am not yet recovered enough to walk without your kind assistance.'

The friends began to make their way to the gate, Arthur's right arm securely around William's waist. The monk could feel the giant's unsteadiness as he helped guide him from the gardens, fully aware that time was a factor in their ability to reach the priory. They had to speak with Prior Vargas before the town's representatives arrived with fear and ignorance as the catalyst for the demands they would surely make.

As they neared the gate Arthur thought about the course of action which should be taken in the face of the powerful motivations possessed by the people of Marghas Byghan. The idea that William should flee the island was out of the question. He had been granted sanctuary and no amount of pressure from beyond the priory's walls should cause this to be rescinded. No, there was truly only one option open to them now. Prior Vargas would have to greet the people with William at his side so they could see for themselves he was no beast, that there was nothing to fear from such a kind and gentle soul.

Arthur opened the gate and the two friends passed through. They walked slowly along the cobbled path to the foot of the steps. The aged monk looked up their steep and long climb as they curved to the left about the rise of the Mount, a frown deepening the wrinkles at the corners of his mouth.

'How is your strength, William?' He looked at his friend's expression, hidden beneath dried blood and facial hair. There was a clear tension, the muscles in the giant's jaw and cheeks taut as he tried to gather himself for the ascent.

'It will not be long until it is restored.'

'Do you wish to begin the climb now or should we wait awhile?'

William looked down at the monk, and though his words had not hinted at his feelings of urgency, the giant detected them in his blue eyes. 'We should begin now,' he replied.

'As you wish.'

They began to make their way up the stone steps, Arthur finding that William used him for support less and less as time wore on, the giant's autonomy increasing as he recovered from the blow he had received and the shock of the sudden event.

38

Arthur dipped the dark cloth into the blood-clouded water as he stood before William. Wringing it out, the sleeves of his cowl rolled to his bony elbows, he then turned his attention back to the patient who sat upon the chair before him. With care, he dabbed the cloth at the blood which still remained about William's nostrils, the giant wincing on occasion as he tried to remain still.

'Why did you not come to teach me today?' asked William from between tight lips.

'I was engaged in duties in the kitchen stores and lost track of time. I am sorry if I caused you concern.' The monk wiped the damp cloth over the thick hair on William's upper lip into which much blood had soaked.

'I am glad there was nothing amiss.'

'We will return to the lessons on the morrow.' Arthur turned to the bowl filled with water that rested upon the table in the giant's room and cleaned the cloth as well as he could. Studying his friend's face, he noted a few red smears on his cheeks which marked the cloth's passage. Arthur wiped at them and checked that none had been missed.

'That is the best I can do for the moment. I suggest you clean the blood from your moustache yourself,' said the monk as he straightened.

'Thank you, Arthur.' William looked up at him with a grateful smile. 'And thank you for your assistance in returning me to my room.'

'You once carried me up those same steps when my need was much greater.' He placed his hand on the giant's shoulder. 'That is a deed I shall ne'er forget.'

The sound of rapid footsteps could be heard in the chapel and they descended the steep steps to the door of William's room. The knock which followed was quick and sharp.

'Come in,' called William.

Brother Cook entered with a flustered look about him, his cheeks reddened by activity. 'I have spoken with Prior Vargas about your suggestion, Brother Elwin,' he said, pausing to catch his breath. 'He agrees that yours is the best course of action. As soon as William is ready he is to go immediately to the prior's rooms.'

'Good.' Arthur turned to his friend. 'If you make the same impression upon those from the town as you have with us then all is far from lost.'

'Let us hope I may make such an impression,' replied William, a touch of nervousness and apprehension in his tone as he stood and stepped over to the small table.

'Try to remain calm and do not speak out of turn and I am sure all will fare well. There is naught in you but goodness and I cannot see how they can fail to see this is so.'

William bent over and gathered water in his hands, splashing it upon his face and rubbing at the hair on his upper lip. He repeated the actions twice more and then turned to Arthur. 'May I have the cloth?'

The monk handed it to him and William rubbed his face dry, the black curls at its edge still glistening with moisture as he looked at his friend. 'There, how is that?'

Arthur studied his features. 'I see no more signs of blood.'

'Good, then it is time for me to go and discover what is to become of me.' The giant looked uneasily at the door where Brother Cook waited.

'Do not worry, William, for my heart is sure all will turn out well and the Lord will be with you.'

He smiled at his friend. 'I am thankful for that, for my heart holds no such certainty.'

'Would you like me to accompany you to Prior Vargas' rooms?'

'That would be a great reassurance.'

'Then let us depart.'

39

The breeze was strong and William's dark hair was tossed to and fro as the small procession descended the steps leading to the entrance hall's rear door. Entering, they found no comfort in its shelter from the elements, only an increase in tension as they neared the prior's rooms. They passed through the door to the left and entered the corridor along which the monk's cells were located. Brother Cook knocked at the first door and they awaited a reply, grateful not to hear unfamiliar voices beyond.

'Enter,' came the stern response and Brother Cook opened the door, stepping aside to allow the others entry before him.

William ducked and stepped into the room with Arthur directly behind him, Brother Cook taking care to shut the door as he followed them into the small study.

Prior Vargas stood behind his desk and there was a moment of silence as he studied William's wounded nose, the window bright behind him and making his features vague and shadowy. 'It looks extremely painful,' he commented, his hands held behind his back.

William nodded, but made no verbal response, a mild feeling of nausea sweeping over him as his stomach churned with nerves.

'I cannot say that I am pleased with the events which have transpired this day, though I understand the blame is not entirely yours.'

'It is not his ...' began Arthur, who was silenced by the prior's raised hand.

'Rest assured, your promised sanctuary here is not in doubt, though it may be that you must be confined to the buildings of the priory and will no longer be able to visit the gardens below.'

William nodded again. 'If you wish it, then it shall be so.'

Prior Vargas looked at William intently. 'Mr Tillbury, I would not wish such a thing upon a man whom I know to love our Lord's creation as you do. The decision will not truly be mine in this matter. If those who come from Marghas Byghan will not see reason and understand you are no threat to them or their families then I am afraid there shall be no choice other than to confine you to the area upon the summit of the Mount.'

'Then I must hope that those who come do so with open minds,' responded William, who was doubtful of a positive outcome. After the years he had spent chained in his master's service he knew how blinded people could be by their own preconceptions, however false they may be. Many people had passed before him, witnessed his captivity, and never had one shown signs of pity or disgust at his foul treatment. He was billed as entertainment and entertainment is what they expected.

There was a gentle rap upon the door.

'Enter,' called the prior.

Brother Stewart entered, a monk who was only a few years the junior of Arthur, but who found age to be much more of a burden, his elderly body filled with aches and pains to such a degree he was no longer able to descend the stone steps and had himself been confined to the summit through no choice of his own. His legs were bowed and his back bent, like an aged servant after a lifetime spent in service to the Lord. 'They have arrived,' he stated, voice croaky.

'Please bring them in, Brother Stewart,' replied the prior, having picked the Brother to be the first to meet with the townspeople because of his advanced years, hoping that his appearance would disarm them to some degree and soften their anger.

Brother Stewart bowed his grey-haired head, the crown of which no longer needed to be shaved, as baldness had set in. He then closed the door as he left to do as instructed, shuffling along the corridor back to the entrance hall.

'Brother Cook, Brother Elwin.' The prior looked at the two monks. 'Please retire to your cells.'

William looked at Arthur with alarm in his eyes, having thought his friend would be given leave to remain.

Arthur smiled at him in an attempt at reassurance, though his eyes betrayed his worry. Brother Cook quickly stepped to the door and opened it, the two monks filing out into the corridor as William's tension increased.

'William, I would ask that you come and sit behind me,' requested Prior Vargas, knowing that if the giant were to stand his height would prove instantly alarming to the folk who would shortly arrive.

William paused a moment and then moved around the desk, spying a simple, low stool which had been placed in the shadows beside the window through which sunlight occasionally spilled when breaks in the gathering clouds allowed. He sat upon it gingerly, fearing its collapse beneath his weight, but found it sturdy and able to bear him with ease.

The sounds of footsteps could be heard beyond the door and William stiffened, only just being able to see over the prior's desk, so low was the stool. Three loud and measured knocks followed.

Prior Vargas moved to stand before his desk and took a deep, steadying breath. 'Enter.'

Brother Stewart opened the door and then retreated to allow two portly, well-dressed men entrance, neither of which William recognised from the incident in the gardens. Their eyes narrowed against the glare from the window as their gazes settled upon the prior and the lead man stepped up to him.

'Prior Vargas, it has been many moons since last I saw ye on the mainland,' he said as they shook hands, the other man wheezing a little as he drew alongside his companion, the effort of climbing the steps having left him breathless, his large stomach heaving beneath his mauve tunic woven of fine cloth.

'I have been kept busy with our affairs of late, Mr Hicks, but it is good to see you.'

'This is Mr Jago. He is a representative of the merchants who use this town and the harbour which lies at the foot of Carrack Looz en Cooz.'

The prior extended his hand as Mr Jago wiped his brow with a white, silk handkerchief. 'I am Prior Vargas. It is a pleasure to meet you.'

The two men shook hands, Mr Jago remaining silent, the expression on his flushed, pig-like face stony and cold.

'I am afraid there is only one chair,' said the prior as he moved to the other side of his desk.

'I will stand,' said Mr Jago, his voice gruff.

Mr Hicks sat on the chair positioned before the prior's bare desk. The fine, mint green coat worn over his pale tunic was vibrant in the sunlight as it briefly shone into the room, only to be covered by cloud within moments, its golden light fading.

'Ye know of the reason for our visit?' asked the sheriff of Marghas Byghan, his dark, bushy eyebrows low as he studied the man before him.

Prior Vargas seated himself opposite the visitors. 'I know of an altercation which unfortunately took place upon the priory's land earlier this day,' replied Prior Vargas.

Mr Hicks leant forward. 'We know what resides here with ye, Prior Vargas, and ye must cast this evil out.'

'Must?'

'Aye.'

Mr Jago nodded his agreement.

'I know not of any evil which resides here. You must be mistaken.'

Mr Hicks' brow furrowed in annoyance. 'There be no mistake. A giant resides upon Carrack Looz en Cooz. It has been seen by many and has threatened the safety of our children.'

'A giant?'

'A giant,' confirmed Mr Jago.

'And you say that it is evil?'

'Aye,' replied Mr Hicks. 'It has struck fear into men's hearts and its black eyes are filled with malice. It is a beast of Satan and I be mighty shocked that men of God, like yourselves, have not discerned such.'

'Could it be that there is no such malice to discern, Mr Hicks?'

Mr Jago huffed and shook his head as anger rose, perspiration still evident upon his rounded face.

'Ye cannot tell me, Prior Vargas, that a creature so loathsome as to strike terror into the hearts of men such as Morgan Pengelly, the blacksmith, is not one of immense evil. The town demands ye cast it out.'

'If you were to be in the presence of this creature would you recognise its vileness, Mr Hicks?' Prior Vargas leant his elbows on the desk and steepled his fingers beneath his pointed chin.

'Of course.'

'Would you feel its evil even if you were not aware of its presence?'

'This is getting us nowhere,' said Mr Jago in irritation as he glanced down at his seated companion.

Mr Hicks shifted in his seat as he continued to look across at the prior. 'Its evil I would sense, of that there can be no doubt,' he stated.

Prior Vargas nodded. 'I see. And you believe such a beast resides with us? This is a poor reflection upon our judgement, do you not think?'

'I ...'

'Mr Hicks,' said the prior, cutting off the sheriff's response. 'Do you truly believe a beast of such evil, one that you could sense even if it were not in sight, could remain undetected amidst us within the priory? Surely we are not so different from other men as to be blind to the creature's terrifying characteristics.'

'It is not my intent to show disrespect to the priory or those who dwell therein. I have the greatest admiration for ye, Prior Vargas, and for the other men of God who dwell here.'

'I am glad to hear it.'

Mr Hicks thought for a moment, shifting on his seat and wiping his clammy palms upon the cloth of his tunic as he tried to find words. He knew what the people waiting back at the harbour expected of him and if he were not to deliver there may be dire consequences. With the lives of women and children at risk he would not be able to stop an angry mob from ascending the steps and doing away with the creature themselves, and he feared even the monks could come to harm if they tried to interfere.

'I am sorry, Prior Vargas, but my hands are tied. Ye must cast this beast out or I will not be held responsible for what comes to pass.'

'That sounds like a threat, Mr Hicks, or are you washing your hands like Pilate?'

He shook his head. ''Tis no threat, only fact. There are a great many fearful and angry people below who will accept nothing less than that which I ask of ye.'

Prior Vargas leant back in his chair and lowered his hands. He sighed and glanced at Mr Jago, whose grey eyes stayed ever watchful. 'What if I could prove to you that this beast is not as you have judged him?'

'It is impossible.'

'Stop toying with us, Prior Vargas,' stated Mr Jago. 'This is an extremely serious matter.'

'Of that there is no argument, but I fear you have already condemned a man without trial or true reason, and that I cannot allow.'

'This is no man of which we speak. This is a beast, a foul creature that has no place here. It should be thankful to escape with its life.' Mr Jago glared at the prior.

'Your words have confirmed what I have said and we clearly have no further room for discussion, so entrenched are you in your ill-conceived opinions. Good day to you both and may the Lord grant you greater wisdom in times to come.' Prior Vargas rose from his seat.

Mr Hicks stared at him in surprise as Mr Jago continued to glare angrily. The townspeople were going to be very unhappy with the news of Prior Vargas' refusal to cast out the beast and if they were to discover the way in which he had treated the matter their rage would be stoked further.

'Surely there must be some way we can appeal to your reason,' said Mr Hicks, remaining in his seat as the prior stood framed in the brightness of the window.

Prior Vargas studied the expression of the man seated opposite him and knew in truth he could not send him back to the people with empty hands. It was clear that William's presence had caused quite a stir and the inhabitants of Marghas Byghan were blinded by ignorance and fear.

'It may be there is a compromise which can be reached,' said the prior as he returned to his seat and the sun briefly shone into the room once again.

'We will not …'

'Mr Jago, I believe this may be our only chance to placate the people below,' said Mr Hicks, turning to his companion sharply. 'I am now certain Prior Vargas will not cast this beast out, no matter how dire the consequences may be. If we wish to avoid what I fear may come to pass then we must hear him out.'

Mr Jago's frown deepened, but he did not voice further protest.

'What is this compromise of which ye speak?' asked Mr Hicks, turning his attention back to the man seated behind the desk.

'There is but one course of action I believe lies open to us,' he began, leaning forward and holding Mr Hicks' gaze. 'We will confine him to this summit upon which we sit. The beast of which you speak will never again descend from these heights.'

Mr Hicks pondered the prior's words. 'And if it should do so?'

Prior Vargas held his hands up. 'Then he is cast out.'

Mr Hicks looked up at his companion. 'What do ye think of this suggestion, Mr Jago?'

'I am not at all sure the people will agree.'

Mr Hicks turned to the prior once again and sighed deeply. 'Your suggestion I will accept, though whether the people will do so I cannot say. I shall do my utmost to persuade them of its wisdom for I have no wish to see trouble brought upon men who have taken holy orders.'

Prior Vargas nodded. 'Then it is settled.' He rose and walked around the desk to shake hands with Mr Hicks. 'I hope that when we next meet it will be under better circumstances.'

'As do I,' replied Mr Hicks.

The prior turned to Mr Jago and held out his hand.

Mr Jago looked at it a moment and then reluctantly took it in his.

'Fare ye well, Mr Jago,' said Prior Vargas without friendliness.

Mr Jago simply nodded in response.

'Mr Tillbury, will you please see that these gentlemen are safely escorted to the steps?' The prior glanced over his shoulder and the two men followed his gaze, for the first time noticing the man seated in the deep shadows to the right of the window.

Their eyes widened as William rose from the low stool. With faces drained of colour, they stared at the giant as he made his way across the small room, the bruising upon his nose and about his eyes lending him a startling visage. He opened the door to the corridor beyond, stepping aside so they could leave.

'May the Lord guide and protect you,' said Prior Vargas, the men glancing at him as if in a daze, the prior displaying the merest flicker of a grin.

After a moment's hesitation, Mr Hicks slowly walked to the doorway, staying as far from William as he could, Mr Jago directly behind him. They quickly stepped out of the room without turning their backs on the giant and the trepidation was evident in their expressions as William followed them into the corridor and shut the door to Prior Vargas' study.

'This way please, gentlemen,' said William, ushering the men towards the door to the entrance hall, surprise registering on Mr Hicks' face when he heard the giant speak, never having thought such a beast could master the art of language and certainly not with such clarity.

Mr Hicks and his companion walked into the entrance hall and hurried through its simple surroundings to the front door through which Brother Stewart had brought them. As the giant approached, Mr Jago hastily opened the door and they nearly tumbled out of the building in their haste to be away from the towering creature.

When he reached the open door, William peered out to find that the men were walking towards the steps at a great pace, constantly glancing over their shoulders with fearful eyes.

'May the Lord be with you,' he called after them as they reached the top of the stone steps and began their descent.

William let out a sigh as he shut the door. Disappointment weighed heavy upon him despite knowing that Prior Vargas had done all he could. At least the prior had managed to secure his sanctuary on the Mount, unless the people below would not accept such a compromise.

'I am truly sorry, William.'

He looked up to find Prior Vargas standing on the opposite side of the small hall, framed in the doorway which led to the corridor where the monk's cells were located.

'There was no other choice open to me other than to offer your confinement.'

'I understand, Prior Vargas. I am sure in time I will become used to it. At least I can still take in the views from on high.'

'That you can, and, possibly, one day you will be able to return to the gardens.'

'I hope that will be so.'

Prior Vargas smiled thinly. 'I must return to my duties, for this day has seen much disturbance.'

'I am sorry for my part in this and would like to thank you for all you have done.'

The prior nodded and then turned away, closing the door to the corridor.

William stood in silence awhile, his mind filled with the day's events, a chaos of images and words which circled like crows above the carrion of the life he had come to savour upon the Mount after so many years of suffering.

The call of gulls in the sky above the priory broke the spell of his reverie and William unsuccessfully tried to clear his mind of melancholic thoughts. His world had unexpectedly shrunk to such a size that he feared he was now within a new cage, one without physical evidence, but a cage nonetheless. He had spent many nights locked in a cage of bars upon the back of a wagon after performing for audiences who cared not about his treatment, only about his ability to astound them with his height and feats of strength. Now, he was caged again.

William walked across the hall to the door where Prior Vargas had been standing and opened it. The corridor stretched before him in shadowy silence, the air grey and thick with emotion as William walked along it towards Arthur's cell in order to share with his friend the events which had unfolded in the prior's study.

40

'William, are you taking note of what I am saying?' asked Arthur as he looked at his pupil, who was staring out of the window to his room, his mind in a distant place.

There was no response and the monk shifted forward to the edge of the chair on which he sat. 'William!'

The giant turned to him with a look of mild surprise. 'Yes?'

'You have not been listening to me for quite some time. Your mind is wandering and I think we should end the lesson for today.'

William looked at the slate and the words written there as he sat upon the straw. 'I am sorry, please continue.'

'What troubles you, dear friend?' asked Arthur as he laid the stub of chalk on the tabletop.

The giant looked into the old monk's eyes for a long moment. 'It is a melancholy which has settled upon me and its reasons I cannot tell. My thoughts turn to my past. They turn to the children, Rachel and Jacob, and the assault which I suffered in the gardens. They turn and turn without my bidding. Maybe tis only the shortening of the days and the onset of autumn which affects me so. I do not know.'

'I think you are still finding it a hardship to remain captive upon the Mount,' said Arthur before coughing a little, hand politely raised before his mouth.

'It is interesting that you use that word, for a captive is how I feel at times, but this sadness runs deeper.' He paused and looked back out of the window at the thick clouds and their miserable shades of grey which held the promise of rain. 'I think of my mother often, wonder at the woman who gave her life in order that I may live.'

William swallowed hard and looked the old monk in the eyes. 'Where was God then?'

Arthur thought for a moment. 'I cannot account for the Lord's actions.'

'It seems no one can. Surely it is the game of life alone and no mighty hand moves the pieces. I hear you thank the Lord for all that is good, but what about all that is bad? You do not curse His name in times of trouble, yet praise Him in times of goodness. Surely He is equally responsible for both or He is responsible for neither.'

'This I cannot say. My faith is not based on the reasoning of the mind, but on the feelings of the heart, like the gifts you gave the children. I feel the truth of the Lord, not as a

191

being set beyond man, but as an existence in every man and in every thing. Within the whole of creation the Lord resides and we each have a share of this divinity.'

William looked at his friend with a sudden expression of wonder. Arthur's simple words brought with them revelation and within his being he knew the truth of what his friend had said. The divine was in the world and all its multitude forms, it was the bond which joined everything.

'God is a unity, a oneness of all things. He is the sum total of all that is,' he whispered as he again looked out of the window with eyes wide and filled with new-found light. 'In separateness we believe we dwell, but in truth we are but part of a wholeness of divine existence. Now I see the truth of it. God is truly everywhere, for God is everything.'

Arthur studied his friend's enlightened expression, had heard the intensity of his words. 'That is your truth,' he said softly, 'but it is not that of others.'

William turned to him. 'Do you not see it?'

'I do not set my mind to these things. Content am I to understand there is a God. There is no desire to know what form He takes or to comprehend His vastness. I feel His existence within and about me, and that is enough.'

'You are God, as am I and all that we see about us,' responded William with continued enthusiasm, his eyes filled with the power of the thoughts which had come to him so suddenly.

'William, do not let any other hear you say things of this nature for they are not as understanding as I.'

'But it is the truth.'

Arthur stared at him with a stern look upon his lined face. 'This is a warning from a friend, William, and you would do well to heed it. Such statements can be deemed heresy and would be looked upon with severity.'

The giant leant back against the cold stone of the granite wall, his eyes filled with the fire that illuminated his mind. 'So I must keep a silence in relation to this revelation?'

'You must. If it is the truth, then surely others will discover it for themselves.'

'They have no need to do so when I can simply tell them.'

'Words are all good and well, but it is experience which moulds a man to the greatest degree. Say nothing, William, and allow them to experience the truth and its awakening for themselves.'

William pondered awhile and then nodded. 'There is much wisdom in your words, my friend, and so I will heed your counsel and hold my tongue in this matter.'

'Of this I am glad, for I would not wish you to be marked out as a heretic and in my heart know this is not the case.'

William smiled at the old monk.

'Now I must leave and attend to my other duties.' Arthur rose from the chair and winced as pain flared in his knees and lower back.

'Will you return to continue with my tutelage on the morrow?'

The monk nodded as he looked down at his most unusual pupil. 'That I will. Until then I bid you farewell.'

'Farewell, dear friend.'

Arthur walked to the door and opened it. Stepping onto the first of the steps which led from the room to the chapel, he paused. 'May the Lord be with you,' he said with a warm smile before closing the door.

William listened as his friend's footsteps faded. The faint sound of waves upon the southern rocks of the island washed into his room and he could hear the cries of gulls in the distance. Staring out of the window, he watched the misty clouds drift by on westerly winds and took a deep breath. Calm began to replace the intensity of the excitement he had felt. It had been the first time since the assault two weeks previous that his melancholy had lifted. Its darkness had crept through him like a thief in the dead of night seeking out all hope and hiding it within its cloak. The darkness had been such that William had started to entertain thoughts which surprised even himself. He had visions of standing atop the southern bluffs and leaping from the great height, his body coming to rest in broken stillness on the rocks below. These thoughts had made him fearful of his own mind and this in turn had sunk him further into the mire of darkness in which he was trapped.

Thanks to his friend something within him had been lit and burned brightly to dispel the darkness and send the thief running from the flames, the warmth of which enlivened him once more. He owed a debt of gratitude to Arthur for the spark of his words and the glory of clear sight it had suddenly granted him. In an instant he had seen and felt the truth, and with such a revelation came an energy as he had never previously experienced.

William smiled to himself and reached for his cloak, which lay to his left upon the straw, balled into a pillow. The sparkle of metal caught his eye beside it and his gaze fell on the rose-shaped brooch which was visible beneath the bedding. His hand moved to it and he brushed aside the straw, picking up the trinket and lifting it level with his glittering eyes.

Slowly turning it in his fingers, his smile grew. The closed rose was not a symbol of a blossoming which could never come to pass, as he had thought, but it was a symbol of its constant potential.

William nodded and gripped the rose tightly in his right hand as his gaze was once more attracted by the passing clouds and a sense of calm filled him in the hush of his room.

41

William stood above the crags of the southern bluffs. The night wind bore with it a chill which marked autumn's arrival. He stared out across the expansive ocean; the full moon hung in the firmament, her light spilling onto the waves like liquid silver.

His features softened by the pale light, the giant settled upon the grass. It was the early hours of the morn and he had been woken by a strange dream of tumbling rocks. In the dream he had been standing beneath the crags looking out to sea on a bright day, the vaulted sky a pure blue with more depth than any ocean. There had been a rumble as if of thunder. A great flock of seabirds circled above, calling out his name in strained rasps, a sense of desperation to their cries, as if trying to warn him of some impending doom. Then a shadow had fallen upon him and he had looked up, discovering to his horror a huge rock tumbling towards him at great speed.

William had woken in a cold sweat just as the rock was about to crush him beneath its weight. The echo of the dream had been strong and remained so as he sat upon the bluffs staring out to sea. Its clarity was unusual in waking life, for he rarely recalled a dream so clearly as this and was disturbed by it.

He took a deep breath of the cool sea air and tried to release the tension in his body, the muscles in his shoulders and neck knotted so tightly they were beginning to ache. There was a feeling of unease which he could not shake however hard he tried.

The ghostly form of a barn owl glided over him in silence as waves crashed upon the rocks below, the white froth of their destruction bright in the moonlight. The wind buffeted him as William absorbed the sights and sounds, pulling his dark cloak closer about his body.

The sounds of soft footsteps upon the grass behind him were only just audible. William could discern that one fell with greater weight than the other and knew it was Arthur who approached.

'Good morning, Arthur,' he said without turning.

'Good morning, William. How did you know that it was I who drew near?' replied the monk as he came to a halt beside his friend and then slowly settled upon the ground.

'Your limp is a clue I could not fail to miss.'

'Then your powers of observation are far greater than mine, though age has had a hand in this, my senses not being as sharp as they once were.' He pulled back the hood of his cowl and felt the breeze upon his shaven crown. 'How are you on this new day?'

'Had I not been woken by a dream I would still be soundly asleep upon the straw,' replied William as he continued to take in the view.

'I judge by your tone this was not a good dream?'

William shook his head. 'Far from it. This was a disturbing dream, the sights and sensations of which I am unable to dispel despite my best attempts.'

There was a moment of silence between them which was filled by the wash of the ocean. Arthur stared up at the moon, fascinated by the shadows upon her surface. 'I once suffered from dark dreams for nearly a year. They came to me regularly, at least once a week. They would take different forms, but always leave me with a distinct feeling of fear and uneasiness,' said the old monk as he craned his neck.

'How did you rid yourself of them?'

'I tried many things, but time was the only cure that finally had effect. They simply came to an end.'

'Did you find a way to cleanse your mind of their images?' William turned to the monk, his face pale and ghostly, the moonlight like fine silk upon his skin and lending him an ethereal quality.

'No, I am afraid I did not.' Arthur looked at his friend. 'Time was again the greatest healer, though on occasion I was able to empty my mind in meditation, but the dream's echoes would stir as soon as I was returned to my normal state of being.'

'No matter how hard I try, I cannot shake the dream from my mind. It brings with it a sense of dread, coupled with apprehension that I would be rid of, for they unsettle me greatly.'

'By the first light of the day they will have faded to naught but vagaries, I assure you.' Arthur smiled thinly.

William did not return the gesture, instead turning his attention back to the undulating ocean beneath the paled night sky, his eyes filled with the borrowed light which lay softly upon the swells. He sat in brooding silence, the sensations of the dream still lingering in his mind as he tried to banish all thoughts.

42

William looked up at his friend as Arthur sat on a simple wooden chair beside him and coughed, hazy sunlight burning through the high cloud and illuminating the old man's face beneath the raised hood of his cowl.

'You should go inside out of the wind,' he said softly.

Arthur shook his head. 'No.' He coughed some more, eyes closing, the pain in his throat like the shallow cuts of a blade. 'It will pass,' he managed, his right hand covering his mouth.

'You are not well, dear friend, and the chill cannot be good for your condition.'

The monk bore a stubborn expression as he glanced at his friend, the coughing becoming more sporadic, his eyes sparkling with tears which had risen in response to the stinging in his throat. 'I will be fine.'

William studied the monk as the old man turned back to the sea. He sighed and wondered whether he should fetch a blanket to warm Arthur as the wind swirled violently about them, seabirds gliding with great speed on the currents below their high vantage point on the Mount's southern bluffs.

The giant turned his attention to the ocean as he sat upon the damp grass, his cloak pulled about him and hood covering his dark curls. It had been two days since the dream and yet he still had not managed to shake the feelings it had given rise to. Though they had lost a great deal of their potency, they continued to linger and made themselves known in quiet moments of wandering thought.

Arthur began to cough again, the chair upon which he was seated rocking with the force of his convulsions as William turned back to him. The old man's hooded head was bowed and body bent almost double, eyes tightly closed and mouth stretched wide.

'You must go inside, if not for yourself, then for my sake,' said William, regretting having brought the chair for his friend, something which had only served to encourage Arthur out into the autumnal winds.

The old monk could barely shake his head as the coughing continued to grip his frail body.

William rose and stepped over to his friend, prepared to carry the wilful monk back into the priory if he would not return to its shelter of his own accord. His cloak whipped and snapped in the wind as he looked down on Arthur, who seemed so fragile and aged in the grip of the convulsions.

The coughing subsided and the old monk looked up at him, eyes pleading with William to leave him be, filled with a deep yearning to remain outside in the arms of nature, whose embrace he loved so much. It had not been long after William's confinement to the summit that Arthur had also found himself confined, but by the circumstances of age rather than those arising from fear and ignorance. His health had been steadily declining, something which the giant had not noticed at first, but of late the change had become more rapid.

Hesitating, William then moved back to where he had been sitting. He could hear the dogs of Marghas Byghan barking in alarm and turned north to look at the haphazard town with a puzzled expression as the sound of cattle lowing also drifted on the wind.

Without warning, the earth suddenly began to shake and tremble violently. William looked at the ground in dismay as he fought to retain his balance. The old monk looked over at him with wide eyes as the chair threatened to topple over.

'What is happening?' asked William, his voice raised and filled with growing panic.

'I do not know,' Arthur called back, his words filled with distress.

The sound of loose rocks tumbling from the southern crags rose on the wind. They shattered upon the tidal rocks below and the noise was terrifyingly loud as it lifted to their high vantage point. William fought to remain standing, his body swaying back and forth in an attempt to keep his equilibrium. He was filled with tension as his muscles and tendons became like bolts of iron and he feared the bluffs would collapse.

He looked over the edge with frightened eyes as the ground continued to quake. Birds flew into the air and battled the wind as they called out in alarm. A huge rock slowly detached itself from the steep crags and began to fall, its speed increasing as it made its descent. It spun over and over and smashed against other rocks, splinters spinning off in all directions like sparks from a flint. It hit the thick grass at the base of the crags and split in two, the pieces bounding over the edge of the island to smash onto the rocks below with fearful violence.

The earth rocked and shuddered as William tried to hold back the urge to run for the protection of the priory. He could not leave Arthur alone upon the bluffs.

The sound of falling masonry rose into the air like a clap of distant thunder and he looked towards the buildings. Over the roofs of the library and monk's cells William saw in horror that the rear of the chapel had suffered a collapse, a plume of dust rising and being torn asunder by the wind.

The shaking of the earth ceased abruptly.

William stood with his legs braced, unsure what he should do, the unsettling dream vivid in his mind as he turned to his friend. Arthur's face was pale and drawn as he remained on the seat, his withered hands gripping its edges with knuckles white. Never in all his years had the old monk experienced such a fearful occurrence and his pulse raced in the wake of the terrifying events.

'I think it has ended,' said William, staring at his friend, who was clearly in shock. 'Arthur, do you hear me?'

The monk slowly turned to him. 'I thought the world were coming to an end, that Judgement Day had arrived and all things were to fall to ruin,' he said in a whisper, his words barely audible above the sound of the wind.

'It is over,' stated William, trying to imbue his words with a confidence he lacked. He worried that at any moment the tremors would begin anew, his muscles tense in readiness.

'How can you be sure?' asked Arthur.

The giant sought words with which to reassure his friend, but could think of none. Setting his will against

200

the trepidation which filled him, he moved to crouch at the monk's side, trying to act without the stiffness of nervous anticipation.

The sound of the church bells chiming in Marghas Byghan lifted into the air as the animals of the town continued to call out. Smoke and dust rose along the hillside and he could see figures moving with urgency about the settlement as crows and gulls circled above, their agitated cries carrying across the bay.

'Why do the bells chime and the beasts make such an uproar?' asked Arthur. 'Be this truly the end of all things?' He stared out to sea, his eyes glazed, his heart fluttering like a caged bird.

'No, I think the bells ring to call for aid,' replied William, looking at the old monk's ashen face. He moved before his friend and took Arthur's hands in his. 'We are safe now,' he said softly, holding the monk's gaze, feeling as though Arthur were looking through him and finding this disconcerting.

'The rear of the chapel has collapsed,' called Brother Cook from the front door of the entrance hall.

William nodded at the young monk. 'I have seen it is so,' he replied with voice raised so as to be heard above the northerly wind. 'Are any thought to be trapped beneath the rubble?'

'All are thankfully accounted for, though Brother Stewart cracked his head upon the floor of his cell when taking a fall.'

'I am glad there is nothing more serious to report,' replied William.

'As am I.' Brother Cook turned his attention to Arthur, who had remained motionless upon the chair during the exchange. 'Is Brother Elwin of good health?'

'He is suffering from shock. He will be recovered soon, of this I am sure.'

Brother Cook nodded at the giant. 'Do you require any aid?'

'No, but I thank you for your offer. I shall take Brother Elwin back to his cell and sit with him until he is returned to his former self.'

'Very well. If you need any assistance please do not hesitate to ask. I shall be with Brother Stewart in his cell.' Brother Cook went back inside the hall and disappeared from sight.

William turned to his dear friend and bent to pick him up. Cradling him in his arms as he had on their first meeting, he looked down at the lined face and the blue eyes that seemed so distant.

'I am taking you back to your room, Arthur. There you shall take rest until you are recovered from this ordeal.'

The monk looked up and his eyes focused on the face which hovered over him, the prominent brow casting pools of shadow about William's eyes. The fog which had clouded his mind began to lift and he tried to smile. 'Thank you,' he croaked, wincing at the soreness of his throat as he heard the bells continuing to peal upon the mainland.

William felt a flood of relief as his friend stared at him, recognition in his gaze. 'Welcome back,' he said softly as the wind messed his black curls. 'Do not try to move or expend your energy for you are suffering from the shock of what has just come to pass.'

'I feel …' began Arthur, his expression turning thoughtful. 'I feel not myself. There is a detachment from all about me which threatens to consume me.'

'Do not worry, dear friend. It will not last and you will soon be returned to full health.'

William began to carry the old monk towards the door to the entrance hall, his pace slow and measured, cloth-covered feet stepping upon grass and weathered rock which had been made bare by the elements.

Quick footfalls could vaguely be heard upon the stone steps which descended to the gardens. The sound drew the giant's gaze and he looked over to see who would come into view from behind the rocks that masked the steps as they curved downward upon the slope of the Mount. He stiffened and his eyes widened as the father of Rachel and Jacob came bounding up, his face flushed and glistening with perspiration, eyes low as he concentrated on keeping his footing.

When John reached the summit he glanced up and immediately saw the motionless giant with the monk in his arms. The farmer ran straight towards him and the giant braced himself for another assault.

The farmer came to a halt before William, his chest heaving beneath the deep green tunic he was wearing, one stained with dirt and dust. He desperately tried to catch his breath, gaze fixed on the creature towering before him. 'The children,' he managed before taking a breath.

William looked at the farmer, his heart rate increasing when he saw the haunted look in the man's eyes.

John wheezed and wiped his brow, his motions quick and filled with urgency, William noticing that his knuckles were torn and bloodied. 'My house has collapsed and the children are inside,' said the farmer rapidly. 'I need your help to dig them out. The stones are too big and there is no one to give me aid, the rest of the townsfolk busied with their own disasters. Ye are my only hope. Will ye come?' John looked at the giant in desperation.

William nodded without hesitation. 'But first I must get my friend to his room so that he may recover from the shock of the event.' He stepped around the farmer and resumed his passage to the entrance hall door, his pace much quickened. 'Wait for me and I will soon return.'

The giant reached the door and entered without shutting it behind him. He moved hurriedly through the entrance hall and entered the corridor beyond.

'Brother Cook!' he called out, his voice filled with tremulous emotion as it echoed off the granite walls. His heart was pounding with renewed vigour as he thought about what the farmer had said. The children were trapped beneath the ruins of their home and in his mind's eye he could see Jacob and Rachel's innocent faces, unable to bear the thought that they may have come to harm.

The fourth door along the right-hand side of the corridor opened and Brother Cook stepped out.

'Brother Cook, I must leave Brother Elwin in your care. There is urgent need of my assistance in the town,' said William as he hurried along the corridor to the young monk.

'I will watch over him,' replied Brother Cook, glancing at the old monk's lined face.

'Set me down, dear friend,' came Arthur's weak voice. 'I am sure I can find my own feet now that the feelings of distress fade within me.'

William looked down at his friend and deep into his eyes. It was plain that Arthur was not yet returned to his usual self, but the giant believed him to be of sound enough mind to know his own strength.

With care, painfully aware of the time that was passing as he did so, William set the old man's feet upon the stone floor and held onto his shoulders as Arthur tested his weight and balance.

The monk took a tentative step and then another with growing confidence. 'There, I told you I could manage.' He smiled at William. 'Now go and aid the children. They are in dire need,' he said.

William looked at his friend for a moment and then spun on his heels, striding back towards the hall as he heard his friend begin to cough violently.

John waited outside without patience, his eyes filled with a fear of which he did not wish to speak as the giant returned and they set off for the town, a silent look passing between them and the farmer seeing the same fear reflected in the creature's eyes as they hurried to the steps and began the descent.

43

They ran along the sand and shingle bar connecting the island to the mainland as a brief squall veiled them in grey rains, passing southward on blustery winds. Their throats burned with the effort and their legs ached after the rapid descent from the priory, hair and faces dripping as the dark clouds rapidly passed over.

Chapel Rock loomed large to the left, rising from the sands. They passed it without pause and covered the remaining stretch of beach with continued haste, the granite walls of the town's sea defences rising before them as the church bells rang out across the bay and the wind ushered ghostly fingers of loose sand across the wide, curving beach.

Climbing the stone steps which led to the town, they entered a scene of chaos. People rushed in all directions and there was a pile of rubble on the other side of the rutted track which had once been a cottage. The sound of wailing lifted into the air with shouts of urgent instruction as townspeople dug at the ruins in search of the occupants of the humble abode. There were looks of alarm as people sighted the giant moving amidst them, their eyes filled with fear and animosity. Many paused in their labours as they watched the creature pass with John Hadden at its side, both with cheeks flushed and expressions of wearied determination.

They rushed up the track which ran the length of the hill, William ignoring the unfriendly glances and occasional pointing, the sight of buildings reduced to piles of earth and stone bolstering his concerns for the children's safety. His loping pace quickened further, John struggling to remain by his side, fire in his thighs and phlegm making his breathing increasingly hard after having already made haste to Carrack Looz en Cooz in order to fetch the giant.

'To the left,' the farmer managed between desperate inhalation as their hurried steps caused a group of roaming chickens to scatter from the track and squawk in alarm.

The men ran up a pathway which branched off up the hill, the steepness of their ascent increasing dramatically and slowing their progress. Frustration began to rise within William, his heart pounding with the effort as adrenalin pumped through his veins and another heavy shower lashed them with rain.

They passed ramshackle cottages, one with its right side collapsed and two people frantically digging at the remains in search of a loved one, clothes sodden, backs bent as they toiled. Then the men passed the upper outskirts of the town and hedgerows rose to either side of the track behind stone walls covered with a growth of moss and ferns. The track curved to the right and the rubble of the farmhouse came into view, a pig sty and its muddied occupants visible on the slope beyond what had once been the children's home.

William glanced at the farmer, his eyes questioning.

John nodded and the giant went immediately to the tumbled cob walls. He scanned the ruins, looking for any sign of the children who lay buried somewhere beneath as the farmer drew alongside him.

John pointed to the left. 'Their room,' he stated as he struggled for breath and doubled over, hands on his knees as he coughed, spitting onto the earth before him, the rain abating and a patch of blue sky allowing the sunlight to rest briefly upon the scene of devastation.

William set to the task at hand without hesitation. His fingers dug into the earth and he quickly uncovered a large stone. He hauled it aside and let it roll onto the track beside the ruins of the south-facing house. He scrabbled in the dank mud, using his large hands as spades to pull it back, its mass falling upon his cloth-covered feet along with smaller stones concealed within.

The farmer moved to his side and began to remove the debris in grief-stricken urgency. They worked with hasty determination, clearing the collapsed cob walls before them. William's fingertips jarred against wood and he began to uncover the roof joists, the far ends of which rose from the rubble like broken ribs rising from the flesh of a corpse.

The sound of moaning caused both men to become motionless. They listened intently until the noise came again. It was Jacob. He was still alive amidst the ruins of the house.

Their efforts redoubled as they sought out the source of the pained sounds. Further joists and beams were steadily revealed, some snapped in the violence of the building's collapse. Cruel splinters like sharpened teeth caught in William's palms as he removed one of the broken roof supports, the giant inhaling sharply with the sudden pain, muscles straining and sweat mingling with rainwater upon his face.

His heart leaping, William spied Jacob's dirtied face through a gap between two of the thick beams which had stopped the rocks and mud from burying the child.

'Will!' the boy exclaimed weakly as he looked up and spied his friend, surprise and hope mingled in his tone, terror fading in his eyes.

'Stay still. We will have you out soon,' said the giant.

'Are ye hurt?' asked the boy's father.

'Not badly. A few cuts and bruises only, I think,' replied Jacob, his voice tremulous.

John felt a flood of relief wash through him.

'What about Rachel?' enquired Jacob as he lay beneath the protection of the beams.

John glanced at William. 'She is not with ye?'

Jacob shook his head weakly as the giant shifted a couple of large rocks which jammed the beams in place above Jacob, his palms bleeding profusely from cuts and the presence of the large splinters which had dug deeply.

With great effort, William lifted the first of the beams. Its far end rose into the air and then the beam toppled to the right after the giant manoeuvred and released it, the timber trembling as it thudded upon the earth.

John moved forward and crouched beside his son. 'Can ye break from your confinement?'

The boy struggled momentarily, his upper torso now revealed, but his legs hidden beneath the second beam. 'No, the beam has trapped my right leg,' replied Jacob eventually.

John looked at the giant, who set to the task of removing the wood without a word. His shoulders strained as he lifted it from the boy with as much care as he could, shifting its weight to the right.

Jacob scrambled from his resting place, his father helping, placing his hands beneath the boy's shoulders and pulling him to his feet. Jacob tested his weight and a slight pain shot up his left leg as William looked for any sign of Rachel.

'Can ye stand without my aid?' asked the farmer as he continued to support his son.

Jacob nodded. 'Though there is a little pain.'

John withdrew his hands and brushed mud from the boy's hair. Then, with tears welling uncontrollably in his grey eyes, he clasped the boy to him. 'I am so glad ye are safe, my son.'

The boy held his father and began to cry, releasing the fear he had been trying to keep at bay as he lay in the claustrophobic darkness as if in a grave, surrounded by wood, rock and mud. His body trembled as his sobs overtook him and the passage of his tears was marked in the dust upon his cheeks.

William began to dig at the rubble again, gripping rocks in his painful hands and flinging them aside. There was no clue as to Rachel's whereabouts and he prayed she had met with the same good fortune as her brother and been afforded some protection from the falling rubble. From what William could discern much of the roof had collapsed first and the walls thereafter, and this afforded him some hope that the girl may still be alive beneath the sheltering beams and mud-covered thatch.

John released his son and rejoined the giant in the effort to discover Rachel's whereabouts beneath the remains of his home. Jacob moved to stand beside his father, wiping tears from his eyes which smeared the dirt upon his face as he watched the progress of the two men and waited in tense anticipation for some sign of his sister.

Time drew out as the men dug side by side, removing rocks from amidst the mud which they pushed away. William grasped great handfuls of thatch and threw them to his left, onto the farm track which continued up to the brow of the hill. New beams were revealed, but he could see no trace of the girl beneath.

With muscles straining, he pulled one of the beams aside and his heart sank. A small, pale hand protruded from the earth before him, its fragile fingers eerily still.

He looked at John, whose face was drained of colour, his gaze fixed on the macabre sight.

'Rachel,' whispered Jacob, his sobbing beginning anew.

William dug at the mud and rocks of the collapsed cob walls, revealing the girl's torso, her chest motionless beneath the old blue dress she was wearing. The giant pulled at a piece of shattered timber and Rachel's face was revealed in a small space beneath, peering up from amidst the mud as if she were being sucked into it, her eyes closed as she prepared to sink beneath the surface. There were no signs of blood or injury upon her peaceful countenance and he could see that though her body had been pinned beneath the weight of the fallen walls, her head had been protected by the remnants of the roof beam.

'Rachel!' her father called out, kneeling on the rubble beside her as William scraped the mud away from the sides of her head, tangles of blonde hair slowly revealed.

'Rachel?' John's eyes glistened with tears as he reached down and stroked her cheeks.

William quickly cleared the last of the rubble from the girl's legs and then turned to look at her face.

'Ye must go and fetch Enid Hyne, the herbalist,' said John without turning to the giant, tears upon his cheeks. 'Quickly!'

William rose as Jacob knelt beside his father and stared down at his sister. With a last glance at the girl's pale and lifeless face, the giant turned and began to run back along the track which descended into the town.

44

William passed the cottages that lay a short distance down the slope and began to seek out the rotund woman whom he had seen visiting the Mount after Arthur had damaged his knees on the stone steps. His tired legs carried him in haste despite their protesting muscles, which burned with the effort.

After moving further into the heart of the town, people again staring at him in surprise and alarm, he finally spied Enid Hyne. She was applying a herbal paste to a woman's arm as the patient sat on a low wall before her with dust caked on her haggard face. The roof of the low cottage behind the injured woman had collapsed and the walls which remained standing were split with dark cracks like petrified lightning.

William ran over to them and came to a halt beside the injured woman. Turning to face the herbalist, he towered over the pair of local inhabitants, who stared up at him with apprehension clear in their eyes.

'I have urgent need of your services.' His words were filled with emotion.

Enid Hyne glanced at the rakish woman seated before her and then turned back to the creature. There was a look in the giant's dark eyes that dispelled any thought of refusal and she slowly straightened, looking the creature up and down with eyebrows raised, noting the blood and dirt caking his huge hands. 'Ye wish me to treat ye?'

The giant shook his head. 'No, there is a child in need of your assistance.'

'What child?' She glanced along the main track which ran between the houses of Marghas Byghan, spying none who seemed injured amongst those milling about the houses and upon the track.

'Rachel, she is a farmer's daughter and her home has collapsed beyond the higher outskirts of the town.'

'Rachel Hadden?' asked Mrs Hyne. 'Is that the child of whom ye speak?'

'I do not know her full name. You must hurry for there is no time to waste in idle chatter.'

'Does she have a brother named Jacob?'

William nodded, glancing back the way he had come with heart pounding and a churning in his stomach as he thought of the girl lying motionless in the rubble.

Mrs Hyne picked up the green bag of herbs which lay upon the ground beside her. 'I am ready.'

'Then go,' said William, his body aching and unable to make haste back to the girl's prone form.

The herbalist hesitated and then began to hurry along the muddy track towards John Hadden's farmhouse.

'You must run,' called the giant, the strength of feeling in his words causing the rotund woman to increase her waddling pace.

William watched until Mrs Hyne disappeared from view and then tottered under the weight of his weariness, almost falling to the track, the woman with the broken arm quickly getting to her feet and scrambling away.

The church bells fell silent as townspeople started to gather at a safe distance, muttering to each other as they stared unkindly at the creature in their midst. William looked at their faces, many of which were darkened by grime, their clothes the colours of autumn's palette. He tried to regain his composure, the dizziness which had come over him after such great exertion fading as he took deep breaths.

'Ye are not welcome here,' called a buxom woman with an ushering motion, wanting the giant to be away from the town.

'Cursed beast,' called a teenage boy as a mangy, brown dog beside him snarled at the forbidding form of the giant.

William straightened, his palms painful, legs and back aching after all his efforts.

'Begone, beast of Satan,' shouted a tall man in dirtied clothes, waving his fist in the air.

William gathered himself up, his dark cloak covered in dirt and dust, a few pieces of thatch clinging to the cloth. He began to walk along the track towards the seafront and the steps which led down to the beach. Those who had gathered there parted to allow him passage as they continued to watch him with unfriendly eyes.

The giant passed as others who had been gathering in the opposite direction along the track joined them, swelling their ranks. They allowed him to move away to what they believed was a safe distance and then began to follow 20 yards behind, shouting taunts as they did so.

'Demon,' a woman called out.

'Heathen beast,' a man shouted, the crowd becoming increasingly agitated as the townsfolk taunted the creature which shambled along the track between the silent, ramshackle houses of the town.

William tried to increase his pace, but his legs were weak, his strength sapped and the rush of adrenalin which had fuelled him having passed, leaving him shaky and without reserves of energy.

'Vile demon.' A stone struck his back and his shoulders tensed in reaction to the sudden pain. Then another hit his head and he stumbled.

'Get away from here,' came another shout from the throng that followed at his back as two more stones hit him.

'Go back to the pit of hell where ye belong.'

William passed the King's Arms hostelry and rounded a bend in the track. The steps to the beach came into view 100 yards ahead. Townspeople who had been busy with tasks of the quake's making stood alongside the thoroughfare, staring at the giant with expressions of distaste.

'It is the beast's presence that has caused this disaster to strike us,' said a man within the mob behind him. 'God is angered by this beast among us.'

There was a murmur of agreement as more stones began to rain down upon William. He put his painful hands to the back of his head to act as protection from the missiles as dark clouds came swiftly over the hill from the north and released a sudden torrent.

Footsteps approached quickly from behind him and he was hit across the lower back with a large piece of wood. William staggered forward with the force of the hateful blow, but managed to keep his footing.

More footsteps sounded and he stopped, turning to those who drew near, rainwater streaming down his face. Approaching were a knot of men, three of which he recognised from the assault in the priory gardens. One carried his smith's hammer, the others wielding pieces of rough timber which dripped as they were held poised in readiness.

They came to a halt a few yards away from William and raindrops flashed in the air between them and the giant. The sound of the heavy drops pattering upon the muddy track filled the temporary hush as the men stared at the object of their anger; the beast who had dared set foot in their town.

'Do him in,' called one of the women in the crowd.

'Leave the beast alone,' came a dissenting voice as a woman in a loose yellow dress moved to the front of the crowd, her hair long and dark.

'To appease God we must be done with the beast,' shouted a man with his hands raised in the air.

The woman moved to stand before the townsfolk, her feet muddied by puddles gathering in the ruts of the track as the rain continued to pour. 'He has done naught wrong,' she said in earnest.

'Are ye in league with the beast, Mary? Do ye wish his fate to be yours also?' asked the man, his thin face marked with numerous warts.

Mary stared at him a moment and then walked purposefully to the knot of men standing before the giant, going to the blacksmith's side at the head of the group.

William watched, a wave of dizziness coming over him as he stood in silence, his body stiff with weariness and tension.

'Morgan,' said Mary as the muscular man turned to her, his hammer held at the ready. 'Ye must not do this.'

'Abomination,' yelled a woman who stood beside the track next to a ruined cottage.

Mary looked into the blacksmith's eyes and put her hand to his cheek. 'Please, let the beast be, he has done no wrong.'

'Kill it,' called the warty man from the crowd.

'Do the beast in,' came a woman's demanding voice.

Morgan looked from Mary to the beast before him and then back to the whore. 'This is not your business, Mary. Stand aside.'

'Please,' she said earnestly.

'Stand aside,' he repeated with greater force, his eyes filled with firm conviction.

'We must rid ourselves of its curse,' said the man in the throng, a chorus of agreement sounding in response. 'It is God's will.'

With a sigh of resignation, Mary took her hand from Morgan's cheek and stepped back to the side of the track as birds continued to circle above the town.

William stared at the men before him, the crowd beyond restless. The rain slowed and then ceased almost as quickly as it had begun. Water dripped from his black curls, his cloak saturated and heavy upon his tight shoulders as the shower moved southward, its grey curtain veiling the ocean.

With a sudden yell, Morgan leapt forward, the other men following suit as the blacksmith raised his hammer and the giant lifted his hands for protection.

The crude weapons beat at William's body as Mary turned from the brutal scene with hands covering her face. The giant bent over as the blows rained remorselessly upon him, his legs beginning to buckle, tears of anguish in his eyes as voices called out.

'Beast.'

'Your end is near, demon.'

A shuddering hammer blow struck William's head and darkness drew its cloak over his mind as he crumpled to the track. The crowd rushed forward with a yell of ravenous desire, puddles splashing at their feet. They surrounded the unwelcome creature within their town, their hands and fists beating upon its still form with the feral violence of fear and disgust.

45

The darkness receded. He could smell straw, its musty scent stirring his mind to vague memories of a small room and a sparrow upon the edge of a table. The sound of waves breaking upon an invisible shore drifted into his emerging consciousness and he could see the faces of two children in his mind's eye, though their names escaped him, as did their connection to his life.

There was a pressure behind him. He realised with lethargic thoughts that he was lying upon a bed of straw.

William Tillbury. The name rose through the fog. He felt recognition and then realised it was his own name, the words others used to encompass all that he was. 'The words William Tillbury are not William Tillbury. They are not tall, with two arms and two legs,' he thought sluggishly. 'They do not change, they do not speak, they are nothing more than a label.'

Into his mind drifted an elderly monk with face wrinkled like shrivelled fruit in summer sun. The monk had kind, blue eyes and white hair about the bald crown of his head. Other monks stood behind him like ghosts gathered at his back, their hands clasped together in prayer as words of Latin rose into the air in a monotonous chant.

He could recall an island and gardens upon it with terraces, vegetable patches and a small orchard of apple and pear trees. There he had sat beneath the sun as nature filled his senses with vitality.

Pain.

He could hear the rattle of chains and felt shackles about his wrists and ankles. Crowds of people watched and he saw their myriad faces. Children with wide eyes pointed at him as they clung to their parents in fright. He heard cheers as he lifted others of abnormality into the air.

The smell of sewage came to him and he remembered rats climbing into a cage in which he found himself when the crowds had gone and night had fallen, rats which he killed for food, so hungry was he. There was a bearded lady with kindness in her pale eyes and a key in her hand.

Pain.

He saw himself upon a rocky bluff as a boulder fell from its steep crags and shattered upon the ground and rocks below. The earth was moving beneath him, rocking back and forth with a fearful trembling motion.

PAIN!

William's back arched as he let out a scream which gave Brother Cook a terrible start as he dozed on a chair beside the giant's bed. He quickly turned his gaze to his patient and saw his mouth was wide, even though the scream had given way to silence. Perspiration dripped down William's face, the skin of which was as pale as snow.

The monk took up a cloth draped over the side of a bowl of water upon the floor and dipped it into the cool liquid. Squeezing out the excess water, he leant forward and wiped the giant's face.

William's breathing was quick as his body settled back to the straw and his mouth closed. The pale grey tunic he wore was saturated with feverish sweat and beneath it his body was marked with such dark bruising as Brother Cook had never seen before and prayed he would never see again. The giant's arms were bandaged, as were both of his legs, which were also in splints in the hope the broken bones would heal.

Brother Cook rinsed the cloth in the bowl and wiped the giant's prominent brow. He was unsure as yet whether

William would make a recovery. Death hovered close and he feared it may still claim the man whose beaten and broken body had been tossed upon the beach from the heights of the town's sea wall, William thought dead by the townspeople who had attacked him with such fury.

Brother Thomas had found him on the shingle beneath the wall after a woman with long, dark hair had come to the priory to inform him of William's terrible fate. The giant's back had been covered in bruises and lacerations from the impact of the fall. It had taken four of the monks to bear the body back to the island and much effort to take William up the steps rising upon the Mount.

At first Brother Cook, who had been quickly summoned, believed William to be dead. Then he had detected the faintest pulse and his treatment had begun in earnest.

He sighed as he looked at the pained expression on the man's face before him.

'Rose!' exclaimed William deliriously, his eyes tightly shut and his lips bloodless.

Brother Cook leant forward and wiped the giant's face as he waited for William to regain consciousness or slip away into whatever awaited the creature beyond the grave.

46

Wistma slowly opened his eyes and stared at the roof beams. His thoughts were hazy and his body ached.

'Welcome back,' came a voice from beside him. With great effort, he turned his head a little to look up at the monk who sat on a chair beside the bed of straw.

Brother Cook smiled down at him, the slight dimples deepening in his youthful cheeks.

William tried to speak, but words evaded him, his mouth dry and moving in silence. His painful muscles tensed and he tried to raise his head a little, its weight proving too great.

'Lay still, William. You have been unconscious for two weeks since the earth trembled and swayed,' said Brother Cook. 'It is only by God's will that you are still alive and we have prayed for you every day.'

The giant tried to speak again, but still found himself unable.

'Do not worry yourself, William,' said the monk, seeing the concern in the man's eyes. 'It will take a great deal of time for your mind and body to recover from the ordeal you have been through. You are weak from lack of sustenance and all reserves of energy have been used to stave off the phantom of death.'

'Arthur?' The word was a mere whisper which William forced from his body like a breath.

Brother Cook's expression stiffened and his smile faded. 'He is unable to attend you at this time,' he said softly. 'We have all been taking it in turns to nurse you back to health and shall continue to do so until such a time as your autonomy is regained.'

There was a knock at the door and Brother Thomas entered with a steaming bowl held in his hands. His gaze settled on William. 'He is awake.'

'Only these last few moments,' replied Brother Cook. 'Is that gruel?'

Brother Thomas nodded, walking over to his Brother and standing beside the chair. 'It was meant for you.'

'William needs it more than I,' he replied. 'You feed him while I support his head.'

Brother Cook moved to the floor, knees resting on the edge of the straw. Reaching forward, he placed one hand behind William's head and the other between his shoulder blades. With careful effort, he raised the giant's upper body into a sitting position and supported it as Brother Thomas crouched beside him.

Brother Thomas blew on the surface of the thick gruel and then lifted the wooden spoon to William's parched lips. The giant opened his mouth and tried to eat, much of the food spilling down his chin and into his dark beard, its heat upon his skin making him wince slightly.

With great patience, the monk continued to feed the giant. Though much of the food was lost, the patient managed to swallow a little, his ability increasing with repetition.

'Do you wish me to take watch now, Brother Cook?' asked Brother Thomas when the bowl was finally empty.

'First, take the implements back to the kitchen and when you return I will take my leave.'

Brother Thomas looked at William, whose eyes were hooded as the strain of wakefulness began to take its toll. The young monk rose to his feet and walked to the door, exiting the room, his footsteps sounding on the stairs beyond.

Brother Cook gently lowered the giant back to his bed. He reached for the cloth resting on the stone floor beside the bowl of water and dipped it in the liquid before cleansing William's chin and beard. As he did so the giant's eyes closed, only to open again a moment later as he tried to fight the onset of sleep. Then, as his lids became increasingly weighty, they finally covered his eyes and did not rise again, the giant slipping into a fitful sleep.

47

There was a knock at the door and Prior Vargas looked up from the documents spread before him on his desk. 'Enter,' he said, his tone one of mild annoyance at being disturbed.

The door opened and Mr Hicks stepped into the small study with an apologetic look and a slight bow of his head. He wore a dark, woollen cloak over his blue tunic and thick, woollen stockings upon his legs to keep off the autumn chill. 'I am sorry to disturb ye, Prior Vargas, and not to have made an appointment in advance, but I much desire to speak with ye.'

The prior looked at him for a moment. 'Please sit down, Mr Hicks.' He nodded at the chair placed before the desk, the day dull and overcast beyond the window behind him.

'Thank you.' The portly gentleman shut the door and stepped over to the chair which had been indicated, noting that the prior made no attempt to shake his hand in greeting.

Prior Vargas settled back on his seat as Mr Hicks sat, the representative of Marghas Byghan feeling uncomfortable beneath the cold stare of the hawkish man opposite him.

'What is it that you wish to speak with me about?'

Mr Hicks cleared his throat, hands grasped together on his lap. 'I understand ye brought the giant's body back to the priory and that he still lives.'

'That is so,' nodded Prior Vargas, 'but I must tell you before you say anything more that I will not hand him over to the townspeople and am disgusted by the ill treatment he suffered at their hands after aiding one of their own number.'

Mr Hicks' rounded shoulders sagged and he sighed. 'The event of which ye speak was very unfortunate.'

'Unfortunate? I think you greatly underestimate the gravity of what transpired, Mr Hicks. It was not an act of civilised people, but one of barbarity which I had hoped would not be possible in this day and age.' Prior Vargas' expression was hard and unforgiving, his jaw tense as he tried to hold his anger in check.

'I cannot turn back time, Prior Vargas. What is done is done, but the people are sorry for their actions and are glad the giant lives.'

A hint of surprise showed in the prior's eyes. 'They are sorry?'

Mr Hicks nodded. 'Indeed they are, and I do not visit with ye now in order to request the giant's release into our hands.'

'Then why do you come?' Prior Vargas leant forward, his anger abating and his curiosity aroused.

'It was only after they had caused the giant's suffering that the people of the town learned of his deeds with regard to the children. Not only do they feel they wronged him in their actions, but also in their thoughts. Through my authority, they wish to inform ye that he is welcome upon Carrack Looz en Cooz, that the restrictions upon him which were wrought at our last meeting may be lifted, if it so pleases ye.'

The prior studied the rounded face of the man before him, hardly able to believe what had been said. 'If what you tell me is true it would please me greatly to lift his confinement.'

'My words are true, as are the townspeople's feelings of regret and sorrow in relation to this matter.'

'It is a shame you did not heed my words during our last meeting.'

'Indeed it is.' Mr Hicks looked down at his hands. 'I can only be thankful that the giant's life was not taken.'

'By the grace of God. He was close to death for a great many days and his recovery is slow. In truth, he will in all probability ne'er fully recover from such an assault.'

'As I have intimated, if it were within my power to take back what has come to pass I would do so without hesitation,' responded Mr Hicks, looking over at the prior once more. 'I realise that our gesture may seem weak after the strength of the attack upon the creature, but what else would ye have us do?'

'He is not a creature.'

Mr Hicks' cheeks were brushed with red. 'My apologies.'

Prior Vargas' expression softened and he took a deep breath. He relaxed against the back of his seat and tried to release the tension he felt within. 'I must apologise also, for I have let my anger guide my words. Your coming here to speak with me on these matters is much appreciated. I am glad you and the people of Marghas Byghan have not been so blinded as to continue your persecution of Mr Tillbury. It is truly good news.'

Mr Hicks smiled thinly. 'Your anger is understood and I would have felt the same should I have been in your position. Our opinions of the giant were not justified and had no foundation. We were too quick to judge and this mistake shall not be made again.'

'This I am glad to hear.' Prior Vargas returned Mr Hicks' smile. 'I am pleased you have come to tell me of this and it will lift Mr Tillbury's spirits considerably, though I think the town owes him a debt of apology.'

'Ye think I should speak with him?' There was a sense of apprehension in Mr Hicks' tone despite his realisation that he had misjudged the giant.

'Not today, for he is still in no condition to receive visitors, but I do think it a courtesy you should extend once he is better healed,' replied Prior Vargas. 'This will also give you the chance to prepare yourself for such a meeting.'

'It shall be done, for ye are right, he deserves a formal apology and there is no other who represents the people of Marghas Byghan as I.'

The prior nodded.

Mr Hicks rose from his seat. 'Now I shall leave ye to your duties.' He extended his right hand.

Prior Vargas looked at it a moment and then got up, stepping around the desk to grasp the other man's hand. 'Thank you for your visit, Douglas,' he stated, using the man's first name in a gesture of friendliness.

Mr Hicks' smile grew. 'The next shall be made by appointment and I shall meet with your guest also.'

'Until then may the Lord preserve and protect you,' responded the prior as they released each other's hands and the portly Mr Hicks stepped to the door.

'Farewell, Andrew. I hope that relations between the town and the priory will now be mended.'

The prior nodded again and Mr Hicks left the study and closed the door behind him.

Prior Vargas moved back behind his desk and retook his seat. The sound of gulls crying outside drifted into the room as he glanced down at the documents before him. There was a thin-lipped smile upon his face, his tension and anger having been replaced with gladness. William would be pleased that his confinement was to be lifted and would again find peacefulness on the bench upon which the prior had often seen him sitting with Brother Elwin.

He nodded to himself and then turned his attention back to the work in which he had been engaged before the disturbance.

48

William waited outside the door to Arthur's cell. His weight rested on a pair of sturdy crutches which had been made especially for him. His body still ached, but his injuries were much healed. It had been nearly three months since the people of Marghas Byghan had attacked him with such brutality and he woke most nights after dreams filled with such terrifying visions as made sleep an unappealing domain. Prior Vargas had brought him the news of the townspeople's repentance with regard to their actions, and for this he was thankful. No longer would he have to fear further violence. He was also thankful for the lifting of the restriction upon his movements, though his health was such that he had thus far been unable to descend to the gardens, where he so longed to rest upon the seat Arthur had constructed many years before.

As his fitness had steadily been restored, so had Arthur's illness grown worse. Brother Cook had revealed to him this truth when he thought William was strong enough of mind to cope and had thereafter informed him of the old monk's condition. This was the first visit he had been able to make, though he had requested to see his friend as soon as Brother Cook had informed him of Arthur's ailment. Now he waited for the young monk to exit after feeding his elderly charge and seeing to any other duties in the nursing of the sick old man.

William was feeling both anxious and apprehensive. He tried to prepare himself for the worst, had been warned by

Brother Cook that Arthur was much faded from the man he had known. The last time he had seen his friend had been when he had carried him to the priory after the earth had quaked. Even then the old monk had clearly suffered from declining health, his coughing worse than ever before and a yellow quality to his skin.

The door to Arthur's room opened and the giant felt his tension rise dramatically as Brother Cook stepped into the dark corridor, candlelight spilling from Arthur's cell, the young monk leaving the door ajar behind him. 'You may go in now,' he said, his expression filled with sadness and grave concern.

William nodded.

'I shall be back shortly to continue my attendance, but if anything untoward occurs please fetch me at once. I shall be in the kitchen.'

'I will.'

Brother Cook sighed and then moved past the giant. He walked along the corridor with his head bowed and a wooden bowl clasped in his hands which was still nearly full of vegetables that he had tried to feed to Brother Elwin, the old monk finding it hard to swallow and unable to consume most of the meal.

William watched until the monk passed into the short corridor off which the library was located, the refectory and kitchen lying at its far end. The silence gathered about him was filled with a sense of foreboding. He peered into the room, unable to see ought but the table which rested beside the bed, a wooden cup filled with water resting upon it. Beside the cup was a solitary white candle with wax drippings upon its sides, the flame flickering softly. His pulse quickened and he tried to calm himself. William wanted to give the impression of normality if at all possible, not wishing to distress his friend, only to raise his spirits through his visit.

He stepped to the door upon the crutches and pushed it fully open. Revealed in the thick pool of light about the bed was a man drained of life beneath dark grey covers, brooding shadows mustered beyond the foot of the cot where the candlelight had not the power to chase them away.

Arthur turned to him and the faintest of smiles fleetingly graced his lips. 'William,' he whispered hoarsely, his left hand loosely falling from the side of the bed as he tried to lift his arm and wave his friend forward.

The giant hesitated momentarily. He stared at the monk's face, the sockets sunken and filled with shadow, cheeks hollow with weight loss, pallid skin pulled tight over his cheekbones and tainted yellow by illness, the sickly colour accentuated by the candlelight. His features were skeletal and the sight was chilling, as if looking upon one who had already tasted death. If it were not for the rasping breath, the faint sparkle of Arthur's dulled blue eyes and the weak movements of his hand, William would not have believed him to be still in the land of the living.

He stepped over to a stool that rested at the bedside, one on which Brother Cook and the other monks took station in order to watch over the old man through these troubled times. William sat and leant his crutches against the table to his right, trying to bolster himself with a deep breath.

'It is good to see you, dear friend,' said Arthur as the giant turned towards him, the strain of talking clear upon his deeply lined face. His hand lifted and he grasped William's right hand with waning strength, the movement taking much effort.

'And you, dear friend,' replied William.

'Do I really look so fearful to your eyes?' asked the old monk, seeing the sadness in William's gaze.

'I ...' The giant tried to find words.

Arthur squeezed his hand gently, his jaw tensing as he did so. 'It is all right, William.' His bloodless lips curled into a tight smile. 'I am glad to see you are recovering well. Brother Cook told me all about your ordeal.'

The giant nodded. 'Soon I will no longer need the crutches, or so I have been informed,' he replied.

'Tell me of the gardens.'

'I have not yet been able to visit them since the day when the earth shook,' said William with a frown.

'No. Tell me of the gardens from the times we sat there during the spring and summer,' said Arthur, coughing weakly.

William sighed sadly and glanced out of the thin window above the bed, stars visible in the dark sky beyond. 'They were filled with vitality,' he began, Arthur closing his eyes as he listened, the flame of the candle caught in a momentary draught, making soft "phutting" sounds as it writhed and fought for life, the shadows in the room dancing like cavorting imps, as if the land of faerie were briefly glimpsed through the fabric of reality's veil.

'The trees bore white blossoms which sailed gently to the lush grass on warm breezes springing from the south. Insects fed upon the nectar of the blossoms and wild flowers which grew alongside the stone walls and about our seat. Birdsong mingled with the sound of the ocean and the colours about us were rich and vibrant.' He stared down at the old monk, his eyes glittering with tears.

'Carry on,' requested Arthur in a whisper, his eyes remaining shut and a vague smile upon his face as his friend's words conjured glorious images in his mind and transported him back to better times.

'Sweet fragrances filled the air as we watched boats coming and going, their sails bulging as they caught the wind. The sun was warm upon our faces as we sat side by side in the gardens enjoying the glories all about us.'

The door to the cell opened and Brother Cook entered. 'Is all well?' he asked as he walked over to the bedside and the candlelight flickered again, the fey shadows swaying about the foot of the bed.

William looked up at him and nodded.

Arthur's eyes opened slightly. 'Those were precious times,' he said quietly. 'Thank you, dear friend.' He managed to give William's hand another gentle squeeze.

'You should rest now, Brother Elwin,' said Brother Cook, noting the fatigue evident in the old monk's expression.

'It has been …' Arthur began to cough, his frail body convulsing beneath the bed cover, which threatened to slip to the floor. His hand gripped William's with surprising strength, his nails digging deep and breaking the giant's skin as Arthur's face became a mask of pain.

Brother Cook quickly reached past the giant and took the cup of water from the tabletop. He perched on the edge of the cot next to William and lifted Arthur's head. 'Here, drink this.'

The tendons in the old monk's neck strained as he continued to cough. His brow glistened and his eyes were closed tight. After a few moments the movements of his body lessened and he managed a quick drink, Brother Cook pouring some of the liquid into his mouth, its coolness alleviating the pain in his throat a little.

The coughing returned temporarily and Brother Cook waited patiently for another opportunity to give his charge a drink, Arthur still gripping William's hand tightly.

After a couple of minutes the coughing finally died away and Arthur managed to drink half of that which remained in the cup, his grip lessening on his friend's hand as the pain abated.

Brother Cook carefully placed Arthur's head back on the pillow and straightened. The old monk's features relaxed and he inhaled deeply, feeling a sense of relief now that the fit was over.

'I think you have visited long enough for today, William. Maybe you can return on the morrow if Brother Elwin has strength enough.' He looked at the giant with sorrow in his eyes.

William nodded. 'Thank you for allowing me to visit with him this evening,' he replied, feeling a sense of helplessness, unable to aid his friend in his time of need, and this in turn giving rise to guilt. He looked down at Arthur's peaceful countenance, the shallow rise and fall of his chest clear beneath the cover which Brother Cook neatened and secured over the monk.

'He sleeps,' said the young monk.

William removed Arthur's hand from his, a little blood apparent where the old man's nails had broken the skin. He tucked the hand beneath the bedcover and then took his crutches from where they leant against the table. Rising to his feet, he looked down at Brother Cook. 'Do you think he will ...?' He could not bring himself to finish the question.

Brother Cook shook his head. 'I do not know. He insists it is an illness arising from autumn's chill, but I fear it is much worse,' he said in a hushed voice.

'How much worse?'

Brother Cook gave him a look which told William all he needed to know. The young monk did not hold out much hope that Arthur would ever rise from his bed again.

'You truly think it that severe?'

The monk nodded. 'And not just I. The butcher's wife from Marghas Byghan has visited on more than one occasion, as she did when you were at your worst, and concurs with my grim assessment.'

'Did she mention anything of a young girl from the town who was buried beneath rubble on the day of the tremors?' asked William, an eagerness to his tone.

'A young girl?' Brother Cook looked up at him in confusion.

William sighed. 'It is nothing.'

He glanced at Arthur's face as the old monk slept and hoped his dreams would be filled with the sights and sounds of the gardens which he had described to his friend.

'Good night, Brother Cook. I will pray for his recovery upon returning to my room.'

'May our Lord preserve and protect you, William, and may He have mercy on Brother Elwin,' replied Brother Cook as William stepped to the door and the young monk took his place on the stool beside the bed.

With a last look at Arthur's sickly face, William left the room and shut the door behind him. He walked along the corridor to the entrance hall, the tap of his crutches on the stone floor filling the silence which pressed from all sides. Instead of walking to the rear door which led to the path and chapel beyond, William crossed the room to the front door and stepped out onto the summit of the Mount.

Turning left, William took great care as he walked to the southern bluffs. He came to a stop above the rocky crags and looked out at the ocean with a heavy heart. On the horizon a storm was passing, forks of lightning visible in the distance, their bright flashes descending to the waves and briefly illuminating the white horses which rode the swells. Faint thunder followed as the giant's eyes were filled with a faraway look and he thought about his friend, praying Arthur's self-diagnosis was correct and all he was suffering from was a severe chill, though fearing Brother Cook and the herbalist's opinions were closer to the truth.

49

William sat on the seat in the gardens, his crutches leaning against it to his right, where Arthur would have been sitting had he been of good enough health to join him. Two monks tended a vegetable patch near the southern wall at the bottom of the gardens as he sat in silence with cloak drawn tight about him, the day cold and grey, a brisk wind toying with his black curls. Upon his legs were a new pair of woollen stockings, dyed a dark grey and made especially for him by some of the women in Marghas Byghan.

Brother Thomas had advised him not to descend the steps, had warned that his strength may quickly wane and he may find himself unable to make the ascent back to the priory, but William had ignored the well-meaning advice. He had been filled with the urge to sit upon the bench where he and Arthur had spent so much time. Though his strength had declined with each step, his grim-faced determination had carried him onward, and would do so on the return journey.

He breathed deeply the cold air. The scent of the sea mingled with those of autumn's last breath as winter closed in. His memory turned to his arrival upon the Mount a year before. The same smells had filled him with a sense of hope as he had sheltered a night beneath one of the evergreens along the south wall of the gardens.

William's thoughts returned to Arthur. He glanced at the emptiness beside him and recalled their first meeting upon the steps in the howling gale. Then his mind's eye was filled with the image of Arthur as he had been during his visit the previous night. The sight had been a shock, despite Brother Cook's warnings. Later he hoped to visit again and longed to see his dear friend in a state of recovery, regaining his strength and his health.

There was a gust of wind and the branches of the evergreen which hung overhead waved with increased violence momentarily, whispering like spirits gathering in readiness to receive Arthur into the next world. William glanced up, half expecting to see the sparrow which he had nursed in the spring, but seeing nothing in the boughs bar emptiness, one echoed by the hollowness opening within.

His gaze turned seaward where a fishing boat braved the rough waters, hidden with regularity in the deep troughs between the swells, a couple of gulls following in its wake as it headed further out to sea.

The giant's brow furrowed and he sensed something untoward, a slight pressure in the air, a whimsical presence. The hairs on the nape of William's neck tingled. He turned to the emptiness beside him and for a brief instant thought he saw the faintest apparition of his friend seated there. He stared at the space Arthur used to occupy, but the fleeting phantom had gone.

His gaze moved beyond the bench, attracted by movement beside the stone wall which ran behind the seat. A blackbird was rooting through decaying leaves in search of crawling sustenance, its orange beak darkened by earth and the death of summer.

He sighed as he contemplated the change within him caused by the quaking earth, an event which was dreamlike in his memory. The feelings of security and separateness he had felt upon the Isle had passed away. Like the rocks which had tumbled from the southern bluffs, they had been shattered by the quake. The island was truly part of the world and the illusion of its independence had been vanquished in the suddenness and violence of the tremor that had shaken the Mount to its foundations and caused so much devastation in Marghas Byghan.

He shifted on the seat, his body aching. Then William caught the faint sound of the gate's hinges creaking as someone entered the gardens and turned to see who it was. His eyes widened and his pulse increased as he spied the farmer coming towards him, father of Jacob and Rachel and the man who had previously assaulted him in the gardens.

He quickly took hold of his crutches and rose, his legs feeling weak as he straightened to his full height.

John halted before the giant and looked up at him. 'To thee I owe a debt of gratitude for your aid after the tremors,' he stated, his expression one of seriousness. 'And after my ill-conceived assault upon your person I am grateful for what ye did for me.' He held out his right hand.

William hesitated, looking at it in surprise as the man's apologetic words sank in. He then grasped it firmly, the two men shaking.

'I have enquired after your health when monks from the priory have come to Marghas Byghan for supplies and this morning was told of your slow descent to these gardens. I am glad to find ye still here and grateful the injuries ye suffered in the town did not take your life, for I feel a great deal of responsibility in this regard.'

'You did not take part,' responded William simply.

'No, but if I had not come and requested your aid ye would not have been on the mainland.'

'It was my choice to accompany you. Besides, there was no way to know that the consequences would be so dire.'

'The people are sorry.'

William nodded.

'As am I. We would make right our injustice.'

'There is nothing for which I ask and forgiveness has already been granted.'

'Then ye are a greater man than I, for such actions I could ne'er truly forgive had they been enacted upon me.' John looked up at the giant with a degree of admiration.

'What of the children?' asked William, barely able to put voice to the question for fear of what the answer may be.

There was a moment of silence and then the farmer turned to the gate, giving a wave. William peered past him and his expression became one of surprise. Jacob pushed open the gate, Rachel behind him, both with beaming smiles upon their faces.

'Will!' called the young girl as the children broke into a sprint.

'Ye are welcome to spend time with my children. Without your assistance they would no longer be of this world.' John smiled warmly. 'All I ask is that ye make sure they return in time for their dinner.'

The children pulled up before William.

'I have missed ye,' said Rachel before flinging her arms about his left leg, holding onto him tightly, her brother following her lead.

The giant looked at the two children embracing him and a tear rolled down his cheek. 'How?' he asked, glancing over at their father.

'Enid Hyne managed to revive her. She said that had Rachel gone undiscovered any longer she would not have survived.'

The children released William's legs and looked up at him eagerly.

'Can we have a piggyback ride?' asked Jacob.

'Me first,' said Rachel, raising her hand enthusiastically.

'He is still recovering and it will be some time before he is able to bear ye upon his shoulders,' replied their father.

'We could play chase,' suggested Rachel with a look of mischief in her pale blue eyes.

'I am afraid I cannot manage such activities at present as I am only able to walk with the help of crutches,' said William.

'Exactly!' she exclaimed with a grin.

William and John chuckled, the giant overcome with a great joy at the sight of the children's good health, his eyes sparkling with tears of happiness as they stood together in the gardens.

50

Sitting on a large piece of fallen masonry, William watched as half a dozen monks busied themselves with clearing the debris of the collapsed rear of the chapel. The work had been taking place since the earth tremor and now that the smaller stones had been piled in readiness for rebuilding the Brothers were straining at larger ones with great weight.

The giant was feeling frustrated that he was unable to help them, but his strength was such that all he could do was watch. Clouds laboured overhead, their darkness growing and threatening rain as four of the monks lifted a piece of masonry the size of a small child, their expressions filled with the strain of their task and brows covered in a sheen of perspiration despite the cold wind which was blowing.

With staggering, laboured steps they moved it from the ruins and took it over to the giant's left, gratefully setting it down beside the piles of smaller stones that rested beside the portion of the chapel that remained standing. They then made their way back to the shattered masonry and roof timbers of the fallen building.

William watched them a moment longer and then turned to look north towards Marghas Byghan, his crutches gripped in his right hand. Smoke drifted from darkened holes in the thatched roofs, creating a grey mist which hung in the air above the hillside town despite the wind's attempts to chase it away. He could make out a few people about the houses and upon the tracks as they went about their daily business, vague figures without definition.

His mind turned to the children and he felt a gladness of heart. The sight of Jacob and Rachel filled with life had given him such joy and he looked forward to seeing them again. Their father had invited him to the mainland to attend a meal of thanks. John and the children were abiding with the farmer's sister while the farmhouse was rebuilt and the children would be sent to fetch him in a week's time in order to guide him to the house. It was due to be a celebration of the children's survival after such terrifying circumstances.

'William?'

The giant turned to find Brother Thomas standing before him, the wind flushing his rounded face. 'Yes.'

'You asked to be informed when you could visit with Brother Elwin again. At this time he is awake and asks that you go to him.' The youthful monk wiped a drop of water from his freckled nose as the rain began to fall.

'Thank you.' William stood and took a crutch in each hand. 'How is he this morning?'

'A little better than yesterday. There is a touch of colour to his cheeks and he is sitting up in his cot unaided.'

'And his coughing?'

'It remains a terrible affliction,' replied the monk as they began to make their way, walking to the small flight of steps which led to the rear door of the entrance hall.

They made their way through the hall in silence, the sound of William's crutches upon the floor echoing around the room. Stepping into the corridor where the monk's cells were located, the sound of Arthur's coughing could be heard.

They walked to his door and hesitated a moment, Brother Thomas raising his right hand and knocking as the sounds died away.

'Come in,' came Brother Cook's response.

Brother Thomas opened the door and allowed the giant entry by stepping back.

William ducked his head and walked into his friend's room. Arthur was sitting, his back propped against the wall at the head of his cot, a pillow between to soften the harshness of the granite and protect him from its chill. A smile graced his lips at the sight of the giant and William's spirits were raised by the simplicity of the gesture.

Brother Cook nodded a greeting as he remained seated beside the bed, turning back to the patient. 'Would you like some more food, Brother Elwin?' he asked, taking an empty wooden bowl from Arthur's frail hands.

The old man shook his head. 'No, thank you. That was plenty. I feel truly full after so long with so little sustenance.'

Brother Cook rose and moved away from the stool. 'Please, sit,' he said to William.

The giant smiled his thanks and carefully sat upon the seat as Brother Cook stepped over to Brother Thomas and they exchanged a few hushed words.

'You seem much better today, dear friend,' said William fondly.

'That I am. My night was filled with heated fever and the chill was sweated out to a great degree.' Arthur looked at his friend, his eyes brighter than they had been before, though skin still yellowed by his illness.

'I am gladdened by your improvement and hope it is not long until you can accompany me to the gardens.'

'I hope for the same. Long have I yearned to sit with you upon the peacefulness of our seat.'

'You will not be allowed out in such cold weather for a long time to come,' said Brother Cook from the doorway. 'Your body would not suffer such an outing for it has not the strength.'

Arthur glanced past William and then leant forward slightly, the strain of the effort showing upon his drawn face. 'They worry too much,' he said in a conspiratorial whisper. 'They would have me in bed for the entire winter even if I were to recover to full health.'

'Yes,' said Brother Cook, hearing the old man's words despite his attempt to conceal them in hushed tones. 'We would confine you to your bed if it were not for your stubbornness to rise as soon as you have a little resilience.'

Arthur's gaze moved to the monks at the door. 'And they have surprisingly good hearing,' he added with a wry smile.

William chuckled, as did the old monk upon the bed beside him. It was this that set Arthur to coughing again and his eyes shut as he raised his hand before his mouth. He leant over as the fit gripped him in its rasping hand and the monks at the door watched with concern. The smile which had appeared on William's face faded quickly and he waited for the coughing to diminish.

'Water,' requested Arthur when he was finally able to speak between the coughs.

William lifted the half-full cup from the table to his right and passed it to the old man. With a touch of horror, he noted the blood upon his friend's lips and a speckling upon Arthur's palm despite the monk's attempt to hide its presence by hastily lowering his hand. It was then that he knew Arthur's claims that he was merely suffering from a chill were false.

The old monk coughed a little more after sipping some of the soothing liquid and then the affliction abated. He drank the last of the water and weakly handed the cup back to the giant, seeing the expression of deep concern upon William's face. 'Do not fear, my dear friend. Let us enjoy this time,' he said, his voice hoarse and knowing that William had noticed the blood.

The giant looked down at his hands, which were clasped on his lap, and wondered how much time they had in truth.

Arthur reached out and rested his hand on his friend's arm. 'Your company is much treasured and I would make the most of it while I may. Talk with me about the children. I understand they visited with you this morn and all is well between their father and yourself.'

William nodded as he looked up at his friend and Brother Cook exited the room with the wooden bowl in his hands, Brother Thomas shutting the door and hovering beside it. 'Yes, Jacob and Rachel came with their father, who spoke with me in the gardens.'

'The gardens,' echoed Arthur dreamily.

'My actions to save the children have brought with them his acceptance and that of the townspeople. It makes me glad of heart, as does the knowledge of the children's continued vitality.'

'They like you very much, and this was plain from the time I spied you carrying them upon your shoulders.' Arthur coughed. 'They see the goodness in you more easily than most adults, I think.'

'That I cannot say, but their friendship is both most welcome and enlivening.'

'And our friendship, William, is one I am glad to have experienced.'

William nodded again. 'As am I. It is of great value to me.' He paused and sighed deeply. 'You are the first true friend I have ever had.'

Arthur looked into the giant's eyes. 'Then I am all the more honoured for having known you and am pleased I was able to show you that not all people are as you experienced them in your life before arriving on the Mount.'

The two friends looked at each other with deep fondness in their eyes. They fell into silence and Arthur turned his gaze to the thin window above the cot, clouds rushing by on high winds as rain fell in grey curtains which veiled the world. William followed his friend's gaze, a melancholy rising from deep within as they shared each other's company.

Brother Thomas watched them from beside the door and felt himself both saddened and given hope by such a bond between men. A thin smile graced his plump lips as he took a deep breath and saw Brother Elwin's eyes become hooded as sleep came upon him.

51

The atmosphere in the King's Arms was subdued, as it had been ever since the quake. The local men stood around the bar in virtual silence as they drank brandy and the fire crackled beside them. Tinker rested her head on her front paws as she lay before the hearth and Jebbit glanced down at her, the farmhand tired after a day of helping John with the rebuilding of his home, the foul weather severely hampering their efforts, but the clearing of the rubble nearly completed. Jack and James Tupp had also been at hand, the twins now standing by the back door at the far end of the corner bar, sharing glances, but no words.

'Let us hope the clear skies of this night last for the morrow,' said John as he set his cup upon the bar, the darkness outside filled with a deep calm now the squalls of the day had blown over.

Richard took a jug from beneath the bar and pulled out the stopper. 'Aye,' he said with a nod.

'Now the wind has died I think it will last,' said Mervin Sallows in response.

'Aye, and my knuckles ache, which is a sure sign of a lasting chill to come.' Morgan Pengelly flexed the fingers of his left hand, cup held in his right as he sat at the table beside the fire. For years he had suffered aches and pains in his knuckles thanks to his tight grip upon his hammer and the prongs he used to hold the metal he was working.

'Your knuckles always ache,' responded John, the others gathered at the bar all nodding their agreement.

'It is more severe this night, as it is whenever a cold spell is on its way.'

They fell back into silence and drank the brandy and mead which brought them warmth and a growing numbness.

The front door opening caused heads to turn and they watched as a man entered, each feeling a sense of recognition. His clothes were of fine cloth and he pulled down the hood of his long, black cloak, the candlelight illuminating his face with greater clarity. The black beard and moustache were recently trimmed and the face healthy and rounded with overindulgence. He stared at the men at the bar with dark eyes as he went over to them, his walking cane clipping on the floor as he did so.

'Greetings to you, gentlemen,' he said with a smile which was friendly and yet set warnings in the men's minds as they watched the stranger and nodded in response to his words.

'Good evening, sir,' said Richard. 'What can I get ye?'

'I will have a pitcher of ale and a room for the night, if you have one.'

'I do,' replied Richard as he put a large tin cup before a barrel which was laid upon its side against the rear wall, turning its small tap and pouring the watery liquid.

The stranger looked from one face to the next, his smile wide and filled with a sense of self-satisfaction. 'I hear of a giant dwelling in these here parts,' he stated, the local men exchanging glances, but remaining silent.

'Did it not aid in the saving of some children and then suffer at the hands of those who dwell in this town?'

'Ye mistake yourself,' said Morgan with irritation before taking a sip of his mead, wracked with guilt over what he had done to the giant.

'Do I?' replied the man with eyebrow raised. 'So none of you fine men know of what I speak?' He looked at them all in turn and each shook his head, their eyes revealing the lie of their actions.

'Then the merchant with whom I spoke only a week ago must have been mistaken.' He lifted the cup which Richard placed on the bar and took a long swig of the drink, wiping his lips with the back of his hand afterwards.

'Does no one here know of this giant and his whereabouts? The merchant seemed to believe the beast dwelt upon the Isle of Ictis.' He noted the slight widening of Jebbit's eyes when he mentioned the Isle and fixed him with his gaze. 'You, will you not tell me what happened here?'

Jebbit felt uncomfortable as the stranger stared at him and turned his gaze to the sawdust about his feet. 'I do not know of what ye speak.'

The man looked about the bar. 'Come now, I have visited before and was not treated in this way,' he said with a wounded tone. 'I passed through a year ago and you were willing to speak with me then.'

'Why do ye ask about the giant?' said John.

'He is a friend with whom I would much like to meet.'

'If he is a friend then why did ye not know of his whereabouts until speaking with the merchant?' asked Morgan.

'We lost contact tis all,' replied the man, turning to the blacksmith.

'What is your name, stranger?' asked Richard as he leant against the bar, his cheeks flushed as usual.

'Baines.'

'Well, Mr Baines, I am afraid I misspoke myself earlier and there be no room in which ye can stay for the night,' said Richard, having taken an intense dislike to the man and his prying.

Baines looked across at the landlord. 'No?'

Richard shook his head.

The stranger drank the rest of his ale and put the cup upon the bar. 'That is a shame for I could pay well. Can you advise me of any other hostelry where I might find a room?'

'Not in this town.'

Baines turned to the Tupp twins. 'And you?'

They looked back at him in silence.

'Do they not have the power of speech?' he asked as he turned to John.

'They do not talk to those they do not trust,' replied the farmer, his eyes cold as he regarded the man.

The stranger looked at him with mock surprise. 'Why do you display such open hostility? I have done naught to offend and only ask about the giant because he is truly a friend who I wish to find.'

The memory of the man's previous visit suddenly surfaced in Jebbit's mind. 'Now I recall!' he exclaimed as his eyes widened and he stared at the stranger. 'Ye were here soon after I had seen the beast upon the brow of the hill. Ye were seeking it with ill intent and told us of its vileness.'

The others stared at Baines as for the first time the mask of friendliness slipped from his face and the smile vanished temporarily. 'Are you all of the belief that this giant is no beast? Have you all been fooled by its behaviour, by the case of the children it supposedly rescued? I tell you now, it is a creature of evil and naught else. From the tale of the townsfolk's actions against the beast I thought you knew the truth of this. Why else would you try to take its life?'

'They were my children the giant saved,' said John, his words measured as he straightened to his full height. 'And if ye look for a creature of evil then ye will not find it dwelling here.'

'Was the story of the brutal assault upon its person untrue? I heard it told that the beast was beaten close to death upon the highway that runs outside this very door.' Baines narrowed his eyes and glared at the farmer.

'It is true,' he admitted after a moment, regret clear in his tone.

'We did not know that it had aided John in the rescue of his children,' said Mervin, his guilt weighing heavy in his grey eyes, George Pascoe nodding sadly, the shadows deep in the hollow of his left eye socket.

'The aid given was not out of any goodness, I tell you,' said Baines, his voice filled with firm conviction. 'The foul beast is trying to lull you into false security, to come amongst you in order to enact some great evil. Heed my words, for they are a warning given out of genuine concern.'

The brothers Tupp looked at John, their eyes questioning. The farmer shook his head in assurance and then turned back to the stranger. 'Ye speak with a tongue which knows only lies.'

'He has deceived you, my friend.' Baines put his hand on John's shoulder. 'Please understand this before it is too late.'

John remained silent as Jebbit glanced at Richard, looks of uncertainty on both their faces as Baines looked from man to man and felt that his words were having their intended effect. Soon the people of Marghas Byghan would desire nothing less than the banishment of the creature upon the Mount.

52

Prior Vargas stood looking out of the window in his study. The day beyond was still and clear, the sky vivid blue and the sea a rich, deep blue, the swell of waves small in comparison to the previous day of autumnal wind and rain.

The sound of footsteps came from the corridor beyond the study and he glanced towards the door as they came to a halt. Two weak knocks followed and he frowned, having hoped for some time in which to find peace.

'Enter,' he instructed.

The door opened and Brother Stewart peered in apologetically, the elderly monk's head bowing. 'I am sorry to disturb you, Prior Vargas, but there is a gentleman come to visit you.'

'On what business?'

'He will not say, though he does tell me it is of the utmost importance.'

The prior's frown deepened. 'You do not recognise him from the town?'

Brother Stewart shook his head. 'He is a stranger to my eyes.'

Prior Vargas fell silent a moment and then sighed deeply. 'You had better bring him in to see me.'

The old monk nodded and shuffled back along the corridor to the entrance hall, the sound of his steps fading as Prior Vargas listened for a moment and then sat on his chair in readiness to receive the guest, irritated slightly by the fact that Brother Stewart had left the door to his study ajar.

A short while later he heard the monk's shuffling return, confident steps and the sound of a cane tapping on the flagstones accompanying him. Brother Stewart appeared in the corridor beyond the doorway. A gentleman then came into view wearing a long, black coat which bore none of the usual grime of travel, a deep blue tunic beneath and fine stockings upon his legs.

'Please, come in,' said the prior.

The man entered, his dark gaze displaying the same confidence as his striding gait, a dark bag slung over his shoulder.

Prior Vargas stood and extended his hand over the desk.

The man, with a self-assured smile, stepped forward and grasped the prior's hand firmly. 'My name is Baines. Thank you for agreeing to meet with me at such short notice.'

'I am Prior Vargas. I was told it is a matter of some importance which brings you here,' replied the prior as he

246

took his seat and looked past the man to Brother Stewart, who was lingering in the doorway. 'You may shut the door and return to your duties now, Brother Stewart,' he called out, Baines surprised by the volume of his voice.

The old monk nodded and closed the door, his footsteps then moving away along the corridor.

'He is a little deaf,' explained Prior Vargas, having noted the gentleman's expression. 'Now, what is this matter of which you wish to speak?'

The man settled upon the chair before the desk and placed the bag on the floor beside him, its metal contents chinking dully as he rested his right hand on the bejewelled top of his walking cane. 'I have journeyed here from Salisbury after discerning the whereabouts of an item of my property which went missing a year ago.'

Prior Vargas looked at him in confusion. 'Your property? I am afraid we have come into ownership of nothing other than foodstuffs in the time of which you speak.'

Baines smiled, a gesture that filled Prior Vargas with discomfort. 'I have it on good authority that my property resides upon the island with you and under your protection.'

'I assure you, sir, that we have not received any items and would ne'er knowingly take ownership of goods which are the result of thievery.'

Baines held the prior with his gaze for an instant. 'Then you have given it a home in ignorance.'

Prior Vargas' expression hardened and his brow furrowed. 'I tell you again ...'

Baines raised his right hand to cut the prior's words short. 'The giant,' he stated simply.

The words brought with them a look of shock on the prior's face.

Baines reached into his cloak and withdrew a rolled document tied with a piece of red ribbon. He took off the binding and placed the paper upon the desk before the prior. 'This is proof of my ownership.'

After a slight hesitation, his expression filled with seriousness, Prior Vargas reached forward and picked up the document. He unrolled it and carefully read the words set before him, his eyes narrowing as he did so and Baines crossing his legs nonchalantly with a look of satisfaction on his face.

Sighing, the prior lowered the paper and set it back upon his desk, his gaze lingering on it with sadness.

'The giant is my property,' stated Baines. 'I will take him away with me today.'

'And if I refuse?'

'You cannot. I am on the side of the law. The beast belongs to me.'

Prior Vargas looked up sharply. 'We have no beast living here.'

'No?' Baines raised his right eyebrow.

'No.'

'You have been persuaded of its humanity?' Baines shook his head and bore a mocking smile. 'I would have thought men of God less easily fooled.'

'Mind your words, Mr Baines.' Prior Vargas' tone left his visitor in no doubt that there was no chance of changing his mind on the matter.

'Very well, you believe whatever fantasies it would have you believe, that does not change a thing. Now, please bring the beast to me and I will be on my way,' said Baines, purposefully using the term of reference which had so annoyed the prior.

'Nothing would please me more than to see you away from here,' replied Prior Vargas, trying to remain calm, but his anger rising with surprising force.

'Then I suggest you fetch it from whatever pit of darkness in which it lurks.' Baines held the prior's gaze.

Prior Vargas was the first to look away, turning his eyes to the document resting on the desk. 'I shall have one of the Brother's fetch Mr Tillbury from his room.'

'Mr Tillbury!' scoffed Baines with amusement.

'The beast, as you call him, is named William Tillbury.' The prior stood and walked around the desk, passing his unwelcome guest as he went to the door. 'You will wait outside the entrance to the priory through which you entered,' he said coldly, opening the door.

Baines looked over his shoulder at the long face of the prior, the monk's expression tense and stern. Pausing a moment, he then reached forward and plucked the ownership document from the desktop, taking his time as he rolled it up and tied the securing ribbon about it, tucking the paper back into his cloak.

He rose slowly and picked up the bag from beside the chair, the sound of metal chinking issuing from within as it shifted. Baines slung it over his shoulder and smiled at the prior as he stepped to the door, passing into the corridor beyond and turning left for the entrance hall.

The prior stared at his back, his gaze seething as the man exited the corridor and was hidden from view by the door closing behind him. Prior Vargas took a few steadying breaths and then quickly headed in the opposite direction until he reached the door to Brother Elwin's room, where he knew one of the other monks would be in attendance.

He knocked once and entered without waiting for a response, Brother Thomas turning as he sat on the stool beside the patient's bed.

'Prior Vargas,' he greeted in surprise, bowing his head slightly.

'Brother Thomas, I have a task for you which is of some urgency,' stated the prior, glancing at Arthur, who lay fast asleep on the cot, his pupils moving beneath his eyelids as he dreamed. 'You must find Brother Stewart and instruct him to take William to the front entrance. As soon as you have given him this instruction, I need you to go to Marghas Byghan and find John Hadden or Douglas Hicks. Tell them that William is in need, that a man has come to claim him and take him away.'

'Take him away?' Brother Thomas looked at the prior in surprise.

'Yes. Do you remember what I have just instructed you to do?'

Brother Thomas nodded. 'Find Brother Stewart, who is to take ...'

Prior Vargas held up his hands. 'I trust in your memory and your ability. I will stay here and watch over Brother Elwin as you attend to this task. Now go.'

Brother Thomas rose from the seat beside the bed and walked briskly to the door. Passing the prior, he then hurried along the corridor to the door which led to the priory's refectory and kitchens, knowing that Brother Stewart was carrying out his duties in the stores.

Prior Vargas watched him leave and then shut the door. Stepping over to the bedside, he seated himself and felt his heart racing. He took deep breaths and turned to the old man.

Arthur groaned in his sleep and shifted beneath the bedcovers as the prior peered down and wondered at William's fate. He was unsure what the reaction of the townspeople would be to the news of the giant's impending departure. They had expressed regret with regard to the beating he underwent at their hands, but would they lend aid in his time of need or would they be happy to see the beast taken from the Mount of St Michael?

He shook his head and sighed. There was nothing more he could think of to do in order to help William and he prayed what he had done would be enough.

53

Villiam followed Brother Stewart, the old man shuffling before him along the path which ran alongside the entrance hall and past the tool shed. The monk's pace suited him, not only due to the crutches he used for support, but because of his current lack of strength. The trip to the gardens the previous day had sapped him more greatly than he would have thought and his legs and hips ached.

He stared at the top of Brother Stewart's hood and wondered at the reason for being summoned as his mud-stained and tatty cloak fluttered in the breeze. The monk had claimed ignorance, that Brother Thomas had asked him to fetch William to the front door of the priory and that he knew nothing more.

They rounded the corner and the giant stopped in his tracks as he set eyes on the man who stood before the priory's front entrance to the left. His heart raced and he felt an additional weakness as a slight sensation of nausea washed over him.

'It has taken much time and effort to find you again, Beast,' said Baines with an unkind smile, accentuating the final word with volume and force.

Brother Stewart, who had not noticed that William had come to a halt, looked over his shoulder with brow furrowed in confusion.

'The others were captured long ago. You are the last, and now I have you again.'

William opened his mouth to speak, but no words were forthcoming.

'The monks have given you up. They no longer want a cursed creature like you abiding in such a hallowed place.'

Brother Stewart stared at Baines, but did not speak after the stranger glared at him, eyes filled with malice, the bent old man taking an involuntary step back.

'Come, I have some old friends to introduce you to.' Baines held up the bag and shook it, William instantly recognising the sounds of the shackles which had bound his wrists and ankles for so long.

'You have no need of them,' said the giant. 'I am in no condition to escape you this time.' He looked down at the crutches.

'Are they the reward for your heroism?' he said mockingly. 'I heard about the events in the town and it is this story which alerted me to your presence here.' Baines walked over to stand before the giant, looking up at his face with eyes sparkling darkly. 'When I heard what the townsfolk did to you, I could not help but smile,' he said, voice lowered. 'I spent much time and money searching for you, Beast.'

He took hold of the bottom of the bag and emptied its contents onto the ground, the old monk's eyes widening when he saw the dull, rusty shackles. 'Put them on,' Baines demanded firmly.

William stared at the symbols of his slavery. They filled him with dread and he could not bring himself to pick them up.

'I said, put them on, Beast.' Baines hit William across the knees with his walking cane, putting as much force into the blow as he could muster.

The giant collapsed to the ground, the crutches falling beside him. His eyes watered with the pain as he rested on all fours before his master. Still he made no attempt to don the shackles.

The next blow was across his back and William fell face first to the rocks and grass.

'Is that really necessary?' asked Brother Stewart timidly as the stranger raised his stick to strike William once again.

Baines turned with his cane still in the air. 'Leave us, old man. Go back to worshipping your absent God.'

Brother Stewart stared at him for a brief moment and then made his way as fast as he could to the hall entrance. 'I will fetch Prior Vargas,' he stated before stepping into the building and hurriedly closing the door behind him.

Baines crouched and picked up one of the shackles. He closed it about William's right wrist as the giant lay still, not wishing to receive another wicked blow. His master took the second shackle and placed it about his property's left wrist, the chain linking the two bonds lying loosely on the ground.

He moved to William's feet after picking up the remaining shackles and the giant's ankles were soon chained together. 'There,' said Baines as he got to his feet. 'And this time there will be no one to set you free.'

The tone of Baines' voice caused William to turn his head and look up at his master. 'What did you do to Elsbeth?'

'That is not of your concern. All I shall say is that she now waits for you in the deepest pit of hell.'

William shook his head and closed his eyes temporarily as he fought back tears.

Baines sniggered. 'She should have known well what reward she would receive for her treachery. If the woman had possessed even a little sense she would have tried to make good her escape with the rest of you.'

'She did not deserve death.'

Baines smirked. 'To your feet,' he instructed.

William shook his head.

His master kicked at his side and the wind rushed from his lungs. 'My patience grows thin and if you do not rise I fear that your reunion with the treacherous whore will come much sooner than previously thought.'

William gritted his teeth and fought against the aches and pains of his body as he rose, towering over his master. Baines picked up one of the fallen crutches and handed it to him.

'You will have to make do with only one for your support,' he stated coldly. 'Now, let us leave this place. There is a long way to travel and I have no wish to linger any longer.'

Baines led the way towards the top of the stone steps and William followed with his head bowed sorrowfully. His master did not bother himself with turning to check on his property's progress, could hear the chink of his chains and felt comforted by the fact the Beast was back in his charge after so long, the sound of his bonds bringing a smile to Baines' face.

They reached the top of the stone steps and William's master began to descend. The giant hesitated and looked back over his shoulder at the priory, spying Prior Vargas and Brother Stewart standing at the door to the entrance hall as a gull flew overhead and let out its mournful cry. The prior raised his right hand in parting and William turned away with tearful eyes.

He stepped down, the chains restricting the movement of his aching legs, and began the long descent. The emotions which arose within him were as powerful as the ocean. Waves of sadness washed through his mind and mingled with feelings of deep despair. The shackles were cold and hard against his skin as the phantom of his past engulfed him in despondent gloom.

The descent was slow and laboured, William having to stop on occasion to recover his strength, Baines always halting a few steps below him and impatient to continue. Hope had been stripped away from William and he began to feel numb. He did not look to the mainland visible above the trees to the left, did not wish to see the undulation of the misted hills rising north and west, the sands of the beach which curved westward or the calm, turquoise waters between the island and the mainland shore. He knew that to gaze upon the panoramic vista would be as torture, for he would never again see its beauty.

They eventually reached the foot of the steps and walked along the cobbles to the path which led to the warehouses and harbour, William hanging his head low, not even glancing at the gate and the gardens beyond before they turned left.

They soon passed between two granite warehouses which loomed to either side. The sound of William's chains echoed off the walls and heightened the giant's misery as his thoughts turned to Arthur and he longed to see his friend one last time. In his mind's eye he saw the old monk upon his bed, a look of restfulness upon his aged face, and hoped his friend could forgive his untimely departure from his side.

Baines led the way along the roadway at the harbour-side, its surface set with stones from the beach. A large ship was moored at the jetty, its hull resting on the sands revealed by low tide and pale sails hanging limply against its three masts. Sailors and deckhands looked over at the strange sight as they readied the ship to sail once the waters returned to the harbour. Like the spectators who had watched William in his master's show of freaks, the seamen stood with eyes wide and looks of both horror and wonder upon their weathered features.

Baines descended to the bar of sand and shingle to the right of the jetty. The giant followed in miserable bondage, his head bowed low and shoulders hunched as he felt the eyes of the audience upon him and rested his weight upon the crutch. The smell of seaweed was heavy in the air, the swells of recent storms having washed it upon the shore, the tide leaving it upon the beaches of Marghas Byghan in snaking piles that followed the contours of the sand and shingle.

As he traipsed slowly along the bar, William's feet sank deeply into the sand and water collected in the indents which were left in his wake. Chapel Rock jutted from the sands ahead and to the left, its dark mass obscuring any view of the steps that led up to the hillside town. Gulls sat upon rocks to the right as wagtails searched for food with wading birds amongst the pools which had been left by the tide, which was now rising and closing in about the bar to either side, waves lapping with a gentle calm as they slowly drew nearer. Further to the east the curving coastline that led to the Lizard Peninsula could be seen and the Greeb rested out to sea, its rocks gently caressed by waves which beat incessantly upon it.

'What is this?' Baines' words intruded upon William's sad reverie.

William looked up and saw a large crowd of people ahead, walking towards them after having come into view from behind Chapel Rock. He narrowed his eyes against the bright, wintry sunlight and noted a few faces he recognised amidst the large gathering of townspeople. Brother Thomas was at the head alongside Jacob and Rachel's father. He also spied the blacksmith who had dealt him such a powerful blow the day he had nearly lost his life upon the town's thoroughfare and the woman who had tried to stop the savagery.

Baines drew to a halt and stared at the approaching throng with a look of uncertainty upon his face as William came to a standstill behind him. The giant watched as the people moved off the beach and onto the sand bar four abreast. Tension rose within him, muscles tightening and pulse quickening as the townsfolk came to a stop 10 yards ahead.

'What is the meaning of this?' called Baines, trying to fill his words with confidence, though his expression showed his sense of apprehension.

John stepped forward from the ranks. 'Ye are going to set the giant free,' he instructed, many of those gathered behind him nodding and making sounds of affirmation.

'It is my property,' responded Baines defiantly.

Douglas Hicks stepped forward. 'Ye are to sign a document which releases Mr Tillbury from your bondage.'

'I will sign nothing of the sort. Move aside so we may pass.' Baines took a step forward, but none in the crowd made any indication that they would allow him passage. His expression softened as he decided to attempt a different tack.

'Have you all forgotten that this creature behind me is nothing but a foul beast with naught but evil within its heart?' he asked, glancing back at William as he stood shackled upon the bar.

'They have not forgotten …' came Prior Vargas' voice from behind William, the giant turning to find him approaching along the bar with Brother Cook beside him. 'Because you cannot forget something you did not already know. There is no evil in Mr Tillbury, of this I can vouch in the eyes of our Lord.'

'You have all been fooled,' shouted Baines, his facade falling away as frustration consumed him. 'This is a beast of deception and evil, I tell you.'

'We hear ye, but we do not believe,' said John. 'Now release him from the shackles and from his slavery to your will.'

'I will not.'

'Ye will, and we shall all bear witness,' stated Mr Hicks.

Baines reached into his cloak and withdrew the rolled document. 'This is proof that the beast is my property,' he said loudly, waving it at those who blocked his way. 'As long as I have this document there is nought you can do, for the beast is legally mine.'

'We will not retreat until your ownership is rescinded,' stated Mr Hicks calmly, Morgan Pengelly crossing his muscular arms over his broad chest.

A silence descended as Baines looked at the faces before him. All bore expressions of conviction and in none did he find hope that they could be persuaded of the creature's malevolence. His frustration grew in conjunction with a sense of defeat.

He shook his head and trembled with fettered rage. Reaching into his tunic with his left hand, he withdrew the key to William's shackles and threw it to the sand.

Mr Hicks approached along the bar flanked by John and Morgan, the trio of local men stopping before Baines.

'This is not lawful,' he complained, confounded by the actions of the townsfolk.

'Ye must hand over the ownership document,' said Mr Hicks.

Baines shook his head.

'I am the local sheriff,' he stated, puffing out his chest a little, 'and ye will do as I say.'

Baines glared at the portly man and then held the document out to him.

Mr Hicks took it and untied the ribbon, letting it flutter to his feet. He unrolled the paper and held it high above his head, turning to the gathered people of Marghas Byghan. With a quick flourish, he tore it asunder. A cheer went up and there was clapping from the crowd as they celebrated the giant's liberty, feeling that the debt they owed him had been repaid and a weight lifting from their collective shoulders.

'Ye will be required to sign a document stating that William is now a free man when we get back to the town,' said Mr Hicks, turning back to Baines, who simply turned his gaze to his feet in miserable defeat.

Morgan reached down and plucked the key from the golden sand. He stepped over to stand before William and crouched to release his ankles. The irons fell away and Morgan threw them aside, where they splashed into a pool of water amidst the dark rocks and vanished from sight beneath the reflected blue of the cloudless sky.

The blacksmith straightened and placed the key into the lock of the shackle about the giant's right wrist. He turned it and a faint click signalled release, the shackle falling away and dangling on the chain which connected it to the metal band still encircling William's other wrist. He moved to release the final bond, but the giant gently took hold of his arm.

'Please,' he said softly, holding out his hand.

Morgan nodded and William let go of him before the blacksmith placed the key upon the giant's waiting palm.

With deliberate slowness, wishing to savour the moment, William released himself from the final shackle and let it fall to the sand at his feet.

Morgan looked up into the giant's dark eyes. 'I am sorry for what I did to ye,' he said quietly.

William nodded and smiled, his eyes sparkling with tears.

'Now ye may leave,' said John, stepping aside from his position before Baines. 'Though we shall meet again at the town hall. There ye will sign a lawful document releasing William from your service.'

The crowd parted, creating a passage along the bar between their massed ranks.

Baines hesitated, turning to look at the giant. Then he began to walk forward, feeling a sense of trepidation as he approached the townspeople and recalled the merchant's tale of how they had beaten the creature they had now helped to gain its freedom. With shoulders hunched and head bowed, he slipped through the crowd and then picked up his pace as he reached the far end of the bar by Chapel Rock. He made his way across the beach towards the stone steps leading up to the town, disappearing from view behind the dark, jutting rock. With murmurings and bright expressions, the gathered people began to drift away.

'Thank you all,' called William, voice cracked with emotion.

'It was our pleasure,' stated Mr Hicks with a smile as he walked over to William and extended his hand.

The giant looked at it momentarily and then clasped it gladly.

'I believe this should be in your possession to do with as ye see fit,' said the portly man, giving the giant the torn halves of the ownership document. The sheriff then turned away and began to head back to the town with the others, Morgan joining him as they made their way along the bar towards the wide curve of the beach.

'I will see ye at my sister's next week,' said John before turning and setting off after his friends.

William stood and watched the people disperse with the remains of the ownership document clutched tightly in his right hand, his heart filled with gladness as Brother Thomas walked over to him. The giant slowly turned to face the prior and Brother Cook, both of whom were smiling warmly.

'I am sorry we could not stop him putting the shackles upon you,' said Prior Vargas.

'You did all you could and have helped bring me my freedom,' said William in response, realising that the prior must have sent Brother Thomas to the town. 'For everything you have done for me I am eternally grateful.'

'Do you still desire to abide with us?'

'If I may.'

Prior Vargas nodded. 'You are most welcome, William.'

William wiped tears from his dark eyes as Brother Thomas drew alongside him. 'Do you need my assistance in returning to the priory?'

'That would be very kind, Brother Thomas,' replied William, turning to the young monk with a smile.

'We must go on ahead of you, William,' said Prior Vargas. 'For we have duties to attend to.'

William nodded and the prior turned back towards the Mount of St Michael with Brother Cook by his side, waves beginning to lap at the sand bar at its lowest point, the tide rising to encircle the Mount once more.

54

The slate rested against the far wall. The words drawn upon it had not altered since before the tremors which had caused so much devastation. They were etched in William's mind and he stared at them as he sat upon his straw bed and leant against the unyielding wall. The feeling of being a free man had not yet fully sunk in after the events of two days previous. He felt as if all that had happened were part of some distant dream. He reassured himself that this was not the case with constant glances at the torn ownership document resting on the table beside the large piece of slate. William had not yet decided what to do with the halved document and until he did it would remain displayed to act as proof of his liberty.

The sight of the townsfolk gathered on his behalf was one which returned to him again and again as he sat in thought. It filled him with happiness to know that his presence had been accepted, that he could live amongst them without fear of persecution.

He took a deep breath and looked up at the window. Thick clouds masked the sun and promised rain as they sped in from the west on strong winds. Winter's grip was starting to close upon the land and the days were cold and short, yet he felt a great warmth within and a lightness danced in his bright eyes.

The sound of quick footsteps beyond his door caused William to turn from the view. Two knocks followed shortly thereafter and he felt himself tense inexplicably. 'Who is it?' he asked, words filled with trepidation.

'It is Brother Cook. You must come quickly.'

William struggled to rise from the straw, the depth of urgency in the monk's muffled tones leaving him in no doubt as to the importance of his visit. He stepped to the door and quickly opened it. 'What is wrong?' he asked, seeing the haunted look in Brother Cook's eyes.

'It is Brother Elwin. He has taken a turn for the worse and you must visit with him before it is too late.'

'Too late?' William's heart faltered.

Brother Cook nodded. 'Come.' He turned and made his way up the few steep steps which led into the chapel, wind ruffling his hair as it gained entry through the collapsed rear of the building.

William ducked out of his room and glanced back at the crutches which lay on the bed of straw. Deciding to leave them, he carefully made his way up the steps with as much haste as he was able.

Following the young monk, who clearly wished the giant could move with greater speed as he continuously glanced over his shoulder, William made his way out of the chapel through the door behind the pulpit which had once been reserved for the prior's use. They followed the edge of the chapel and passed the ruined rear of the building, soon after descending the steps which led to the rear door of the entrance hall.

Within a few minutes they reached the door to Arthur's room and William's tension rose as Brother Cook knocked and then entered without awaiting a reply. The giant bowed his head and followed after him, seeing Brother Thomas and Brother Stewart beside the bed where his friend was gripped by a horrific bout of coughing, blood and saliva dripping from his lips and chin, mouth stretched wide as if letting out a scream of agony. The old monk's eyes were tightly closed and tears ran down his face as he clutched at his stomach, doubled over as he lay beneath the covers that hung over the side of his cot, his thin body only partially covered.

'There is nothing we can do,' said Brother Thomas with a look of desperation towards Brother Cook as they all gathered at the bedside bearing sorrowful expressions.

William winced as the coughing became worse, his friend struggling for breath. Then the affliction began to die away and his body slowly sank back to the bed, perspiration glistening on his face as Brother Stewart dipped a cloth into a bowl of water placed on the table beside the head of the cot.

As Arthur settled, his coughing finally dying away completely, the other elderly monk tenderly wiped his lined face with the cloth.

'How long has he been like this?' asked William.

'Since the middle of the night,' replied Brother Thomas, turning to him, his eyes shadowed by a lack of sleep.

Arthur's eyes opened upon hearing the voice of his friend. At first he could not focus, the faces hovering over him indistinct. He blinked a few times and finally gained clarity of sight, staring at William sadly.

With all the effort he could muster, the old monk tried to raise his left hand, but it fell limply back to the cot. He tried again and met with an equal lack of success, intense frustration apparent in his expression as his frail body refused to bend to his will. Opening his mouth, he attempted to find the power of speech which had evaded him for the past few hours, but it did not return, pain searing his throat.

William bent closer to Arthur and took up his hand, clasping it tightly in both of his. 'I am here, dear friend,' he said softly as he looked upon the monk, who had become a shadow of the man he had known, a wraith bereft of colour or physical power within the world to which he clung.

Arthur tried to nod as Brother Stewart moved aside and William sat on the stool next to the bed, the smell of body odour and sickness filling his nose as he looked upon Arthur and felt a great sense of helplessness.

Arthur tried to speak again and William leant over to try and hear should a word be uttered. The old monk was filled with despair as words remained elusive and closed his eyes as he tried to summon the will to overcome his inability.

'Friend.' The word was barely a breath, but William heard its soft whisper.

The giant looked upon Arthur as the old monk opened his blue eyes and the faintest of smiles touched his bloodless lips. He coughed once and the strain was evident upon his face, his cheeks hollow and eyes raw.

They looked at each other with profound fondness, one communicated in the thick silence of death's approach. In the old monk's gaze William saw the glimmer of an unspoken farewell blurred by tears of mournful departure. He squeezed his friend's hand in a gesture of comfort, his heart aching with agonising grief.

After a few moments Arthur's expression softened. The tension in his emaciated body faded with the light in his eyes as his final breath was released in a sigh of passing. As the monk's chest fell still the first drops of rain began to fall out to sea, descending in brief flashes to rejoin the ocean from which they had come.

William began to weep as he continued to grasp the old monk's withered hand. Tears streamed down his cheeks and their salt waters glistened in his beard as Brother Cook leant over the still form and gently closed Arthur's eyes to the world that he had loved so dearly.

55

Illiam hobbled along the Mount's summit through sea mist so thick that it gathered upon his hands like gauntlets of fine jewels. The air was still, only the cries of gulls and wash of the ocean filling the paleness. The vague forms of the priory buildings rested to his left as he moved to the southern bluffs with cloak about him.

He came to a halt and looked at the torn pieces of the ownership document held in his hand, the droplets of mist on his skin cool and glittering. A wind rose from the north and the air stirred.

He looked into the well of mist falling away before him, his expression filled with loss. Lifting the pieces of the document, he tore them again and again, finding little solace in his actions.

Taking a deep breath, William cast the shreds out over the bluffs. They circled and danced gently as the wind buoyed them momentarily. Then they began to tumble playfully, losing definition in the mist until they faded into nothingness, as if making a journey into another world. Did Arthur rest in the mists somewhere beyond his sight? Did his friend's spirit watch from the next world?

The giant sighed, his dark shadow motionless as he stared into the mist, which was thinning as the wind grew in strength. With the whip of his cloak, he turned and began to make his way across the grasses and bare rocks. The buildings to his right whispered with memories as he passed and, in his mind's eye, he saw Arthur seated in his room giving his lessons on reading and writing. The kindly monk had possessed much patience as his strange pupil stumbled over words and found himself clumsy with the chalk at first. There had been laughter when they joked together and Arthur had smiled when William showed his quickness of mind and studiousness. William recalled the mystery of the slate and Arthur's indulgence in secrecy, the old monk smiling when its use was finally revealed.

The giant reached the stone steps and began to descend awkwardly, beginning to regret leaving his crutches in his room. He found that the mist-veiled steps whispered in the same melancholic voice as the priory. They conjured images of his first meeting with Arthur, the squall raging about them as the giant had lifted the monk into his arms and borne him to the summit, blood soaking into his cloak from the old man's wounds. He recalled segments of conversations they had shared while descending or ascending the steps, ones filled with the monk's insight, wisdom and gentle humour.

The mist grew thinner as William struggled with the descent. He passed beneath the blanket of paleness and felt as though he had journeyed between two worlds, one of myth without substance, the other the world of men with its immediacy and physical presence. He stopped and looked up towards the summit, which was wrapped within the pale embrace, hidden from sight.

He slowly descended the last of the steps as the wind toyed with his dark curls and the mainland was hidden from sight by the trees rising to his left. His legs and hips ached and were filled with a growing weakness, but he went on, an expression of determination upon his face, large brow knotted and teeth gritted against the pain which grew with each footfall.

William walked into the gardens as the wind began to usher away the mists hanging about the Mount, the rising crags revealed beyond the western fringes of the garden.

The sound of the gate hinges creaking brought with them a faint and fleeting smile as his mind turned to the times he and his dear friend had spent in the walled confines. He walked slowly along the northern terrace, limping as the pain increased.

His thoughts were filled with recollections. He had attended the old monk's burial that morn and now wanted to spend some time with him, thinking of no better place to do so than the bench upon which they had spent so much time in each other's valued company.

He reached the seat and came to a halt, staring down at it. William remembered the trepidation he had felt when first approaching and requesting with a nod to be seated beside the wizened, white-haired monk. He recalled the nervousness which had plagued him after he had made the decision to talk with Arthur. His stomach had knotted and twice he had lost the courage to give voice to all the words which buzzed in his head like a swarm of hornets trapped and maddening in their incessant restlessness. When he had finally spoken with Arthur the sense of relief had been great. They had shared so much upon the bench, both in silence and in conversation. William had revealed himself for the first time and found such great reward, such a wonderful friendship for which he would be forever grateful.

The giant smiled thinly as his fingers closed about the implement tucked in his tunic, one which had been borrowed from the priory's tool shed. He withdrew it slowly and moved to crouch before the right-hand side of the bench.

William began the task he had set himself, again remembering the reading and writing lessons which Arthur had conducted in his room and the gift of the slate which had been such a mystery until the old monk had revealed its purpose with a bright smile.

The giant worked with care as the gentle breeze brushed against his face and the tree whose branches hung over the bench whispered softly. William's eyes glistened as he tried to concentrate. Wood chippings fell to the grass and his tears bowed the leaves at his feet.

When the task was complete, he straightened and stared at his work for a moment, slipping the tool back into his tunic.

Sitting on the left side of the bench and keenly feeling the emptiness beside him, William looked out over the gardens, the mist above now gone, chased away by the northerly wind to reveal the majesty of the Mount. No other was present and for this he was thankful. He took a deep breath and pulled his cloak closer about his frame as his gaze wandered out across the waves to a distant ship, the sails of which fluttered as it made for the horizon and distant lands.

Epilogue

Rachel entered the gardens with her youngest son wrapped in swaddling and clutched to her chest. Her third son, Elijah, followed with a large, yellow shell in his hands. It had been found on the beach that morning and he thought Uncle William would like it, the 4-year-old's expression filled with joy at the thought of seeing the giant whom he loved so dearly.

They walked along the northern terrace towards the seat. William had taken to spending most of his time upon the bench in the late years of his life, and there, like on so many occasions before, he sat facing the sea, which was calm beneath the grey washed clouds that promised rain.

'Will,' called Rachel, her long, blonde hair tied back from her face as the gusting wind blew in from the ocean and the front of her green dress rippled gently.

The giant did not respond or even turn to her approach as he sat dressed in a brown tunic made for him in Marghas Byghan.

'Will?' She spoke his name more softly than the first time and her pace slowed as she noted the fixed expression on the giant's face. Her heart skipped a beat when she saw the stillness of his eyes, a smile set upon his face which told of a peaceful and contented passing.

'Elijah, ye must stay here,' she said, crouching before her son.

He looked at her in confusion. 'Why must I, Mummy?'

'Because I think Uncle William may be feeling unwell. Ye do not want to catch a bug, do ye?'

Elijah shook his head after a moment's thought. 'No,' he replied simply.

She patted his curly hair lovingly and then rose. Preparing herself, she took a deep breath and then walked the short distance to the motionless figure on the bench.

Stopping before him, Rachel shifted the weight of her baby. She sighed and smiled sadly at William's pale face, an expression of tranquillity softening the lines of age. His right hand lay open upon his lap, the silver crucifix she had given him so long ago resting on its palm, its tarnished chain hanging loosely over the side and swaying in the wind.

Rachel bent forward. Her hand moved to his and she felt the cool lifelessness of his leathery skin. Her pale, slender fingers closed his hand about the silver trinket as they had when she was but a girl and her eyes glistened in the soft light.

'Goodbye, William,' she said softly as she straightened and her youngest gurgled in her arms.

She briefly glanced down at the babe's ruddy face and then her gaze moved to the word carved into the back of the seat beside the giant. 'Friend,' she whispered, the roughly etched letters green with age.

Rachel remembered William telling her that the word had been carved in memory of one of the monks from the priory, an old man with white hair whom she could barely recall. Many times William had spoken of the old monk and always with great fondness. Now it was his turn to slip into memory, become the giant who once walked the island and who had saved her life after the earth had trembled so fearfully.

Rachel turned to the ocean view with tear-clouded eyes. Gulls wheeled and turned, dark against the grey sky as they soared in the wind. She watched them dreamily as they glided swiftly and then banked over the white-capped waves, their wings beating as they ascended to heaven.

END

Afterword

Though the story upon these pages is fictional there are a few facts contained within which the author would like to draw your attention to:

1. The name Marghas Byghan means "Little Market". The town of Marghas Byghan is now known as Marazion (pronounced Maraz-eye-on), and looks out over St Michael's Mount in western Cornwall, England. (1)

2. A castle is now situated upon the Mount, but a Benedictine priory once rested there, its chapel and a few other remnants still remaining.

3. Outcasts from society, sometimes due to their abnormal appearance, often sought sanctuary in monasteries or priories.

4. On 11 September 1275, an earthquake struck western Cornwall, causing part of the original Benedictine chapel to collapse, the rebuilding of which was completed in the fourteenth century.

5. Finally, the skeleton of a man said to be 7 foot 6 inches or 7 foot 8 inches, depending upon the source, was discovered on St Michael's Mount early in the twentieth century. This skeleton was found beneath debris in a small anteroom connected to the Benedictine chapel. The skeleton was removed and given a Christian burial in the island's graveyard, though the site of this burial was not marked.

Reference
1. Various – The Charter Town of Marazion, p. 7, Marazion Town Trust, 1995